ACTS OF LOVE IN FARAWAY PLACES

RICK TALBOT

FARAWAY PLACES TRILOGY
BOOK 1

ACTS OF LOVE IN FARAWAY PLACES

FARAWAY PLACES TRILOGY, BOOK I

BY RICK TALBOT

Copyright © 2022, By Rick Talbot. All Rights Reserved.

Published by Chainreads

ISBN: 978-0-9881371-7-2

This is a work of fiction. All the characters and events portrayed in this book are fictitious, and any resemblance to real people or events is purely coincidental.

MAJOR LOCATIONS IN THE STORY

THE MOONS OF URANUS

Name	Diameter	Composition	Terraform Status	Inhabited
Miranda	471.6 KM	Ice	N/A	No
Ariel	1167.8 KM	Rock/Ice	N/A	No
Umbriel	1169.4 KM	Rock/Ice	N/A	No
Titania	1576.8 KM	Rock/Ice	Yes, within Adriana, Lucetta, and Bona colony domes.	Yes
Oberon	1522.8 KM	Rock/Ice	Yes, within Hamlet colony dome.	Yes

THE MAJOR PLANETS

Name	Diameter	Composition	Terraform Status	Inhabited
Earth		Rock	God-created	Yes
Mars		Rock	Fully	Yes
Venus		Rock	Fully	Yes
Mercury		Rock	Partial on dark-side colonies	Yes

NOTABLE EXTRA-SOLAR COLONIES - NEAR CLUSTER

Name	Distance l.y.	Notes
Alpha Centauri	4.2	Nearest star to Earth
Gliese 447	11	Mount Sinai II
Gliese 832	16.1	Quarantined by order of Stellar Corp
Lacaille 8760	12.8	S.C. Protectorate
Epsilon Indi	11.8	S.C. Protectorate
Gliese 784	21.8	S.C. Protectorate
Gliese 682	16	S.C. Protectorate

NOTABLE EXTRA-SOLAR COLONIES - FAR CLUSTER

Name	Distance l.y.	Notes
Epsilon Eridani	10.5	Cats.
Luyten's Star	12.4	Luyten's Corp
GJ 2066	28.6	Planet Fabulous

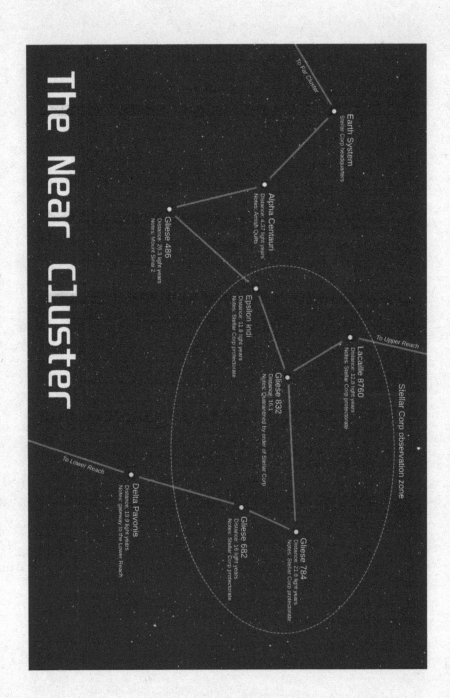

ACTS OF LOVE IN FARAWAY PLACES ∞ iii

The Far Cluster

GJ 2066
Distance: 26.6 light years
Notes: Planet Fabulous

GJ 205
Distance: 18.5 light years
Notes: Unmatched

Wolf 294
Distance: 18 light years
Notes: unmatched

GJ 229
Distance: 18.8 light years
Notes: brown dwarf companion

Luyten's Star
Distance: 12.36 light years
Notes: Luyten's Corp

Epsilon Eridani
Distance: 10.5 light years
Notes: cats

Earth System
Stellar Corp headquarters

To Near Cluster

ARCHIVIST'S NOTE

This document was created in part from notes provided by Stellar Corp Archivist Ashley Chung. For readers without Stellar Corp security clearance, a limited declassified collection of notes is viewable at the following address: www.ricktalbot.com/wiki/

Prologue

IN THE YEAR 2715 – or somewhere thereabouts – the secret of interstellar travel was finally discovered. Travel to other stars at faster-than-light speeds became common-place. This meant that interplanetary corporations could finally go interstellar. Exotic goods, such as fine quilts made with Amish silk from Mount Sinai II (which are absolute must-haves) could now be imported faster than the fifteen years it took for the robotic barges to make the trip. This alone made the expense of faster-than-light worth it – at least for those who followed the latest in interstellar fashion.

N.B. In 2775 the term *superlight* was chosen as the official ISO standard, meaning "travel at faster-than-light speeds."

1

Adriana Colony, Titania, a moon of Uranus

Bailey shouted across the canyon, "Echo!"

(Echo, echo, echo....)

"This is awesome!"

(This is awesome, awesome, awesome....)

"You're such a baby," Shep said. He slapped her on the shoulder. "Baby."

"You're such a killjoy," Bailey replied. She stuck out her tongue.

Balraj was on the far side of the canyon, looking down into the crevice.

"I don't know guys, it's pretty deep."

"C'mon Balraj, we already did it. It's only thirty meters. Just run and jump," Shep said.

Balraj backed up a bit, then ran forward and jumped. He flew up and across the thirty meters of the canyon, passed by Shep and Bailey, and landed awkwardly on a pile of garbage. Dust filled the air.

"You okay? Balraj?" Bailey asked.

Balraj picked himself up from the garbage heap. He looked down at himself, and then looked back at his friends who were running toward him.

"I tore my jeans."

He pointed at the left pant leg, which had a rip from the knee all the way down to the ankle. It seemed that somehow he had not been hurt. "My mom is going to kill me."

2

S.C. APPLEGATE, IN ORBIT OVER TITANIA, A MOON OF URANUS

Perspective is everything when you look down at the world that you're supposed to be protecting, and you see nothing.

The three colonies on the moon Titania were nearly invisible from orbit. Adriana, Lucetta, and Bona were nestled in their namesake craters for protection from the elements: from solar radiation, from Uranus's magnetic field, and from rogue meteorites.

Aboard the S.C. Applegate, Captain Jeremy Bach sat staring out the bridge window, idly scratching his leg. The window was actually a large computer display, currently showing a view of Titania as seen from one of the ship's cameras.

"Captain, Engineering reports everything is normal," Smitty said. Smitty's civilian outfit, a jean jacket with dark jean pants, contrasted with the official Stellar Corp uniform worn by the rest of the crew: a light-pink suit in the traditional Indian pajama style. The color was meant to project strength, but not aggression, to the citizens under their protection. Stellar Corp staff wore no rank insignia as a rule, to prevent officers from being identified in the rare event that they encountered a hostile adversary.

(Scratch, scratch, scratch.)

"Captain."

"Huh?" Jeremy asked. He paused for a second. "Thank you, Smitty. Umm, okay." Jeremy looked at Smitty, nodded at him, and then returned to staring at Titania on the display.

"Everything okay Captain?" Smitty asked.

"Fine."

The two sat for a while in silence. Jeremy stared out at space as Smitty stared at Jeremy, wondering what his captain was preoccupied with. The pilot, Jerry Mulligan, who sat nearby, busied himself with data on his console.

"You know Smitty," Jeremy said, as he tapped his fingers on his chair. "Hmm..."

"What, uhh, what is it Captain?"

"Smitty, I'm really fucking bored."

Smitty said nothing for a moment.

"Oh..."

Jeremy Bach: captain of the least interesting patrol in the history of the universe. In the window, the drab gray surface of Titania lay revealed before them, surrounded by the endless dark void, just as it had been every day for years now.

3

Hamlet Colony, on Oberon, a moon of Uranus

Steven Wang, president of Hamlet Customs Brokers, was enjoying a glass of Scotch whiskey when a flash of light brightened his office for an instant.

He activated the intercom on his desk.

"Did you see that?" he asked.

"Yes, Steven. What was it?" Carol replied.

"I have no idea. I thought I was imagining it."

He rushed to the window to see if he could spot anything out of the ordinary. His view of Hamlet was substantial – he could see all two-hundred kilometers of the colony from end to end – and it all looked normal. He sighed in relief. Then he looked up. A dull red glow, something resembling a coal ember, was moving across the sky. Steven ran back to the intercom.

"Carol, something in orbit just blew up. See if you can get hold of Stellar Corp for some info."

"*Shit, Steven, okay. I hope it's not one of ours.*"

Steven poured another glass. His hand trembled slightly, and a splash of the rare vintage drink spilled onto his desk.

"Fuck," he muttered.

This was not good news. There were too many safety protocols; ships did not explode, ever.

4

HORATIO STATION, STELLAR CORP, IN ORBIT OVER OBERON.

Commander Tajiki watched the bright fireball as it moved across the orbit of Oberon.

"Is this a threat to us?" she asked.

"No, we're safe. It's moving away."

"Okay. How about the colony?"

"Hold on," Wayland Hauer said. He brought up a map on the main display. He calculated the trajectory of the fireball and overlaid it on the display. "Oh, oh no. There's a very high chance that it will land on the colony."

"Are you sure about that?" Lauressa asked as she walked toward the display.

"Commander, look at those projections. If the remains of that ship don't break apart, then the whole thing will land on Hamlet. If it does break apart, then there's a chance it could overshoot."

"Thanks Wayland. Could you call up the nearest ship please? We need to destroy that wreckage."

Wayland hit a few buttons. The nearest Stellar Corp ship was located, and communications were established.

"S.C. *Johnson* here. Go ahead Horatio Station."

"S.C. *Johnson*, this is Commander Tajiki. I need a firing solution for that wreckage."

"*We're already following it.*"

"Our projection of its path shows it landing on Hamlet if we do nothing. S.C. *Johnson*, you have permission to fire on the wreckage. Obliterate it."

"*Acknowledged, Horatio Station.*"

The ship accelerated toward the smoldering hulk and opened fire with all lasers. Eight nearly invisible beams – just barely observable because they fried any bits of dust that crossed their paths – dashed instantly forward with a dull blue glow. The beams converged on the center of the wreckage. The red-ember wreckage turned white-hot under the laser barrage. Then it blew apart into thousands of tiny fragments.

Commander Tajiki jumped. "Woo! That was sudden!"

Wayland calculated the trajectories of all the new tiny bits of ship.

"It looks like none of it will hit Hamlet."

"Good. Good. Now we need to find out how that ship blew up in the first place. It's been a long time since there's been an accident like this," Commander Tajiki rubbed her stomach. "It's going to be a long night. I'm going to get a quick bite to eat, and then I'll get to work on this. Can I get you anything?"

"I'm fine," Wayland replied. Commander Tajiki had started for the door when a message notification chimed at Wayland's console.

"Commander, it's the president of Hamlet Customs Brokers."

Commander Tajiki sighed.

"Fine. Patch him in."

Wayland hit a button. "This is Horatio Station. I have the Commander here. Go ahead."

"Lauressa? It's Steven. What's happening up there?"

"Hello Wang, I'm kind of busy," Commander Tajiki said.

"I just want to know what's going on. Is it one of ours?"

"We don't know yet. Have any of your ships missed a check-in?"

"Not yet, but the way they're staggered, it could take a week before they all check-in with us."

"Okay, send me your itineraries. I'll compare your schedules against the station's sensor records."

"Lauressa, this isn't good. It's been... I've been on Hamlet for almost two hundred years. The last time anyone lost a ship was – it's been so long that I can't be sure exactly – I think it was a hundred and twenty years ago."

"At least a hundred years for sure. These things are not supposed to happen. I've got to get back to work. I'll let you know if it's one of yours."

"Alright Lauressa, thanks."

"It's Commander Tajiki during office hours, Wang. Bye."

Lauressa Tajiki walked out of the command center. Steven Wang was still talking; drawing out his goodbye. Wayland cut the connection as soon as the Commander had left the room, and the room fell pleasantly silent.

Outside the station, thousands of glowing embers spread out in orbit over Oberon. They were like sparks from a campfire, reaching up toward the heavens.

5

Aboard Horatio Station

Lauressa Tajiki closed the door to her quarters and let out a long sigh. Steven Wang had always managed to get under her skin; to insinuate himself into her life in some way. It was bad enough that she had made the mistake of spending that drunken weekend with him (decades ago!), but did she have to pay for it for the rest of her life?

Wang just seemed like he'd never moved on. She was endlessly mean to him, so terribly mean, but he wouldn't let go. Lauressa wondered if the people who had cured disease and aging – the people who had turned humans into demi-gods five-hundred years ago – had ever taken into account the misery of having one lost weekend follow you forever? If they had, then maybe they would have put in some kind of self-destruct mechanism, instead of dooming us to wait for war or disaster to finally do the job.

Lauressa let her hair out from the tight bun that it had been pinned into. She poured a glass of wine. *No drinking on duty – fuck, under the circumstances, who cares?* She took a drink – it was dry and dark – and she let out another long sigh. Her order to open fire was the first given in seventy-five years. There'd be hell to pay. *So much paperwork! I'll be doing paperwork for months because of this shit.* But as long as she was investigating the accident then she wouldn't need to file any forms. *Oh well, back to work.*

Lauressa grabbed some bread and headed out of her room toward the Research Center.

* * *

Lauressa entered the access code, and the doors to the Research Centre opened. The room was dark. Rows of lights flickered on overhead as soon as she stepped over the threshold. Someone was hunched over a desk on the far end of the room.

"Are you okay?" Lauressa asked. The person didn't move. She walked closer, placed a hand on the woman's shoulder, and gave it a shake.

"What?" the woman asked. "Oh..." she said as she put a hand to her head.

"Are you okay?"

"I, uh, I must have fallen asleep." She turned to look at Lauressa. "Oh, Commander!" She tried to stand and got about a quarter of the way up before sitting back down. "Oh, my head."

"You don't look so good," Lauressa said. "I don't think we've met."

"I'm Ashley Chung. I just arrived two days ago. I'm a research archivist."

"Okay, Ashley. Why are you in here sleeping?"

"I was, uh..." Ashley stopped and rubbed her temples. "I feel sick. My head is pounding."

"Have you been drinking?"

"No. I wouldn't do that at work. But I feel hung-over. I don't understand why."

"Okay, let's get you to the infirmary."

Ashley stood up and took a few steps. She fell to her knees, mumbled, "Oh my god," and vomited all over the floor.

"Sure you haven't been drinking?"

"I'm sure." She wiped her sleeve across her mouth. "I don't know if I can get up on my own."

Lauressa reached down and took a firm grip on Ashley's arm.

"Ready? Here we go. Let's go get you checked out." They walked carefully out of the Research Centre, then down the hall to the elevator. Ashley vomited against the elevator door as they waited. The door slid open and the vomit squished up against the doorframe.

"Well, now I'm quite concerned." Lauressa watched a glob of vomit drip down to the ground. Lauressa entered the elevator, carefully avoiding the vomit. Ashley followed, barely able to stand. They were relieved to reach the infirmary without further incident.

The doctor examined Ashley. He went through the list of symptoms: found passed out, headache, vomiting, difficulty walking, and a general 'hangover' feeling.

"And you're sure you haven't been drinking?" Doctor Poisson asked as he shone a light into one eye, then the other.

Ashley held up a hand to block the light. "Oh! That hurts! No, I haven't been drinking."

The doctor shook his head.

"Okay, it could be anything. Toxic shock from food poisoning, a stroke, an aneurysm." Ashley's mouth opened slightly. "Don't worry, it's probably none of that. Most likely, you drank so much that you can't remember it. But I'll run some tests anyways." He took a quick blood sample from Ashley's arm and placed it into the Analyzer. The machine whirred for a few seconds, began a countdown on its screen, and then chimed when it was done.

"Oh, this is strange. Have you been using drugs?" Doctor Poisson asked.

"No. Why?"

"You've got phenobarbital in your system." He passed the analyzer to Lauressa. "Look at the chart."

Lauressa looked at the display: a graph at the top and a series of numbers below.

"I don't see it."

"The spike there on the graph. That's the phenobarbital. Ashley, do you take this for seizures?"

Ashley shook her head.

"I don't take any drugs. I'm not on any medication."

"And I wouldn't expect you to. It's not frequently used now, and it's never been a recreational drug. Hmm, this doesn't make sense. You said you found her passed out at a desk in the Research Centre?"

"That's right, about twenty minutes ago."

"Ashley, what's the last thing you remember?" Doctor Poisson asked.

"I went into the Research Centre to start reviewing the last twenty-four hours of orbital sensor data and prepare it for the archives. That's it," Ashley replied.

"That's it?"

"I don't even remember sitting down at my desk."

"Do you remember what time it was?" the doctor asked.

"I think it was five o'clock."

"That's over six hours ago. You're lucky the dose wasn't higher. But you'll have to stay here overnight until it leaves your system completely." The Doctor walked over to a small room with glass walls and opened the door. "Go ahead and sleep it off in here. You'll feel a lot better in the morning."

Ashley nodded and walked a little drunkenly into the room. He closed the door behind her.

"What do you think?" Lauressa asked.

"I think that she either uses drugs recreationally, or she was drugged on purpose."

"On purpose?"

"This isn't the most common drug to run across. She either brought it onto the station, or someone else did."

"You don't have any?"

"I don't stock it. There are better alternatives available. Sure, you'll find it in some of the smaller colony hospitals, because it's cheap to manufacture and it works. But if you've got the resources you'll stock the newer drugs. Less risk of overdose."

"She'll be okay?" Lauressa asked.

"She'll be fine. She'll sleep it off. I'll advise her to take it easy for the next twenty-four hours."

"Okay, good."

"Lauressa, we've got to figure out how those drugs got on the ship."

Lauressa nodded. This was just what she needed. An exploding ship wasn't enough – now she had a drugged civilian crew member to worry about.

"Doctor, can you look into it?"

"I have to report this to Stellar Corp anyways, so I'll see what I can find."

"Thanks Doctor. I'll be in the Research Centre."

6

Adriana Colony, Titania

"Let's go to the Arcade," Shep said.

Balraj shook his head.

"Your pants are really not torn that bad."

"No way, I'm already in trouble. I need to go home."

"You're already boned, so just come with us to the Arcade."

"Fine," Balraj replied. He shrugged his shoulders and let out a deep breath. "I guess you're right. Let's go."

"Guys, this is going to be so fun," Bailey said. She hopped in excitement.

Shep laughed, pointed at her, and said, "You're like a dumb floppy puppet. Bouncing up and down."

"Suck it, Shep." Bailey turned and ran in the direction of the Arcade.

"You're such a dick," Balraj exclaimed with a sigh. He started off after Bailey.

"Whatever...."

Shep watched as the two of them kept running.

"Hey guys, wait for me!"

They made their way past the colony garbage dump. Flies and other insects, attracted by their body heat, buzzed around, trying to make themselves at home on their clothes and in their hair. The three of them walked a while longer until they got to the industrial area. Rows of prefab buildings lined both sides of the street. Trucks headed both ways, delivering or picking up whatever it was that the factories made.

"That's Titania Carbonics over there," Shep said. The Carbonics buildings were all the same – five stories tall with a series of smoke stacks on each roof. The stacks alternated between sucking in the air – capturing the carbon dioxide in flexible polymer lungs – and letting out the by-products, which were oxygen, water, and some ozone. The polymer lungs sat on top of the buildings. They looked like the kind of bellows that were used back in those archaic times when homes were heated with fireplaces. The lungs inflated and deflated every few minutes. The Carbonics factory produced multiple carbon-based products – reinforced cables, plastics, filters, concrete, inks – anything that could be made with carbon. Other industries in the colony were allowed to vent their carbon dioxide directly into the colony atmosphere. Levels were maintained so that the overall carbon dioxide produced was equal to the amount consumed. Excess carbon dioxide could be vented outside the dome, but this was something to be avoided, since shipping in fresh atmosphere was expensive.

The kids walked a few blocks further, until they stopped at a local store for a drink. It was a run-down place. A layer of dust seemed to cover every item on the shelves. An old, wrinkly, and sickly-gaunt Martian expatriate sat slumped in a chair behind the counter. A faded flag hung on the wall behind him.

"Hey kids, welcome to Tom's Place."

"Hi. That's a flag from Mars."

"That there is the Free Martian States. Those stars along the top of the flag are all the colonies on Mars. The four stripes along the bottom are the orbits of the first four planets. The black line across the third stripe is the symbol for our independence from Earth."

They'd studied it in history class. The Free Martian States had been overrun by Earth almost five-hundred years earlier.

"Were you there?" Balraj asked.

"Was I there? Was I.... Wait, how old do you think I am?"

"I can't tell."

"Well I was there. Not only was I there, but I was one of the poor ones. The ones who didn't have the benefit of all that anti-aging technology stuff to keep us all supple and soft and young looking." He stared off into the distance. "There's not many of us left now. A lot of us died in that war. And those that were left, without the medicine when we were young, we just don't live as long, most of us." He rubbed his chin. White stubble peeked out from between the wrinkles. "Five hundred and, uh, twenty years. Good genes I guess." The trio just stood there, looking at him – a relic. "Alright, are you gonna stand there or do you want something?"

"Oh, just some drinks," Balraj replied.

"Well tap your hands on the scanner so you can register. Then take whatever you like and it'll get billed to you when you carry it out. Pretty high-tech for an old guy, eh?"

They tapped their fingers against the console on the counter. It read their biometrics and displayed their basic info for the shopkeeper – name and credit balance. They picked out some drinks and some snacks. Balraj got a Titania Cola and some chips. Shep got an imported Coke, which was an Earth luxury item. Bailey grabbed an ice-pop and a pack of cookies. As they left the store the system detected what they carried out and took the money from their personal credit accounts.

A little ways down the road, the three kids found a hill to sit on. From that hill they could see most of the buildings up to a few kilometers away.

Balraj sipped on his Titania Cola. "I'm so glad I came."

"I told you. You could be at home, or you could be here, looking down at half the colony," Shep said. He took a drink of his Coke. "I don't know why you bought a Titania."

"Umm, your Coke is like triple the price, Shep. How can you afford it?"

"I save up for it."

Bailey shook her head. "You two are too much. You know there's really no difference between the two. It's all the same company."

"I know, but the recipes are different."

"Sure."

They settled in and relaxed. Overhead, the stars were slightly visible through the colony dome and the rings around Uranus glowed faintly in the sky. They sat, looking up, munching on their snacks, and enjoying their drinks. They noticed a faint red light stretching from the ground up to the sky.

"Guys do you see that?" Bailey asked.

"What?" Balraj asked.

Bailey pointed at the sky. "I'm talking about that red light, over there."

Balraj looked to where Shep was pointing.

"Oh, I see it. Is that a laser?"

"That's what it looks like to me."

"Looks like it's coming from the weather observatory."

"Maybe they're doing some sort of Uranus weather experiment with the laser."

Shep jumped up. "Oh, I almost forgot, I have my binoculars with me." He pulled them out from his shoulder bag and peered through them, pausing on a faint red beam in the sky. He followed it downward, until he reached the ground. "Hey, yeah, it's the weather observatory." He adjusted the focus. "I think I see someone." He zoomed in more. "Yeah, I have a clear view. There's someone there with a tripod."

"Hey, let me look," Balraj said. Shep passed the binoculars to Balraj. He traced the laser down to the ground, focused, and zoomed in. "Yeah I see him." Balraj zoomed in more. "He's wearing all black. I think he has a beard."

Shep took the binoculars back from Balraj and looked again.

"Yeah, it looks like a beard. I guess he works at the observatory."

"Let me see," Bailey said. She snatched the binoculars from Shep. "Oh, I see him. Yeah, he probably just works there."

"Yeah, probably. I just never knew that they used lasers at the observatory."

"Another thing you don't know, Shep."

"Wow, thanks Bailey."

They got tired of watching the man with his laser and started talking about other things – like who was the best ballplayer in the colony. They sat for a while longer, until they had finished their snacks. Then they packed up their garbage and continued on their adventure.

"In another fifteen minutes we'll be at the Arcade," Bailey said.

Balraj smiled. "Oh, I love the Arcade."

"I'm going to play poker," Shep said.

"Do you even know how to play poker?"

"A little. I've tried some online games."

"How much is the starting bet?"

"Not sure. But I think there's a free table at the Arcade, for beginners."

"That sounds like a smart way to start," Bailey said.

"Yeah. I don't want to just waste my money."

"At least not at first."

"Gee Bailey. You're always so sarcastic."

"Not always. Just around you."

Shep headed straight for the free tables as soon as they arrived at the Arcade.

"You guys know where to find me."

Bailey and Balraj wandered around together. There were all the old classics – fishing games, mole hitting games, shooting games – and a few newer games specific to the colonies, like Colony Raider, Independence Fighter, Astro Chicken, and low-G bowling. There were rows of stalls with merchants selling imported goods like Amish silk from Mount Sinai II, furniture from Earth, and cats from Epsilon Eridani.

They had just finished browsing the stalls and were heading back toward the games area, when the building started shaking. A few seconds later, a loud thundering sound arose and then quickly subsided. Bailey and Balraj took off running to find Shep. There was no weather on the colony, so thunder never happened. Something was seriously wrong.

7

ABOARD S.C. APPLEGATE, IN ORBIT OVER TITANIA

ARCHIVIST'S NOTE: *The Ojibway word 'miigwech' is recorded as being used with some frequency among English speakers beginning in the early twenty-first century. The practice began in Canada when that nation grappled with its genocidal past and had begun a long process of embracing its Indigenous peoples and cultures. Miigwech, which means 'thank you', became used by non-Ojibway in the same way that non-Italians use 'ciao' — as a drop-in replacement for a word. The practice is more widespread among Canadians, who have adopted dozens of Indigious words into every-day English.*
    --Ashley Chung, Archivist

"Fuck! Come about!" Jeremy Bach screamed. The pilot turned the ship toward an unknown vessel that had just launched a missile at Adriana colony. It had just come in from the far side of Titania less than a minute before. They were in the process of attempting to open communications with the ship when it had fired on the colony.

They had just finished their turn when Smitty yelled, "Incoming chaff! Hard to port!"

The pilot spun the Applegate to the left as quickly as he could and fired the engines to start it moving away from the chaff. About five seconds later the barrage of chaff passed behind the rear of the ship. A few pieces impacted the ship's armor plating, but most of it sped by harmlessly.

"We're hit!" Smitty yelled. "Wait. We're okay."

The pilot fired thrusters, steadying the ship after the impact as it spun slightly on its axis.

"Turn and fire lasers," Jeremy said.

The pilot spun the ship back, keeping it on-course.

"Ready now, Captain."

"Fire!" Captain Bach yelled. The beam launched toward its target. Suddenly they all realized that the target had vanished. "What the fuck! Where did it go? Did they flash?"

"Captain, it's gone." Smitty brought up an x-ray spectrum view on the screen. "Look at that trail. They went superlight just as we fired."

"Well that's fucking great."

"The chaff was a delay tactic to give them a few seconds to flash away. Hold on... we're receiving multiple messages from Adriana colony. They've got fires."

"Mister Mulligan, put us in low orbit right over the colony. Keep the lasers powered up in case they return."

The Applegate turned and its engines throttled up, sending it toward the colony. Once it got to the correct altitude, it spun around so that the main guns were pointed out into space.

"I'm running a trace on the x-ray field," Smitty said. The computers scanned the space in front of them for x-ray remnants and began to run different scenarios. "If we're lucky we'll be able to tell what direction the ship was headed when it flashed away."

"Good thinking."

Jeremy scanned through the messages originating from Adriana colony. Most of them were meant for the other colonies, Lucetta and Bona. Among the jumble of messages was a distress call from the Governor of Adriana Colony:

This is the Adriana colony on Titania. We've been attacked from space. There are multiple fires in the city. We request help from anybody who is able to assist. We need firefighters, doctors, and medical equipment. If you're able to assist, contact Adriana port traffic control for landing clearance.

Jeremy put the main radio display on the screen. He typed in the contact details for Adriana's traffic control. After a few seconds a voice came through on the loudspeakers.

"This is Adriana port traffic control. Go ahead."

"This is S.C. Applegate – Captain Bach here. We're in low orbit over the colony now, in case the attacker returns."

"We see you on our scanners S.C. Applegate."

"I can send down a shuttle with supplies and personnel. We can be down there in twenty minutes."

"Miigwech. We really appreciate it, thank you so much," the traffic controller said. The line went silent for a moment, except for some background murmuring. "Captain Bach, I'm holding bay twenty-nine open for you for the next hour. Land as soon as you're ready."

"Roger that, traffic control. S.C Applegate out."

"Smitty, I'm taking a team down to the surface. You're in charge while I'm gone."

"Right, Captain."

"Smitty, do you think I can take twenty people with me?"

"Half the crew? I don't think we need all hands. They won't be back."

"If they do come back, do you think you can handle them?" Jeremy asked.

Smitty nodded. "Sure, we're combat certified for as few as 10 personnel. So yeah. But I really don't think they'll be back."

"You seem pretty sure of that."

"Chaff isn't the kind of thing used by someone who wants a fight. They did what they came for – whatever it was – and now they're gone."

"That makes sense. You've got more experience than I do in these areas."

"That's why I'm here. Now go get your shuttle loaded up. Hopefully by the time you get back I'll have finished figuring out where they were headed."

"Okay, let me know when you have something. I'll let you know when we're unloaded on the surface."

Jeremy pressed the elevator button. A few seconds later the doors opened and he walked off the bridge. Smitty went back to work. He brought up a tactical interface on one of the screens beside him, just in case.

* * *

"Captain, this is our entire supply of adrenaline. And morphine. And burn patches," Doctor Smith explained. He pointed at the two crates of medical supplies that sat on a sled on the hangar floor behind him. "If something happens up here we won't have anything for the crew."

"When was the last time something like this happened? Five hundred years ago, right?"

"More or less," Doctor Smith replied.

"Okay, so let's do what we can to help out."

"Fine. I suppose you'll want me to go down there too." The doctor folded his arms and his biceps pressed against his shirt sleeves. Most men from Eridani had thicker than usual muscles and bones because of the higher gravity on their colony.

"Yes, but you won't be alone. I'm going with you, and I've got another fifteen volunteers on the way."

"Volunteers. Right."

"Something bothering you, Doctor? This is what we do."

"No, no, it's fine. It's just that..." Doctor Smith paused and rubbed his hand through his hair. "We're emptying out the ship for people we don't know, which is fine, except we're putting ourselves at risk."

"I know that. But we're the closest thing to real emergency help that's out here. So we're going down and we'll do our best."

"Okay, Captain. Alright. I'll finish packing and load up the shuttle."

Jeremy nodded and Doctor Smith went back to work.

Several of the crew walked into the hangar Jeremy looked at the entire team – Doctor Smith, two medics, an engineer, a Mechanic, and ten marines – a total of seventeen including himself.

"Okay, now that we're all here, let me just take a minute to reiterate our job. Adriana has been attacked. A single missile was launched at them by an adversary who then fled. We don't know the full extent of the damage, but the colony government reports multiple fires. We're going to go down there to help in any way that we can. The engineer and Mechanic are going down because we have to make sure structures are safe before we enter. The medics will be with Doctor Smith. Marines, I'm relying on you to provide assistance to the Doctor and the engineers wherever required. We'll know more once we reach the surface. Let's help the colony, and make them proud of Stellar Corp. Let's go."

Jeremy walked into the shuttle. The rest of the crew followed. The sleds of supplies were loaded and the side hatch was sealed. Jeremy sat down at the pilot station and activated the radio. One of the marines sat at the co-pilot's position beside him.

"This is Applegate shuttle, requesting permission to disembark," Jeremy said.

"Shuttle, this is S.C. Applegate. Permission granted," Smitty said over the intercom.

Jeremy activated the departure program. The hangar doors opened and the shuttle lifted off and flew out of the hangar.

"Good luck, Captain Bach."

"Good luck, Captain Smitty."

As they got closer to the colony, they could see smoke rising in the center of the city. Several ships were flying in from the other colonies. The shuttle activated its communication protocol once they were within range of Adriana's port, bringing up a line with Adriana's traffic controllers.

"This is Adriana port traffic control, go ahead," the traffic controller said.

"This is Applegate shuttle. May we have permission to land at landing bay twenty-nine?"

"Permission granted Applegate shuttle. Proceed, and, uh..." Again there was murmuring on the other end of the connection. "Uh, Applegate shuttle, a team is going to meet you at the landing bay to escort you to the attack site."

"Understood traffic control."

A small group of men waited for them at the landing bay. The first one stepped forward toward Jeremy and raised his hand – it was more a wave than a salute.

"I'm Chief Volaris Gollari. The Governor asked me to meet you and escort you to the attack site. My staff can help you unload your shuttle. We have a truck waiting just outside."

"Thank you, Chief Gollari. How bad is it?" Jeremy asked. His marines were already at work unloading the supplies onto dollies. Volaris' men went over to assist.

"It's bad, and call me Volaris. The weather observatory is completely destroyed and at least five buildings around it have collapsed from the shockwave. There are several others that look at risk of collapse as well. There are also multiple fires, mostly from ruptured gas lines."

"That's not good at all. Hopefully my engineering team and medical team can help. If there's anybody to rescue... or dig out.... Whatever it takes, whatever we can do to help."

"Thank you, Captain. As soon as the truck is loaded we'll drive straight there."

Once the last of the supplies were loaded they drove away from the port. Volaris pointed to pillars of smoke rising in the distance.

"The atmospheric scrubbers are working at emergency capacity, and the carbon-sequestering factories are running at full tilt. They're just dumping raw carbon powder into the street right now so they can make room to absorb more. We'll worry about what to do with it all later."

"How long can they run like that?" Jeremy asked.

"A few days. But Lucetta and Bona are sending additional scrubbers, and we'll have them set up later today. That will give us some more, um, breathing room, ah, no pun intended, to get the fires out."

"That's good news."

The truck abruptly stopped. A smoldering piece of metal was sitting on the road. The truck reversed to the previous intersection and went a different way.

"There's bits of debris all over the colony. So far they haven't caused any significant damage, so we're focusing our effort on the immediate area around ground zero," Volaris said. They continued down the road toward the impact zone. There was debris scattered on either side of the road. "We're only a few kilometers away now. Looks like the road has already been cleared for us. Probably the first response teams."

The damaged buildings became visible as the truck turned the corner. The four or five buildings closest to them had lost all their windows. Further down the street there were several smoldering piles – buildings that had collapsed from the shockwave. Those piles formed a kind of ring of rubble, and in the center there was a crater about twenty feet deep where the observatory had been.

Volaris pointed at a trailer, about fifty meters down the street, that people were coming and going from. "That's the command center. And over there are the search & rescue tents. We'll unload here. Your doctor can take his supplies to the search & rescue tent."

"Doctor Smith, take the medics and five marines with you," Jeremy said.

"Okay, I'll get to work. Let me know if you need me." The doctor began unloading supplies from the truck.

"Volaris, I suppose we should go to the command center."

"I was just going to say that. You'll be able to speak with the site commander there. I'll introduce you."

They walked over to the command center. The engineers and Mechanic followed behind them. The five remaining marines took up the rear, towing the non-medical supplies behind them.

"Governor Shull, this is Captain Bach, from the S.C. Applegate," Volaris said.

"Captain!" the Governor declared excitedly. He jogged toward him from the other side of the trailer. "I'm so grateful for your help. Miigwech! I hear you brought medical personnel with you."

"Yes, they're already at work. I've also brought engineering and mechanical expertise."

"Great. Great! We've had a tough time with the buildings closer to the attack site." He turned to Volaris. "Deputy Chief Gollari, would you help the engineers get set up? Show them which buildings we're trying to secure."

"Certainly, as long as it's okay with Captain Bach, I'll take his men and get them started."

Jeremy turned to his engineering team. "Go ahead. Let me know if anything needs my attention. Take three marines with you." The engineer, the Mechanic and the three marines left with Volaris.

"Captain, our space port control told us that you were fired upon by the ship that attacked us?"

"Yes, they launched chaff at us."

"Chaff? That's an odd tactic."

"It is. It turned out to be a great way to buy themselves some time before flashing to superlight."

Governor Shull learned closer to Jeremy.

"We should talk in private."

"Of course. Marines, please wait outside." The marines saluted and left. There were some people at the other end of the trailer, but nobody was within earshot. Still, the Governor spoke quietly into Jeremy's ear.

"I don't know who to trust. Something seems wrong here."

"What do you mean?" Jeremy asked.

"This ship, it comes out of nowhere, fires a single rocket at a weather observatory, and then runs. Right?"

"That's correct."

"So this single building was attacked. Why?"

"I don't know. It doesn't make sense."

"Exactly. Something is going on here."

"But what?" Jeremy asked.

"The timing is strange too," Shull said. "It's Sunday afternoon."

"What's strange about that?"

"The observatory was closed today, and most people in this neighborhood were already out at the market. There have been very few casualties so far."

"That's a good thing."

"I agree, but the timing of it is either a lucky coincidence or it was planned this way."

"Planned this way?" Jeremy asked. "Do you think someone here on the colony could have been involved?"

"Maybe. At least someone who knew the best time to make their move if they wanted to minimize deaths."

"Hmm. What can I do to help?" Jeremy asked.

"Look around, see if you can find out what really happened here. I'm hoping I can trust you. I have to trust you. If this involves people from the colony then I have to be careful."

"All right, I'll go talk with my team and we'll let you know what we find."

"Thank you, Captain Bach."

Jeremy walked out of the command center. The two marines were waiting outside.

"You two stay with me at all times from now on. Let's go find Doctor Smith."

They walked down to the Search & Rescue tent. Doctor Smith was checking on a patient, the medics were changing bandages, and the marines were helping to clean up the area.

"How'd it go?" Doctor Smith asked.

"Can I talk to you in private, when you're done with your patient?" Jeremy asked.

"Sure, I'm actually finished now." The doctor put his hand on his patient's shoulder, and said, "Keep your arm in the sling for the next two weeks. Take it off to sleep and bathe. After two weeks go back to your regular activities, but don't lift anything too heavy at first. Take it slowly."

The patient left.

"So?" Doctor Smith asked.

"Notice anything strange?"

"Other than the crater in the middle of the colony? No."

"The governor is worried that someone in the colony was involved. He thinks the timing was too good to be a coincidence – most of the people in the area were at the market at the time."

"Now that you mention it, there aren't a lot of injuries or casualties."

"Exactly. With an explosion this size...."

"That's true. Maybe it's just luck."

"Maybe. Keep an eye out for anything strange. Keep it between us. Oh, and keep the marines near you, just in case."

Jeremy walked out of the Search & Rescue tent and went over to the Engineering and Mechanical area. The engineer was looking at blueprints of buildings and comparing them to live structural scans. The Mechanic was looking at electrical and robotic schematics of the city infrastructure. The marines were leaning against a long table. They stood at attention when they noticed Jeremy enter.

"Relax, guys. Any luck?" he asked.

The engineer – John Dvorak – handed a data tablet to the Captain. "We've completed scanning seven of the damaged buildings. Two need to be demolished, the rest can be repaired."

"That's good news."

"Now take a look at this." He tapped an icon on the tablet, and the display changed to a topographical radiation map. "David discovered this. David, you can explain this better than I can, could you come over here?"

David, the ship's Mechanic, came over and pointed to the pad. "This is a plot of the impact zone and everything within two-hundred meters of it. See the red areas? Those are traces of carbon-14. The warhead was nuclear."

"Nuclear? You're sure?" Jeremy asked.

"Absolutely, that's the only kind of warhead that creates carbon-14."

"Okay."

"But look at the area outside of the impact zone. There's no red – no carbon-14."

"Well that doesn't make sense. Radiation doesn't just stop like that."

"It doesn't. Someone either cleaned it up – which you can't do in only a few hours, or there was a force-field used at the time of the blast."

"A force-field? Who raises a force-field just before an attack like that? You'd have to know when and where it was about to happen."

John Dvorak traced a circle on the screen around the impact zone. "The destruction was worse near the impact zone because the force-field contained the blast. It kept most of the energy locked up inside it." He zoomed out to a wider view of the colony, and drew another circle. This larger circle was about twenty-five percent the size of the colony. "This is how far the damage would have spread without the force-field. That force-field saved a lot of people."

"Have any of you talked to anybody about this?" the Captain asked.

"No sir, nobody."

"Okay, let's keep it that way. Something's not right here. We don't know who was involved. Keep collecting what you can, and we'll decide what to do later. Don't talk to anyone. Keep the marines close."

"Got it."

"I'm returning to the ship. Make sure to let me know when you're on your way back."

Jeremy got a drive back to the space port, accompanied by two marines. Once in space, he turned the shuttle toward his ship, and radioed ahead.

"S.C. Applegate, this is Applegate shuttle, requesting permission to dock."

"*This is S.C. Applegate. You have permission to dock.*"

"Miigwech, S.C Applegate. Tell Smitty that I need to speak with him right away. And get a pilot ready to take the shuttle back down. I don't want my people down there any longer than necessary."

8

ABOARD HORATIO STATION

Ashley Chung was sleeping soundly in one of the small glass-walled private rooms in the infirmary. Doctor Poisson could hear her snoring, even through the walls. He was busy preparing his notes on the incident – he was required to report any drug overdose to Stellar Corp. His report included all the details of her medical history, all of the scans that he ran on her, and detailed logs about the station's own drug inventory. Phenobarbital was available on some of the colonies, but the fact that it wasn't stocked in the infirmary led the Doctor to the only possible conclusion – that it was smuggled onto Horatio Station. He specifically mentioned this in his report.

Lauressa Tajiki was in the Research Centre, scanning through the ship manifests and itineraries that had been sent over by Steven Wang. Some of Ashley Chung's vomit was on the floor – thankfully it was far enough away that she couldn't smell it from where she was sitting. There were a few hundred ships to review, each with its own itinerary and cargo manifest. This was going to take all night – or longer. Lauressa tried excluding any ship that wasn't scheduled to be at Oberon in the prior twenty-four hours. This cut down the list of ships to a few dozen. Then she realized that just because a ship didn't have Oberon on its itinerary didn't mean it couldn't be the ship in question. Any ship could have flown in from anywhere and gotten itself blown up. She'd have to go through all of the ships in the Hamlet Customs Brokers itinerary, one by one.

Lauressa scanned each itinerary line-by-line, looking for anything that seemed out of the ordinary. Everything looked normal, and after the fiftieth ship and eight hours of searching, she began to doubt that this method of investigation was even worth it.

The sensor logs! Why didn't I think of that first? Horatio Station's sensors recorded all ships coming and going. There could be hundreds, or even thousands of ships in the logs for just one day. But at least it would eliminate the cargo ships that hadn't arrived that day. That would narrow the search down tremendously.

The Commander loaded the sensor logs onto her primary display. She started with the past week of logs – over ten-thousand ships had come and gone in that time. She narrowed the data down to just the past twenty-four hours. Twelve-hundred ships. The ships were categorized by type – based on their size and shape as detected by the sensors. There were more than ten military frigates – the kind designated with an "S.C." in front of their names, a few dozen local patrol vessels, and hundreds of various types of cargo ships, passenger transports, luxury liners, and diplomatic and trade vessels.

Lauressa narrowed down her search further by excluding everything that wasn't a cargo ship. The list was now down to two-hundred-twenty vessels. She ran a comparison against all of the ships on the Hamlet Customs Brokers itinerary. All accounted for. Every ship that was supposed to be at Oberon in the past twenty-four hours had arrived without incident. She ran the comparison in reverse to look for ships that the sensors had picked up but that weren't on the itinerary. Nothing out of the ordinary – no mystery ships to be found.

This didn't look promising. All the ships were where they were supposed to be and they were all on the itinerary. Lauressa hunched over and put her head in her hands. *When was the last time I slept?* Some time the previous day it seemed. She looked at the clock on the wall and figured she'd been awake for more than twenty-four hours at this point. She needed to rest, but she needed to make some progress on this. *The first person to fire on another ship in seventy-five years?* That took precedence over sleeping.

She stared at the display for a few minutes, almost falling asleep. Then, Lauressa noticed something peculiar about the display. It had all of the cargo ships on it, and each new arrival was time-stamped accordingly. The quantity of ships arriving followed a pattern, a kind of an ebb and flow. It worked out to a ship every five to ten minutes. But there was an oddity. There was a gap between two of the ships of about a half-hour. Lauressa zoomed in on the gap. It was probably just an abnormally long lull in cargo traffic. Just to be sure, she had the system display all ships, not just cargo ships. But the gap was still there. It seemed as if not even a single ship had arrived during that time – which was just not possible. There was a hole.

Something had happened to the sensor logs. But there weren't any extra ships on the Hamlet Customer Brokers itinerary. What's going on? Lauressa queried the computer for suspicious activity. The computer's security logs did not report anything odd. They had just installed new real-time sensor backup software a few days earlier. She checked the size of the backup for that hour – it was 10 Petabytes. But according to the current logs, there were only 7 Petabytes of data. Someone had definitely deleted information, even though the security system didn't know it.

Lauressa began a data restore operation, which the computer indicated would take four hours. Well thank God for backups. She went straight to her bed and set an alarm for four hours later. She passed out as soon as she hit the pillow. She started to dream about Steven Wang. Damn it! He wouldn't leave her alone during the day and now she had to deal with his unwanted advances at night? This wouldn't do at all. She tried to convince herself to wake up in her dream. But she was so tired that her body wouldn't let her. Instead, Wang began to caress her arm. He soon moved down to her thigh. Oh no! Lauressa found herself making mad, hurried love to Wang. She loved it, but she felt dirty and disgusted at the same time. He was so revolting to her, but still she loved onward, harder and faster. It went on like this for thirty minutes or more, until the dream faded away into a deep sleep.

* * *

Doctor Poisson was enjoying a nap on the couch in his office. He had sent his report to Stellar Corp and was waiting for their reply. Dealing with a drug overdose was stressful – now add on top of that dealing with the various crew who came in with their own stress due to the whole ship-blowing-up incident, and the Doctor was a little on edge. So instead of actually going to bed, he had decided to just recline on his couch and drift in and out of sleep as his anxieties nipped at his mind. He heard someone walk in.

"Doctor?" Ashley asked.

The Doctor opened his eyes. "Oh, hi there, Ashley. How are you feeling?"

"Better, I think. How long have I been asleep?"

"The better part of twelve hours."

"Wow, I must be a mess."

Doctor Possion smiled. "I've seen worse, don't worry about it."

"My stomach is upset."

"It's probably a bit of a hangover. Come, sit here. I'll get you some soup to eat. It should help settle your stomach."

Doctor Poisson left the room for a few minutes. Ashley reclined slightly on the couch with her eyes closed. She leaned her head back against the wall. The Doctor came back with the soup. He stopped at the doorway and watched her for a moment. She was pretty.

"Ashley, here you go."

"Oh, thanks, Doctor," Ashley said. She swallowed a spoonful of the soup. She waited a few seconds to make sure she felt okay, and then took another spoonful. "This is good. Oh wow, I'm hungry!" Ashley finished the rest of the soup hurriedly. "Oh, that hit the spot."

"You don't have to stay here now. You can go back to your quarters. But make sure to rest for another twelve hours."

"I'd feel better if I stayed here for a while. So why are you sleeping here?"

"I can't sleep. It's been a stressful day, so I was just lying down, trying to de-stress."

"I hope I didn't cause all this stress."

"I'm concerned that someone has been possibly running around the ship drugging people – and I'm glad you're okay. Also a ship got blown up, which frankly has everyone stressed out, and they're all coming to me."

"Oh, that's no good, you need to rest. Why don't you sit down?"

Doctor Poisson sat on the couch beside Ashley. She looked at him. She reached out and put her hand gently against the side of his face.

"Thank you."

"Ashley. What..."

She ran her hand through his hair. "Handsome man."

He didn't think of himself as handsome, although he'd heard gossip to the contrary. Doctor Poisson closed his eyes. This wasn't proper. He wasn't supposed to allow this kind of behavior. But she was quite lovely. And he had been alone for some time. The feeling of her hand against his skin felt electric. He couldn't help himself. He reached out with both arms and embraced her and drew her in close. Her body felt hot against his.

They made love – deep, slow, love. The couch could barely fit the two of them sitting side by side, but somehow they now had more than enough room to do as they pleased. They became entwined: her thighs pressed against his waist and their arms wrapped around each other's backs. She was admirably athletic for someone who had just recovered from being drugged.

Afterward, Ashley said 'thank you' again, and went into the glass-walled room to rest. The Doctor reclined on the couch. A smile grew across his face. He fell into a deep sleep, still smiling.

9: Educational Material

A Brief History of the Labian Empire

ARCHIVIST'S NOTE: *Labian culture is in some ways quite different from what we see as 'normal' in human cultures. Much of this is due to their extreme circumstances. However, some of our reactions to their social order may say more about us, than about them. This is especially true when we read about their history of violence, including sexual violence, as presented here.*
-- Ashley Chung

The Labian Empire began as a colony on one of the moons of Gliese 832b. The colony was established around 2575, during the first wave of multi-generational colony ships that reached out to dozens of stars within 20 light years of Earth.

The colonists adhered to the belief that humanity would be perfected through genetic engineering. They began the process on Earth and continued it during the 75 year trip to Gliese 832b. Four generations of children were born - each stronger and healthier than the last. Muscle mass, bone density and neurological resilience were all increased. Most common medical issues, such as hardening of the arteries, had been eliminated from the population.

And so, the first generation to arrive at the colony was suited to the intense manual labor required to build their new home. These colonists survived and thrived, and went on to build the largest and most populous colony outside of the Sol system. The colonists excelled at science, art, and feats of physical prowess.

Around 2605 the colony introduced a fatal genetic modification: one of the new planned genetic improvements had an unintended interaction with another previous modification. A generation of babies was then born with a virus embedded in their DNA. The virus was carried by the female babies, but it spread rapidly throughout the entire population. All males were killed within days.

The Labian scientists struggled to find a cure, but they were unable to remove the virus. Attempts at doing so resulted only in children with severe mental handicaps. Older women who did not have the modification were also, sadly, unable to have male children, since they had also become infected with the virus. And so, the colony was reduced to being only female and being able to give birth to only females.

The Labians were forced to find men from other colonies in order to become pregnant. These men would invariably get sick, though they would eventually recover from the effects of the virus. The children from these pairings were always female, and unfortunately always carried the responsible viral DNA, which resisted attempts at being bred out of the population.

Word of the illness eventually spread, and in time people avoided mating with Labians. Stellar Corp placed a quarantine on the colony, and Stellar Corp employees were forbidden to consort with Labian females on or off of the colony. Spurred by fear that the viral DNA could spread to other colonies, as well as a practical issue of not wanting their soldiers to be sick and unfit for duty, the quarantine was rigorously enforced.

The Labians learned to become stealthy in their approach to mating. Some began to take jobs as strippers or prostitutes, in order to seduce men, and would then flee as soon as they had mated. The men would show symptoms a short time later, but too late to do anything about it.

This strategy was inefficient, and the population kept shrinking until it had become dangerously low.

Out of desperation, the Labians turned their physical superiority to their advantage. They deployed a series of raiding parties to the four nearest colonies around the other planets in the Gliese 832 system. They went into the homes of the colonists and forced themselves upon the men. They went in pairs, so that one could hold back the man's wife when necessary (which was often), or help hold down the man when necessary (which was not often).

Their physical perfection meant that few men put up more than a token show of resistance for the sake of plausible deniability.

"Dear, I'll just lay down here until they're done. For your sake," was the common sentiment. "To keep you safe."

One practical problem was that the men became desperately ill and useless to their wives for about a month afterwards. Therefore, the Labians became despised by the women of the colonies. The men had decidedly mixed feelings about the whole thing.

(N.B. *This depiction is based on historical interviews of the men at the time, and from our contemporary perspective, we may find it odd or disturbing. It is possible that they reported their experiences in this way to 'save face' during a time when men were expected to always want sex, and to admit otherwise was to appear to be weak.* -- A.C.).

These raiding parties occurred on a monthly basis. Calls for help were sent to Earth. However, due to the speed of interstellar communication, it would take around 16 years for a message to get to Earth, and around 30 years for the fastest ships to arrive with military support (if they arrived at all).

The Labian population quadrupled within a few years, each woman having an average of 4 daughters. This created a different problem – a lack of genetic diversity since the size of the other Gliese 832 colonies was small. The scientific minds of the Labians set out to find a solution, and found it in the invention of faster-than-light travel in 2655. This allowed them to take ships to planets outside of their own system. They traveled to the four nearest colonized systems. These colonies had no defenses, and so were easy targets to find new breeding stock.

After twenty years there were four times the number of adult women of child bearing age, and there was not much for them to do. Around this time, the leadership saw that it should be a priority to hone their stealth, combat, and raiding capabilities. They put more women into combat training and built up a sizable research program on weapons and ships.

The local colonies and four distant colonies were now suffering quadruple the number of raiding parties. Virtually every man was 'used' every few months. The economies of the colonies began to collapse, due to a lack of healthy labor. They became dependent on the Labians for food and supplies. The colonies existed now to serve only the needs of the Labians.

The leadership realized this, and by the end of 2675, the Labian Empire was born. For some unknown reason, the leadership adopted old Latin terms to describe themselves. The Emperor called herself Imperatrix. Leaders who had driven the raids on the different colonies added the colony names to their last name. For example, a Leader named Sarah Jeffries who had commanded the raids on Lacaille 8760 now gave herself the honorific name Sarah Jeffries Lacaillus.

The Empire went undisturbed until the invention of superlight travel on Earth. It was after this that Earth finally answered the calls for help with a military response – over 75 years after the first calls had arrived. In 2730, a task force of four ships arrived at one of the colonies. The Labians were ordered to withdraw by the authority of the United Nations Stellar Corp.

The Labians ignored this order, and were fired upon by the Earth ships. The Labian ships – of which there were only 2 – destroyed three of the Earth ships within minutes. The fourth retreated via superlight. Several more battles like this took place, each time resulting in Earth ships destroyed, or disabled, and their crews taken captive for mating purposes. This series of battles has been termed The First Labian War.

However, Earth learned from these losses, and it wasn't long until they were able to create ships fast enough and with weapons powerful enough to match the Labians. In one final battle in 2740, which is now called The Second Labian War, Stellar Corp attacked all four colonies simultaneously, and pushed the Labians back to their home system.

These colonies were introduced to interstellar commerce via superlight. The Labians had a change of leadership and gave up on their ambitions of dominance. The Empire had fallen.

The Labians still needed to reproduce, and so they adopted a new strategy – payment.

During the days of the Empire they had built significant wealth. Now, men were offered the chance of a lifetime: live for a year among the Labians in the lap of luxury; have a different strapping young Labian woman on your lap daily; receive massive doses of medication to keep the virus symptoms to a minimum; and try to tolerate the constant stream of young, fertile warriors.

Each year a few thousand new men would take this contract, and twelve months later they would leave, worn-out but satisfied. And pampered like kings.

This is how the Labians function to this day.

- From the Files of Ashley Chung, Archivist

10

Labia Minor, on Gliese 832c

"It has been three hundred and sixty-five years since our defeat at the hands of the men of Stellar Corp," Consul Shauna Lone said to the assembled Senators. "Three hundred and sixty-five years of being limited to our system alone. Three hundred and sixty-five years of paying – paying! men for the privilege of mating with us. Beyond the borders of our little Gliese 832 system we're a laughing-stock. We're a joke. Do you know what the latest joke is? I'll tell you: A man, a woman, and a Labian walk into a mechanic's shop. The mechanic sees the Labian and shoots himself. That's the joke. We're the strongest and most beautiful women in the galaxy. But now we're a joke. It's time we did something about it."

Proconsul Reanne Jensen Lacaillus pounded her desk and laughed.

"You're such a drama queen Shauna," Proconsul Reanne said. "The women of Gliese 832 are happy and at peace with the world. We get up in the morning and watch the sunrise. At night we survey the stars. During the day we make pottery, paint, run, play tennis, wrestle, and do archery. We take our turns with the hundreds of men that we host, and honestly we take turns with each other sometimes too." There was some muted laughter in the Senate. The Proconsul smiled. "Can you blame a girl? We are the most beautiful women in the galaxy, after all. But a joke? No, we're not a joke, and we don't miss the old ways."

Shauna Lone stood up, bringing her lean six-foot figure to its fullest height.

"Pottery? Painting? Look at me. Does this body look like it's meant for leisure? Our ancestors built us to be strong, intelligent, and energetic. Those ancestors – a few of whom are still alive and here in the gallery watching today – wanted us to be powerful; to be warriors and rulers. Not a girl, as you just called yourself. What we've become is a shadow of the promise and hope that they've invested in us."

"Yes, you are beautiful. I love how your hair flows over your shoulders, by the way. You're chiseled. You're young. You're a living statue. You also lack experience. Look at me," Reanne said, standing up and displaying herself to the Senate. "My hair has greyed (it used to be chestnut like yours once) and I'm not quite as chiseled as you are – age has a way of doing that – but I'm still strong and I'm still powerful. And I wear the Labian toga with pride. The Empire of our youth is behind us. We've matured, we've learned some lessons, and we've moved on. Things are better now. No war, no dying, no suffering. And what's wrong with that?"

"What's wrong, Reanne? What's wrong is you learned some lessons and then you stopped. Our defeat ended the Empire and our self-respect. We've stopped growing, we've stopped reaching higher, and we've stopped trying to become more than we are. We're stagnant, Reanne. We need to expand. We need living space for our desires."

"Living space? Many men in history have used ideas like that to do all kinds of horrible things."

"We're not men. We're better. We're women. We're Labians. Three hundred and sixty-five years of Republic has gotten us nowhere. I move to vote now, to end the Republic and bring back the Imperial system. Who will second my motion?"

A voice from the back of the room announced, "I will."

"Who will vote with me?" asked Shauna. A dozen yays called out.

"Who will vote against me?" Shauna asked. A chorus of nays filled the Senate, larger and stronger than those of her allies.

"You need to relax Shauna. As you can see, the vast majority of the Senators enjoy peace."

"It's unfortunate.... You're relieved of your duties."

"What? That's a poor joke, Consul Shauna."

"I'm not joking. You're relieved. Guards!"

The doors to the Senate swung open and dozens of armed women ran into the room.

"Escort Proconsul Reanne to her apartment, and keep her there. Same for the rest of them," Shauna Lone said. The guards forced the Senators out at gun-point, except for the dozen that had voted in her favor. Shauna Lone walked over to the ceremonial throne, which was occupied by the Speaker of the Senate, the white-haired Sarah Jade Gliesus. "Your dedication to the old Empire and the Republic is respected by all. But we don't require a Speaker anymore. You may go home, or stay to watch. However, that is my seat now."

The Speaker got up slowly and reached for her cane. Her back was hunched and the skin on her hands was drawn tight around the bones. "I hope you know what you're doing," she remarked. She put her hand on Shauna's shoulder. "It wasn't as Romantic as you imagine it to have been."

The speaker hobbled out of the Senate. Shauna Lone sat on the throne.

"After living aimlessly for far too long, the Labians have a purpose once again, and an Imperatrix to lead them. We will be respected once more," Imperatrix Shauna Lone said.

11

The Arcade, Adriana Colony, Titania

"What's happening?" Bailey asked. The windows of the Arcade had shattered and people had fallen everywhere.

"I don't know," replied Balraj. "That was loud, and huge. Maybe the Carbonics factory."

Through the broken windows they could see the sky. It was getting darker. "What's that, a cloud?"

"I think it's smoke. That's not good," Balraj said.

"Hey, where's Shep?"

"I don't know. He was... he said he was going to look at the cats from Eridani."

Bailey raised her hands and shrugged. "I don't know why people love those cats. They're *just cats*."

"They're cute, and soft, I guess. Let's go find him."

Bailey and Balraj walked toward the other side of the Arcade, toward the booths that belonged to the dealers from Epsilon Eridani. Some merchants were straightening up their booths, and sweeping away glass. Some were helping customers – or being helped – and tending to scrapes and bruises.

As they got near the cat dealers they saw cats wandering everywhere. They had gotten out of their cages.

"Here, kitty," one of the dealers said. He was holding out a treat, trying to coax one of his cats to come to him.

"Do you know what happened?" Balraj asked.

"No, kid. But it sure felt like an explosion." The cat dealer looked under a table at a cowering kitten.

"No way. There's too many safety protocols, on everything. Our teacher told us there hasn't been an accident in something like a hundred years," Bailey explained.

"Well, that's what it felt like. Felt just like when the cat food plant blew up back home."

"How could a cat food plant blow up?"

"Nitrogen, apparently. They were importing it as fertilizer, to put on the crops that they use to make cat food. The whole pile just went up one day. Boom!"

"I don't think there's that much fertilizer on Adriana."

"Is that so. Hey, can you kids help me round up my cats?"

"Sure," Balraj said. "But we have to find our friend first, then we'll be back."

They moved on, through the different dealer's booths, looking for Shep. They called out for him, but heard nothing in response. Then, after a few minutes – after they'd got close to the windows – they heard a voice calling back.

Shep called out, "Over here." His voice seemed weak.

They started running toward him. They found him sitting against the wall. "Oh no!" cried Bailey. "What happened?"

"When the rumbling happened I went to the window to look. Then the window broke all over me." Shep turned his head slightly. He had cuts everywhere. There were a few shards of glass sticking out of his skin.

"We have to get you help, hold on to us." Balraj and Bailey each took an arm and hoisted him up. "Let's go, we'll get you help."

They guided Shep outside. A large cloud of smoke was growing and moving toward them slowly. The dome over the colony reflected an orange glow.

"Fires," Balraj said.

Injured people were all around, sitting or lying on the sidewalk. The uninjured tended to them, mostly cleaning wounds and talking to them. There seemed to be mostly cuts and bruises, but a few people appeared to be more seriously hurt.

Emergency vehicles were racing by, but not stopping to help the injured. They all headed in the direction of the smoke.

"What do we do?" Bailey asked.

"I don't know. This is bad. Nobody's coming to help," Balraj said.

"Can I sit down, guys?" Shep asked. They helped Shep sit down on the sidewalk. They sat on either side of him and propped him up.

"Thanks guys. I feel weak."

"You'll be okay," Balraj said. "I have my handheld with me, I'll see if I can call my mom."

Balraj pulled out his handheld, and entered in his mom's number. Nothing happened.

"This was supposed to be a no-handheld adventure. But try my parents' number," Bailey said. This got the same result — nothing.

"Communications must be down."

The three of them sat on the sidewalk, along with all of the other injured or confused people. There didn't seem to be anybody who could help, or anybody in charge. Meanwhile the cloud of smoke was still growing.

A security guard from the Arcade came outside. "Everyone, please come inside. There's been an explosion. We'll be safer inside." He was waving his arms, motioning for them to come in. "The communications network is down, so I've called for medical help on my emergency radio, but they won't be here for a while. I have some first aid kits inside, and food and water."

Balraj and Bailey helped Shep up and moved him back inside. The other people came in too. The less injured helped the more seriously hurt.

The security guard began to hand out first-aid kits. "We've got five kits. Please share them."

Bailey went to get what she could. She brought back some gauze, a sterilized towel and some water. "We'll clean your face up. The water might hurt."

Bailey poured the water across Shep's face. It washed away some of the blood and dirt and the smaller pieces of glass. Shep cringed.

"You'll be okay. It's not looking as bad, now that it's cleaner," Balraj said.

"But we have to pull the glass out," Bailey added.

Shep started to cry. "Oh it's going to hurt. Okay, just do it."

Bailey grasped the first glass shard and pulled. It came clean out. Shep's breath quivered. She took hold of the second piece and pulled. It was crooked, and it tore at his skin.

"Oh Bailey, oh Bailey!" he cried.

"Sorry Shep, hold on." She wiggled the piece of glass and it came out. "There."

"Any more?" Shep asked.

"Two more," Bailey replied.

"I want Balraj to do it."

"Okay."

Balraj pulled out the last two pieces of glass. They came out cleanly. "All done," he said. "I'm going to clean your face again. Hold on." Balraj poured water over Shep's face. More blood and dirt and tiny flecks of glass gave way. Shep was shivering.

"You're okay, Shep," Bailey said. She took off her jacket and put it around him.

"Am I? I feel cold."

"You're fine, you're just scared." Shep just looked at her, unblinking. "You're okay. Okay?"

"Okay. Can I lay down?"

"Sure."

Shep laid back and put his head on her lap.

"Thanks."

The deeper cuts were oozing, but it didn't look as bad as before. Balraj's hands were covered in muck. He wiped them on his pants.

"You're pretty tough," Balraj said.

Shep smiled and looked up at him with heavy eyes. "Tougher than you. But I don't want to do that again."

"Okay champ, I'm going to go look for some food for you."

"Get something sweet. It's supposed to help," Bailey said.

"Okay. I'll be back."

He took off toward the security guard.

"Can I have some sugary food for my friend? He's shivering and weak."

"Sure kid. Sounds like he's in shock. Keep a close eye on him."

"Okay."

The guard handed Balraj a small wrapped item.

"Here, take this. It's mostly sugar. It should help. I don't have training for this, but come get me if he gets worse."

"Thanks, where are the medics?"

"All gone to the observatory."

"The observatory?"

"Yeah, that's what I gather from the chatter on my radio. The observatory is gone. Just gone."

Balraj was confused. He stood beside the guard. He could see the big cloud of smoke through the window. It was ominous, and almost at the Arcade.

"Hey, go give that to your friend. I've got other people to deal with."

Balraj snapped out of his inaction and ran back to Shep.

"I have a snack here. Shep?"

Shep raised his head slightly.

"Oh, thanks." He took it and tried to unwrap it. His fingers were clumsy and heavy. "I can't..."

"Oh, here. Bite a piece off," Bailey said. She took the treat, unwrapped it, and held it near his mouth.

Shep took a piece and slowly ate it. Balraj handed Shep some water. He was able to hold the bottle and drink on his own. He took another bite, and another, and another.

"I'm starting to feel better. Less weak. My head doesn't feel all noodley."

"That's good. The sugar counteracts the stress. That's what I've read," Bailey said.

"Help me sit up?"

Balraj took one of Shep's arms and gently pulled, while Shep pushed himself up with his other arm.

"Thanks. Thanks guys," Shep said. He started to cry a little.

"It's okay Shep. You're fine," Bailey said. She hugged Shep, careful not to touch his face.

"Thanks. Okay, I'm okay."

He could smell her hair. It smelled good.

"So, what the hell happened?" he asked.

"I talked to the security guard," Balraj announced. "And he said the observatory is gone."

"What?"

"It's gone, he said the whole thing is gone."

"That guy with the laser. I wonder if he was there?"

"Who knows. I think we're stuck here for a bit. All of the ambulances went that way. Who knows how long until someone comes to help."

Shep smiled. "You know, on the way to see the cats, I passed by a booth with some home medication products. Think they have carbonic bandages?"

"I'll go look. That would be great!" Balraj said. He jumped up and ran off in search of the booth.

"Bailey..."

"Yeah Shep?"

"You smell nice."

"Uh.... Stop smelling me!" Bailey yelled.

"Okay, fine. I was just making it up anyways."

"Oh, thanks!"

She was just about to push him, but realized that he'd probably just fall over and cry in his current state. A few minutes later Balraj returned.

"I found some! Here, I'll put it on you."

He sat down in front of Shep and squirted a bunch of the carbonic bandage into his hand. He then dipped his fingers in it and applied it to all of the cuts on Shep's face.

"Ouch! That stings."

"Yeah, but it will be healed by tomorrow."

"Yeah, dad put it on me before, on my knee when I fell and cut it open on a jagged rock. There's no scar or anything. But I still don't like the stinging."

"It probably won't sting for long," Bailey said. Shep smiled at her.

"Yeah, it's already starting to feel better. So now what?"

Balraj pointed out the window. "Let's stay here for now. It's not safe outside."

The smoke cloud began to pass over the Arcade. Smoke came in through the shattered windows, but it wasn't too thick to breathe. The security guard came over.

"You kids stay on the floor, the air will be easier to breathe down there. We're patching up the windows." The guard walked off toward a group of men at the windows. They were putting up plastic sheeting and had already made their way around most of the building, but smoke was still getting in.

One of the vendors walked over and handed them three mouth inserts.

"These are scrubbers for colonies with bad atmospheres. Just put them over your mouth."

The vendor walked over to the men patching the windows, and handed them some scrubbers as well.

"This is great. I'm covered with cuts and now I have to put this thing on?" Shep asked.

"I'll help you," Balraj replied.

"No, I can do it." Shep pulled the scrubber out of the box. He stretched the elastic bands around his head and secured it over his mouth and nose. "Oh, that stings!"

"You look awesome."

"Better than you... Oh great, now we sound all deep and muffled."

"At least we can breathe okay," Bailey noted.

"Yeah that's true. So, now we sit around?"

"Yeah. It'll be a big walk to get home with all this smoke and debris and stuff. I'm fine with waiting until the smoke gets better."

"Okay," Shep said.

"Okay," Balraj said. "Hey, I saw some board games at one of the tables. We can play something while we wait."

"Sure, but I might be a little slow. I'm still not feeling super awesome."

Balraj went and found a board game – Astro Chicken Adventures – and the three of them played for a few hours. It was a game meant for little kids, but it was better than nothing.

12

Aboard S.C. Applegate, in Orbit over Titania

Captain Jeremy Bach looked up when the doors to the meeting room slid open. Doctor Smith, head engineer John Dvorak, and David the Mechanic walked in and gathered around the tactical table. A photo of the impact zone, taken from the ship, was projected onto the table.

"Welcome back, let's get started. I've been reviewing what we know with Smitty," the Captain said. "David, go ahead and present your assessment on the carbon-14 you found."

David pressed a button on his tablet computer. A topographical map appeared on the surface of the table.

"This is the radiation map that I showed the Captain earlier. See how the carbon-14 only exists within this circular area? We found strong evidence of gamma and x-ray burns within the impact zone."

"People?" Smitty asked.

"Cats," David said.

"Cats?"

"Yes sir, cats. A lot of people have been buying cats from the Eridani traders. They had just set up in the market in the past few weeks."

"And they were burned."

"Burned right up. Third degree burns over their entire bodies. Not from heat. From ionizing radiation. And their bodies are somewhat radioactive now."

"That's just sad. Were they all within the impact zone?" Captain Bach asked.

"Almost all. We also found some cats and people with burns just outside the impact area, but only within a few meters of the force field."

"There's that force field idea again. Are you sure?"

"I'm pretty sure of this."

"So am I," John Dvorak added. "It's the only thing that fits the pattern. Here, take a look." He touched his tablet computer. New data appeared on the table, overlaid on the map. "These dots are where all the burned cats were found. Inside the impact zone, all dead from burns. But look at this." He added another set of data onto the map. "These are all of the cats and people with burns outside of the impact zone. All within less than thirty meters from the impact zone, and all minor burns."

"Nobody died outside of the impact zone? No cats? No people?" Smitty asked.

"No sir. Outside the zone we only found minor burns. First degree at most, and only within that thin thirty meter ring. Beyond that, nothing."

"I think you're onto something. If the burns were severe just inside the impact zone, and then were minor literally on the other size of the street – well that doesn't follow the laws of physics. Radiation doesn't just drop off like that, unless something is blocking it."

David laughed – "ha ha!" – and then paused. "Sorry. This is just exciting. I mean, it's not exciting as in 'fun'. This is serious business. It's exciting, as in, 'we're on alert and trying to figure out what's going on, and we're in the middle of something huge'. That's what I mean by exciting –"

David realized that everyone was staring at him. "Sorry, I'll shut up."

John touched his hand-held computer again.

"This is an overlay of different kinds of force fields," John said. Concentric circles of different sizes appeared on the map. "There are three different force fields that match in terms of size and transmissive properties."

"Which transmissive properties are you selecting for?" Smitty asked.

"You know a lot about force fields, Smitty?" the Captain asked.

"This is right up my alley. I spent my youth in mining and colony construction. Two jobs that rely on force fields."

"We selected for three properties," John began. "Physical impact resistance, radiation transmission, and rigidity. First, if we look at physical impact resistance, we know that it had to be virtually totally resistant to physical impact, since there was no carbon-14 or any other material that got thrown out of the impact zone. Second, when we look at radiation, less than ten percent of the radiation that reached the edge of the impact zone went beyond it. At least based on the severity of burns, ten percent is a reasonable assumption."

"Or less. The burns outside the force field were more like sunburns. Nothing to worry about. It's the shock-wave that really caused the injuries outside of the impact zone," Doctor Smith explained.

"That's the third piece. The shock-wave. There's a large area of shattered windows, cracked building frames, and blown-over signs. This force field wasn't rigid enough to keep all of the energy in without flexing. So when the explosion hit the force field at full speed, the force field flexed rapidly outward and then back inward, causing a shock wave outside the impact zone that moved outward in all directions."

"This all sounds like a small ship-mounted force field," Smitty said. "A colony builder's force field would be too big, too powerful. But a mining ship would have a force field that's just about the right size. In mining we're worried about small asteroids and solar radiation. That's about it. We aren't worried about attack. We don't need the kind of resistance to radiation or physical impact protection that you would need if you were concerned about when the next attack on your colony is going to happen."

"A mining ship force field is one of the three that match. The other two are types of portable tactical defensive force fields – Stellar Corp issued," John said.

"Stellar Corp force fields are hard to come by, so it was probably taken from a mining ship. But where is it now?" Captain Bach asked.

"Captain?" David asked.

"David."

"I think that it's underground. The shape of the carbon-14 and the impact zone are both identical. The force field had to be underground, right under the exact place where the bomb was planned to be detonated."

"Wait, it could still be there. We need to find it," Smitty said.

"It's not safe. The explosion damaged a lot of the infrastructure in the area. Our survey shows some deep underground tunnels that survived, though they could collapse at any minute. But, we could send a robot. I have a conduit crawling robot that we could use. We just need to be at the tunnel entrance and we can remotely control it from there."

"If we can find the force field unit, then we might be able to trace it back to its owner. Or at least the person who owned it before it was stolen from them," Smitty said.

"Okay, we'll go looking for it. Now what about the weapon they used?" Captain Bach asked.

"We know it was fired from that ship," Smitty replied. And it was a missile, not a bomb. According to the sensor data it had maneuvering ability."

"That doesn't make a lot of sense. Nuclear missiles haven't been manufactured in at least three hundreds years. They're not exactly common," David added.

"So that's not something you want to just shoot for no good reason. You probably aren't finding a replacement."

David looked at the data on his hand-held, and said, "You know, based on the radiation profile and the yield, this could be a really old weapon."

"How so?"

"It appears that the amount of x-ray and gamma rays are high, relative to the size of the blast. So this was a small blast, and it was fission only. No fusion."

"You've been reading up on nuclear weapons?" Jeremy asked.

"I studied the history of weaponry at the Technical Academy," David said. "Anyways, the nuclear weapons manufacturers switched to fusion-only weapons nearly five-hundred years ago. They made a bigger explosion and produced very little radiation.

That made for a better weapon at less size and cost than could be done before. So this missile could be five-hundred years old, or older."

"So we've got a five-hundred year old missile and a force field unit from a mining ship. And they decided to blow up a weather observatory. What the hell. It just doesn't make sense," Smitty said.

"And Governor Shull said he suspected something, and that he didn't know who he could trust," the Captain said.

"Maybe he's just paranoid."

Doctor Smith shook his head. "I'm not so sure. Something is wrong with that Volaris guy. I don't like the look of him."

"You don't like the look of anybody at first," Smitty said.

"Well that's true. But something really doesn't sit right with me about him."

"Hold on there doc, just because a guy looks like –"

The Captain interrupted. "We don't know if we can trust anybody. Let's see if we can get down there and go look for that force field unit."

"Well, good luck. The computer should be finished by the time you get back. It should have figured out the most likely origin and destination of the attacker," Smitty said.

"Good, good. We'll go looking for that ship as soon as we get back then. David, get your robot ready. We're going to sneak down to the surface as soon as you're prepped."

13

ABOARD HORATIO STATION

Commander Tajiki hit her head against the table. Not hard. Just lightly, out of tiredness and frustration.

Fucking backups! What's the point of backups if you can't read them after recovering them? The backups took several hours to recover, and then... Nothing. No way to read or view them. Just a big hunk of useless binary. Lauressa had tried everything that she knew to try: text file viewers, binary editors, log parsers, but nothing helped. Finally she asked the station computer to analyze the file. It told her that she had to take the entire station mainframe off-line in order to re-integrate the backup into the live system.

But if she did that then Horatio station would be vulnerable – basic systems like life support and short-range sensors would work fine, but everything else would be inoperative. They'd be blind to the world beyond about 5 kilometers, for however long the recovery would take. An hour? Longer? *I shouldn't do this. But I need to.* Lauressa needed engineering help. She went to the bridge.

"Mister Hauer, can you call the head engineer up here?" She asked Wayland.

"Yes, Commander.... Oh, she's not here. She's on leave for the next month. The acting head engineer is Petty Officer Davis."

"Petty Officer? How new?"

Wayland brought up the engineer's personal information.

"Just graduated last month. Transferred here to relieve the head engineer."

"I was sent a totally green engineer to replace... well that's stupid. He won't be at all familiar with the station systems. Are there any other engineers? Maybe with a little experience?"

Wayland did a search and retrieved one name.

"Dr. Poisson has an engineering degree."

"Really? Why didn't I know that?"

"I don't know, but he's been the station doctor for ten years, and this was from when he was younger. From a hundred years ago, when he... well this is interesting: he trained here as an engineering student, during the station's construction."

"Really? That's quite a convenient coincidence. Can you ask him to meet me at the Research Center please? I'll be down there."

Commander Tajiki made her way to the Research Center. She stopped briefly in the cafeteria on the way.

Lauressa was nursing a coffee in the Research Center when Dr. Poisson walked in.

"Hi Lauressa," Doctor Poisson said.

"Hi Doc, how are you? Oh, and how is your patient?"

"Oh! Oh... she's okay. Fine, fine."

"Good. You always take good care of your patients."

"Thank you – so what did you want me to meet you here for?"

"Okay, so here's the thing, I understand you're an engineer."

"Well, I do have an engineering degree, but that was a long time ago. I'm no longer certified."

"But you're familiar with the station. You did some of your training here."

"Yeah, I did. I had an internship and I shadowed one of the engineering teams during the construction."

"Good, that's why I'm hoping you can help me."

"With engineering."

"Yes, I need help with recovering some sensor backups. The computer says I'll have to take most of the stations' external functions off-line to do the recovery."

"That's the new backup system. I have no experience with that. But I'm pretty familiar with the internal mechanics of the rest of the station."

"That's good, because I need those backups."

"Okay, we'll need to check the Manual Room."

"The what?" Lauressa asked.

"The Manual Room. You know, the room with all the manuals.... Follow me," the Doctor said. They left the Research Center and took an elevator down to the station's bottom floor – sublevel zero.

Sublevel zero looked incomplete. The ceilings had no drop paneling and the walls had exposed beams. There were bits of wire hanging in random places and all of the doors were unmarked except for small numbers on them.

"This is disgusting," Lauressa complained as she brushed a dangling cable away from her face.

"You've never been down here?" Doctor Poisson asked.

"No."

"These are the bowels of the station, in a way. It's not meant to look good and it's cheaper to leave it unfinished."

She followed him down the hall, around a corner, and then around another corner.

"Here we are. Let's go," Doctor Poisson said.

He pressed a button on the wall and the doors slid open. A dark space opened before them. The Doctor stepped through the threshold and lights began to flicker on. Rows of shelves became illuminated one at a time. First the row closest to them, then every row one at a time after that. The room looked like a library. The shelves were completely filled with printed paper manuals.

"Welcome to the manual room," Doctor Poisson announced with a flourish. "Good luck," he added. He turned as if to leave.

"Woah, you're not leaving me here!"

"No, of course not. I'm just kidding. This place is kind of overwhelming, eh?"

"Just a little," Commander Tajiki said.

"Let's get started, I'll show you how to navigate the shelves."

"This is enormous. Is that *paper*?"

"Hard copy. But not exactly paper. It's fireproof, cold resistant, radiation proof, and really hard to tear."

"But why so much?"

"It's everything you'd ever need. Every schematic, every documented valve, conduit, and pipe. Every replacement part down to the bolts. It even has a hard copy to reprogram the computer for basic functions in case of a total failure."

"That sounds impractical."

"In a big way. But the bureaucracy required it at the time."

"I've never seen anything like this before."

"I suppose most people haven't."

"So what do we do now?"

"We retrieve the data we need."

Dr Poisson went to a console with a keyboard.

"We can access any document from here. This computer instructs the robotic system to go to the appropriate book and return it to us. We just need to reference the index."

He pulled out a gigantic book from underneath the console. "What are we looking for?"

"How to shut down the mainframe so that we can restore the logs."

"Ok, let's see. Mainframe," Doctor Poisson said. He flipped to 'mainframe' then scanned down multiple pages. "Shutdown.... Here it is."

Dr Poisson typed in the code provided by the index. A whirring sound could be heard as the robot moved across the room, then up one shelf. It grasped hold of a book and then traveled to the console.

"Here we go. Mainframe Shutdown and Recovery Procedures."

The manual was a few thousand pages.

"Oh great. I just need those logs recovered," Lauressa said. She sighed at the sight of the thick manual.

Doctor Poisson flipped through the pages.

"It's not that bad really. There's about a hundred pages of actual procedures. The rest is troubleshooting in case there's a problem. We can do this."

"Alright then, where to now?"

"We can do it all from the mainframe room. Easy."

"Okay, we can..." Lauressa's voice trailed off.

"Lauressa?"

"Huh?" she asked absently.

"Okay Lauressa, you're wiped out. You need to get some sleep."

"But we need to–"

"No buts, get some sleep. You're useless if you fall apart."

"I'm responsible, I need to–"

"Give it a break. You've got nothing to prove, now go and get some rest. I've got to review this manual anyways, so take advantage of that."

"Alright. Fine. I'll take a nap."

The Commander and the Doctor left the Manual Room. They made their way back through the industrial jumble of sublevel zero, then went their separate ways. Tajiki went straight to bed. She felt like she didn't need any sleep, but as soon as she sat down she passed out.

Dr Poisson returned to the infirmary. His patient had left. There was a note on his desk. It read, "Dinner?"

A light was flashing on his display. It was a message from Stellar Corp: Drug overdose report reviewed. No further investigation warranted.

* * *

Lauressa slept hard for five hours, until she was awakened by the alarm she had set. She felt groggy and struggled to sit up. She had been dreaming. *What was it about? Wang? Great.... You dream about a guy you don't even care about. Get that guy out of your head, Lauressa! And don't worry about it, it's probably just because you're so tired anyways.* She walked over to the mirror. Her hair was bunched up at the back of her head, and quite frizzy. *You look amazing, like you've just spent the last month working in a mine.* Lauressa had a quick shower. She put on a tiny bit of makeup, just to cover the circles under her eyes. She unsteadily got dressed and went down to the cafeteria for some more coffee. She took a sip of the coffee. The hot, bitter drink made her feel slightly less exhausted. But her head still felt like it was stuffed with cotton balls. Still, it was an improvement.

Lauressa went into the infirmary. Dr. Poisson was pacing and mumbling to himself. His face was red.

"What happened?" Lauressa asked.

"Those fucking douche-bags think they can tell me what to investigate?"

"What? Who told you–"

"Those assholes at Stellar Corp!"

"Okay, calm down. What did they do?"

"Take a look for yourself," he said. He turned his display toward her. "Look at that!"

Lauressa read the message ordering the doctor to not investigate any further. "This doesn't make sense," she said.

"Damn right it doesn't make sense! Not a bit of sense! How can they tell me to drop it like that?" he asked, his voice shaking.

Lauressa didn't answer.

"A person was poisoned by a drug on my station, Lauressa."

"I know."

"On my station. I'm the Doctor. I'm responsible for her, I'm responsible for securing the flow of drugs. Someone smuggled it in. Could have killed her. And I'm supposed to just drop it?"

"No," Lauressa said.

"Damn right, so what the fuck is wrong with Stellar Corp?"

"I don't know."

"I'm going to get to the bottom of this one way or another. Nobody drugs someone on my station."

"Okay. Let's just keep it between us, okay?"

"You don't think I should file a protest?"

"Why bother. Why rouse the bureaucrats? Anyways, as long as I'm in command I have the final say. So we'll just look into this together and see what we can find."

"Thanks Lauressa," Doctor Poisson said. He took a deep breath. The red in his cheeks receded. "Those idiots back on earth think they know better.... Alright, just the two of us. Speaking of the two of us, I've reviewed the manual. Ready to give the backup recovery a try?"

"Sure, let's do it."

Lauressa and Doctor Poisson left the infirmary. They went down a few levels, and then walked toward the center of the station. The Mainframe Room was circular and ten meters tall. Catwalks ran around the room at different heights to provide access to various levels of server equipment.

"According to the manuals we can do everything from there," Doctor Poisson said. He pointed toward some consoles in the center of the room.

They each sat at a console. Lauressa logged on and brought up the backup systems. The backup file was in front of her on the screen. Doctor Poisson logged into his console, and brought up the Mainframe controls. A text-only interface appeared, where he could type in commands manually.

"Okay, this should be really simple. I'm going to shut down enough of the mainframe systems for you to start the recovery. Ready?" Doctor Poisson asked.

"Ready."

Doctor Poisson entered the first command: *sudo notify shutdown*

An automated computer voice spoke through the intercom. "The mainframe system is being shut down for maintenance. Please stand by."

Then the Doctor entered additional commands:

sudo shutdown external systems .... [shutdown complete]
sudo shutdown internal systems ... [shutdown complete]
sudo shutdown communications ... [shutdown complete]

The station was now operating on minimal systems. Life support, short-range sensors with visibility to 5 kilometers, and basic power were all that was on-line.

"Okay, you should be able to recover the backups now," Doctor Poisson said.

"Okay, here we go."

Lauressa asked the computer to begin the restore. The system notified her that it would take twenty minutes to complete. "That's not bad," Lauressa remarked. "Thanks for helping me with this."

"Of course. My pleasure."

"You know, how long have I known you?"

"Four years. We met the day you first arrived on the station, to take your command."

"We've spent so much time together, but I never knew you were an engineer. You think you would know someone after a few years."

"It's not a big deal, it was part of my youth, but it's not important now. I don't think it means you know me any less."

"Oh, that's not what I meant Doc. What I meant was. Well, with how long we live for, how many times can someone change their entire identity? We live so long, but a hundred years is still a hundred years. Am I the same person I was then?"

"You're in a philosophical mood."

"I was just thinking about it. Something that you did a hundred years ago, engineering, is coming full circle now. And I'm thankful for that. But I wonder if our past is something that will always follow us around, and the longer we live the more there is to follow us, and it can either be a godsend or a... or a real problem," Lauressa said.

"I don't know. I'm only a hundred and twenty five. I don't know if I have enough experience to say for sure," Doctor Poisson said.

"Well I've got you beat there."

"Oh that's right, you're one-hundred and eighty three."

"Shhh, you don't know who could be listening. I don't want people to hear that."

"Why not? You still look like you're thirty, or at least what thirty used to look like when age mattered. Are you feeling self-conscious?"

"No, not really."

"This isn't about us, is it?"

"Oh, no Doc."

"Good, because I'm quite happy that we're friends and all."

"Friends."

"Of course. I mean, those first few months were special. You know I was a little heartbroken when we broke up. But I think we're really better off for it. I really treasure our friendship, I really do. I don't think I ever told you that. So if that's what you're thinking about, you can stop worrying."

Lauressa smiled. *Here's a real gentleman, not like that damned Wang.*

"You're the best. I'm not worried at all," she said.

"Good. I'm beginning to think that the most important thing in life isn't passion, isn't love, isn't sex. It's friends. We can live forever, and the only way to survive that is with a true friend by your side. So there."

"Now who's philosophical," Lauressa said.

"You brought me there."

The two of them talked for a while longer. Then Lauressa's console beeped.

"The recovery is complete," Lauressa said.

"I'll bring the mainframe back online."

Doctor Poisson entered the commands to bring the systems back on-line:

    sudo start external systems .... [start complete]
    sudo start internal systems ... [start complete]
    sudo start communications ... [start complete]
    [error during communications start-up]

"Everything is back up, except there was an error during communication startup. Let's see what the troubleshooting manual says."

Doctor Poisson leafed through the manual.

"Oh, it says to restart communications."

"Just try turning it off and back on again? Okay, give it a shot," Lauressa said.

The doctor entered the shutdown command followed by the startup command:

    sudo shutdown communications ... [shutdown complete]
    sudo start communications ... [start complete]

This time there was no error.

"It's fine now, it must have been a transient error. I guess now that you have the data recovered you can go do that research," Doctor Poisson said.

"I'm going to do that now."

"Sounds good. I'm off to meet my dinner date. In the morning I'll start looking into Ashley's drugging in more detail."

"Sleep sounds like a good idea. I'm still exhausted, so as soon as I've finished looking at those logs I'm going to get some sleep too."

Lauressa and Doctor Poisson left the Mainframe Room. Lauressa went back to her quarters to pick up her coffee mug. While there, she made the mistake of deciding to rest for a few minutes on her couch.

Doctor Poisson went back to the infirmary. He sat at his desk, and pulled out a small makeup kit from the drawer. He flipped up the kit's built-in mirror, applied some concealer under his eyes, and then added a light dusting of foundation across his face to even out his complexion. He rouged his cheeks, put on some eyeliner to emphasize his eyes, and finally applied some tinted lip gloss.

Ashley walked in as he was placing the kit back in the drawer.

"So, you clean up nice. I've been thinking about you," Ashley said.

"I've been thinking about you too."

"What do you want to do for dinner?" Ashley asked.

"The cafeteria has some great Standard Portions."

"That sounds lovely. Afterward, if you're nice, I'll show you my cabin."

"That sounds wonderful, Ashley. I'm so happy to see you again," Doctor Poisson said. He reached out to Ashley and touched her hair gently. She pressed herself up against him and put her arms around him.

"Let's go," she said.

14

Aboard S.C. Applegate, in Orbit over Titania

"Ready to go?" John Dvorak asked. He was standing at the doorway of David's cabin. "Jeans? Good choice for blending in down on the colony."

"Thanks. And we're ready," David said. He pointed to the equipment case in his right hand. "Crawler hasn't been used in a while, so it's excited to be going." David left his cabin and they headed toward the hangar.

"Interesting. You're not the first Mechanic I've worked with who reads human emotions into his robots," John said.

"They're not human emotions, but I do get a sense of feeling from it. Like it's alive. Crawler's neural cells want new experiences."

"But it's still a robot. It doesn't think."

"I'm not so sure about that. I've seen them do things that they weren't programmed to do. There's a sense of self-preservation that some of them have. I've seen them retreat from a fire – literally turn and run. I've only ever seen that in robots with living neural cells. Never in traditional computerized robots."

"I don't know, David. But I'm kind of excited to watch it perform."

They entered the hangar, where Captain Jeremy Bach was waiting for them. Two marines were with him.

"Okay, we're all here. Let's be on our way," the captain said.

Jeremy walked into the shuttle and the marines followed after him. John Dvorak and David followed. John pressed a button on the inside of the shuttle and the hatch closed. Jeremy sat down at the pilot station and activated the communication system. One of the marines took up the co-pilot's position.

"This is Applegate shuttle, requesting permission to disembark," Jeremy said.

"*Shuttle, this is S.C. Applegate. Permission granted,*" Smitty said from the bridge of the Applegate.

The hangar doors opened and the shuttle lifted off and flew out of the hangar.

"This is Applegate shuttle, going dark," Jeremy said.

"*Acknowledged shuttle, go ahead.*"

Jeremy entered in the commands for stealth mode. The communications systems turned off entirely. Interior lights, exterior lights, and active sensors such as radar were all switched off. The shuttle was now invisible to most detection instruments. There was always a chance that they would be spotted visually, but space was so large compared to the shuttle that the risk was minimal.

"Uh, Captain, how were you planning to get through the colony dome without asking their traffic controllers to open it?" David asked.

"We're not going through the dome. There are suits and bikes in the storage compartment."

"We're driving in?"

"That's right. Hope you're ready for some off-roading."

Jeremy piloted the nearly-invisible shuttle toward the colony. He guided it to within a few hundred meters of the colony's edge, then set it down behind a large boulder that obscured it from the view of anyone inside the dome.

They put on their EVA suits, then inspected each other's suits for diagnostic issues. Next, the inside of the ship depressurized and the shuttle hatch opened into the almost-vacuum atmosphere of Titania.

They mounted their bikes, which had battery packs large enough to travel a few hundred kilometers. They drove the short distance to the colony dome, then followed the edge of the dome north.

"We should come across an airlock in a moment," Jeremy said.

They came to an old manually controlled airlock only a few kilometers away. Jeremy pressed a button on the airlock and the outer door opened. They rode in. Jeremy went to the inner door and pressed a second button. The outer door closed. Air was vented into the airlock, and the inner door opened. They rode into the colony and Jeremy signaled for them to stop.

"Let's get out of these suits. There's nothing more suspicious than a bunch of guys in space suits."

They removed their suits and stowed them in the back of the bikes.

"John, why don't you lead us to the nearest entrance to the underground tunnels," Jeremy said.

"My pleasure. This way."

John Dvorak rode at the head of the group. He led them about twenty kilometers, in the direction of the impact zone where the weather observatory had once stood. The entrance to the tunnels were a few kilometers north of the devastated area.

There was a ramp down to the tunnel entrance. A metal door secured the entrance to the tunnel. John drove down the ramp, and the others followed.

"This is a pretty good spot. Nobody can see us unless they're looking directly down the ramp."

David opened his utility case, and Crawler hopped out. Crawler fixed its lenses on him.

"Are you ready, Crawler?" David asked.

Crawler hopped once.

"Good. Just hold on a minute while I get a signal from your camera."

David adjusted his hand-held computer until the view from Crawler's lenses appeared.

"Okay, I've got you. Go ahead and go down that tunnel. Just run through and try to get as close to the impact zone as you can. I'll be watching, and I'll tell you if there's anything I want you to stop and look more closely at."

Crawler hopped, turned around on its eight legs, and started running for the tunnel entrance. It crawled through a vent on the bottom of the door and then stopped. It turned around and pointed its lens at David for a second, and then dashed off into the tunnel. David looked at John Dvorak, who shrugged.

They watched the video on David's hand-held computer. Crawler was moving quickly through the tunnel, faster than any human could move. It jumped or crawled over most obstacles. At one point it crawled up the tunnel wall to get over a pile of rubble.

"Van der Waals forces?" John Dvorak asked.

"Exactly," David replied.

"Just like a gecko. That's a good ability to have in tight spaces."

"Hold on, what's that?" David asked.

"What?" John asked.

"Crawler, go back," David said.

Crawler turned around and started to retrace its steps. A crate appeared on screen.

"Crawler stop. Go to that crate."

"What is that on the crate? A flag?" Jeremy asked.

The flag grew as Crawler got closer to the crate.

"That's a martian flag," David said.

"It sure is," John Dvorak said.

"That crate is a relic. I wonder how long it's been there," Jeremy considered.

Crawler got to the crate, crawled up one side, and peered inside. It was empty.

"Okay Crawler, false alarm. Back on course," David said.

Crawler turned and started running toward its original destination. It wasn't long until Crawler made its way to a large chamber which was centered almost exactly underneath the impact zone. Suddenly Crawler's lights turned off.

"Crawler, I don't see anything. Are you okay?"

A night-vision view appeared on the screen. Crawler began to transmit audio to David's handheld. Two figures, visible as red against a mostly black background, were moving on screen and talking.

"*Did you hear that?*"

"*I didn't hear anything.*"

"*I thought I heard something. And for a second I thought I saw a light, like someone's down here with a flashlight or something. Anybody there? Hello?*"

"I don't think there's anyone down here. They'd be all worried about the tunnels collapsing."

"I could swear."

"Look, let's just get the unit out of here, just in case it really is dangerous down here."

"Okay."

"Crawler, can you get a better image?" David asked.

Crawler moved forward into the open. The dull light of the two men's worklights were just barely enough to see them with. They were lifting a large object onto a motorized sled. It must have been heavy, because they were wearing portable exoskeletons to help with the lifting.

"That's a force field unit," David said.

"We need a better image. Can you get a good closeup? If we can get the manufacturer information or serial number we'll have a chance of tracking this thing down," Jeremy said.

"Crawler, I need a brighter image."

Crawler didn't do anything.

"Okay Crawler, try the infra-red light first," David said.

Crawler turned on an infra-red light, which flooded the men and the unit in non-visible light. Crawler switched back to night-vision mode, and now everything was clearly visible.

"Good Crawler. Now get closer. We need a really good view of the unit they're carrying."

Crawler crept forward slowly.

"Is it getting warm in here?"

"Yeah I feel it. Weird."

"They're feeling the infra-red lamp. Just a little bit closer, Crawler," David said.

Crawler moved closer. One of his legs snagged on something on the ground, and it caused a scraping sound.

"What the hell was that?"

The men swung their flashlights in the direction of the sound. They saw Crawler, which was standing motionless.

"A robot? Shoot that thing!"

The men pulled guns from inside their jackets and aimed them.

"Get out of there!" David yelled.

Crawler threw up a flash of light and then took off running. The flash startled the men, who fired wildly.

David watched as Crawler scurried down the long tunnel back toward them. The image on screen changed to a very sharp image of the men and the unit they were carrying.

"Great work David, look at that image. We can see the serial number," Jeremy said.

"I didn't do that. It was Crawler."

"No way, it's a coincidence," John Dvorak said.

"Look at the image. I didn't tell him to use his lights as a flash. He did it and got that image, and now he's showing it to us," David said.

"Maybe it was a pre-programmed crisis reaction."

"It's a conduit crawling robot. It doesn't have that kind of programming."

"The results speak for themselves. Crawler got us what we needed," Jeremy said.

David nodded, and said, "Good work Crawler. When we get back I'm going to take you on a walk around the whole ship."

The image on the screen switched back to a live view from the crawler's lens. A door was visible. Suddenly Crawler slid out from the vent, ran toward David, and jumped at him. David caught it in his arms. Crawler weighed only a little over a kilogram.

John Dvorak jumped back.

"What the hell?"

"I told you, the ones with living neural networks act... differently. Okay, go in your case, Crawler. We're going back to the ship."

Crawler walked into its case and powered down. David closed the case and picked it up by the handle.

"I'm ready to leave if you are," David said.

"John, care to lead us back to the shuttle?" Captain Bach asked.

"Absolutely, Captain," John Dvorak said. He hopped on his bike and started driving. David and Jeremy Bach followed. The two marines took up the rear.

There were no surprises on the trip back to the shuttle. The flight back to the Applegate was uneventful – they had not been detected. Upon their return, Smitty was waiting for them on the bridge.

"Captain Bach, welcome back."

"Thank you, Captain Smitty. You're relieved."

"Miigwech. It was fun, but command can get monotonous. Any luck?"

"We got very lucky, thanks to that conduit crawler. Take a look."

Jeremy went over to a large display and tapped a button on his hand-held tablet computer. An image appeared on the display.

"Crawler took this image."

"Wow, caught in the act. We can run those two guys through facial recognition," Smitty said.

"Good idea. Now look at this," Jeremy said. He zoomed in on the force field unit. "We can see the serial number."

"Let's run it right now," Smitty said. He recorded the serial number from the image on screen and entered it into the ship's computer. It searched the database and returned one result. "Look at that. From a mining ship. Registered to a company from Mars. More than five hundred years ago."

"Mars? Are you sure?" David asked.

"That's where it's from. Doesn't mean people from Mars are using it. It just means that's where they could have stolen or purchased it from."

"I hope so. A five-hundred year old force field generator from a mining ship, and a five-hundred year old nuclear missile...." Jeremy said.

"Extremists. We saw that old crate with the Martian flag down there," John Dvorak said.

"It's all coincidental right now," Smitty began to say. "We're talking about stuff that's five-hundred years old. That's not a reason to suspect —"

"My grand-parents died in that stupid war. I really hope it isn't the start of something like that again," John Dvorak said.

"We'll report what we've found to Stellar Corp. Just the facts. We're really just speculating on the rest," Captain Bach said.

A console on the bridge beeped, accompanied by a flashing icon on the screen.

"Speaking of facts, we just got some. The computer just finished calculating the attacker's likely origin and destination," Smitty said.

"Bring it up," Jeremy said. Smitty touched the display in front of them and a chart of the moons of Uranus appeared. A red dot flashed over Miranda, a small moon close to Uranus, lying just beyond its ring systems. "That's odd."

"It's what the computer thinks is both the origin and destination of the ship," Smitty said.

David touched the display to zoom in on Miranda.

"There's nothing there, it's too small, too close to the rings. John, what do you think?" David asked.

"I agree. I wouldn't build a structure on a moon that small, and so close to the rings. You're just asking for an accident. A stray asteroid from the rings. Or the moon gets hit, and if the impact is hard enough your whole structure gets ejected into space."

"We'll check it out. I'm going to report this to Stellar Corp. Let's head to Miranda as soon as we hear from them," Jeremy said.

Jeremy left the bridge. Smitty turned to John and David, and said, "Let's get this ship ready for action. Next time we run into an unfriendly, I want to make sure we're ready to unload a few lasers into their side. Let's go."

15

ABOARD HORATIO STATION

It was early morning on Horatio Station, about 5 AM on the station clock. Commander Lauressa Tajiki sat at a table in the corner, cradling some oatmeal and a coffee. About a dozen other crew were eating breakfast or just sitting quietly. She looked around. A man in the corner – she wasn't sure who he was – noticed her and did a half-wave-half-salute. Lauressa nodded and smiled, then turned back to her oatmeal. Things weren't going well, by her estimation. It had been twenty four hours (or was it forty-eight hours) and so far all she had managed to do was recover the logs. At least she had gotten a few hours of sleep. She finished her oatmeal and got up with some effort. The crew ignored her as she walked out, which was for the best. They all knew what was going on and they could see how exhausted she was. *This isn't good for my skin. Keep it together – I've got more important things to worry about than whether all this stress is prematurely aging me.*

Lauressa went down to the Research Center. She noticed that the vomit had been cleaned. *Did I notice it earlier when I met Doctor Poisson down here? I can't remember. At least it's gone.* The air held a faint citrus smell. She sat at one of the consoles and brought up the sensor data.

A dot flashed on screen where the recovered data had been re-inserted. Now instead of a gap of thirty minutes in the logs, she could see the typical pattern of continuous space traffic. Lauressa zoomed in on the log. She adjusted the display so that only cargo ships were visible during the thirty minute window. Five cargo ships had arrived during that time, and their identification codes had been correctly captured by the sensors. She compared these codes to the itineraries that Steven Wang had sent up from Hamlet Customs Brokers.

One ship stood out. According to Wang's manifest, it had arrived on-time in orbit. However, according to automated records transferred from Titania, it had arrived late at Titania by sixteen hours. They had offloaded their cargo on Titania, skipped shore leave, and then got to Oberon on time. This alone wasn't alarming – ships were sometimes late to one or more destinations, and adjusted their schedules to compensate. The alarming part was that of the five cargo ships that arrived at that time, four of them existed in further sensor logs. This ship, however, had just vanished. It was as if it had been blown out of the sky.

Lauressa set up a connection to Hamlet Customs Brokers. Steven Wang's executive assistant, Carol, picked up the line.

"*Hamlet Customs Brokers, Mr. Wang's office.*"

"This is Commander Tajiki, can you put Steven on please?" Lauressa asked.

"*I'm sorry, Mr. Wang is very busy, can I take a message?*"

"Go and tell him either I talk to him now, or I send some marines down there and arrest him for smuggling."

"*One second,*" Carol said. The line went silent for about ten seconds. "*I'm putting you through now.*"

"*Hi Lauressa.*"

"Wang," Lauressa said.

"*You didn't have to threaten me. I just told Carol I was busy, it wasn't aimed specifically at you.*"

"What are you busy doing?" Lauressa asked.

Steven sighed. "*You're always so suspicious. I'll have you know that I've been going through the itineraries, trying to figure out which ship I lost.*"

"I've found it. It was definitely one of yours. A ship named Bollox. It arrived only a few minutes before that cargo ship exploded, and it hasn't appeared in any of the sensor logs since. According to Titania's sensor logs it arrived sixteen hours late, did a quick unload, and then raced over here."

"*Hmm, ships can be delayed,*" Steven said.

"Of course. Under normal circumstances it happens and you wouldn't think twice. But that ship blew apart. So I have to investigate why they were late. I have to suspect that they were smuggling something volatile."

Steven brought up the manifest for the cargo ship. "I have the manifest here. Bollox was the ship, right?"

"Right."

"The manifest says they were delivering iron ore to Titania, and then loading some consumer goods to bring to Oberon. Titania cola and the like."

"Cola isn't very explosive," Lauressa noted.

"So you think they were smuggling something? Weapons? Explosive chemicals?"

"It makes sense, doesn't it?"

"It does. Lauressa, I wish we could talk about something other than this. When this is through I'd like to –"

"Wang... Steven. Look, I, uh. I can't think about this right now," Lauressa said. *Don't be so mean. Try to let him down easy.* "Once this is over, then we can have a chat, okay?"

"Okay, thanks. I know I can be a little much. After three hundred years.... Well, never mind. I'll let you get back to work."

"Thanks. Steven, be careful," Lauressa said.

"I'm always careful, I haven't made it this far by being careless. I know something is wrong here. Watch your back, okay?"

"I will. Okay, I'm off to report this to Stellar Corp. I'll let you know what happens next."

Lauressa disconnected the line between them. *Are you confiding in Wang now? He seems concerned though, and kind of sweet, for once.*

* * *

Lauressa spent the next hour or two compiling her report for Stellar Corp. She detailed the explosion of the cargo ship and explained how she had been forced to shoot down the wreckage. She reported on the missing logs, and that once recovered, it had indicated that the Bollox was the lost vessel. She recommended that they research its history, to try to determine if it had been smuggling anything.

Her answer came back thirty minutes later: Accident report reviewed. No further investigation warranted.

16

The Arcade, Adriana Colony, Titania

Bailey, Balraj, and Shep played Astrochicken Adventures for a few hours. They got tired. It looked like it still wasn't safe to go outside, so they had decided to sleep in the Arcade. They had made a makeshift bed out of rugs and quilts that they'd found at the stalls. The merchants didn't mind, since they were all stuck in the Arcade as well. Everyone was lending to everyone.

The kids slept under one of the dealer's tables, just in case some new explosion caused things to fall down around them. The sun came up, but it wasn't really the sun. It was the colony dome illuminating the colony on schedule. Dusty beams of light filtered into the Arcade. Balraj sat up and wiped his eyes.

"Oh man, I hope we can go home today. I hope I'm not in trouble."

Bailey opened her eyes and yawned.

"I'll bet your mom understands. Hey Shep, wake up," she said.

Shep was lying motionless on the quilts, face down.

"Shep, wake up. Are you okay?"

He didn't answer.

"Shep!" Bailey yelled. She started shaking him.

Shep woke up with a start and sat up.

"What? What? What's going on?" he asked.

"Shep!" Bailey said.

"Shep, your face!" Balraj said.

"Oh, no, what's wrong? Am I okay?"

Balraj laughed and hugged him.

"You're fine, your face looks almost completely healed!"

"Wow, that carbonic bandage stuff works pretty good," Shep said.

"Sure does."

Bailey touched his face. His former injuries were now smooth new skin.

"All better. Let's see if we can get out of here," she said.

Bailey went over to the nearest doors. She opened them and stepped outside. The area was littered with debris. But there were no sirens, and no emergency vehicles were driving by. There were faint wafts of smoke in the sky, but otherwise things seemed to be peaceful and quiet. She went back to her friends.

"Guys, it looks safe outside, I think we can go home."

"That's good. But let's get something to eat first," Shep suggested.

The three of them went to the food stalls to get some breakfast. There wasn't a good selection of fresh food, but there was still a surplus of freeze-dried meals and packaged treats. They feasted on ramen imported from Japan, drank Titania Cola, and helped themselves to sweet candies brought in all the way from Planet Fabulous.

They set off from the Arcade in search of a way home. They soon found that entire streets were closed. In fact, the normal route home to their neighborhood – past the industrial area and the Carbonics factory – was completely blocked. They'd have to take the long way around.

"This sucks," Balraj said.

"Hey, we'll still get home in pretty good time, it will just take twice as long because we have to go the long way around, through down-town," Bailey said.

"I know. I just know my mom is going to kill me."

"You worry too much. Your mom's going to be really happy you're alive."

"She'll be happy, and then she'll slap my head. Just watch."

"Guys, cut it out," Shep said. The other two looked at him with surprise. Shep was usually the instigator, but now he was complaining about their banter. "I'm still not feeling great. Can we just figure out how to get home?"

"Alright," Balraj replied. He pointed to the right. "Let's go downtown."

The trio walked for an hour or two, toward the middle of the colony.

They reached the center of downtown. Dozens of tall buildings – some more than fifty stories tall – were packed into a few square blocks. Some of them were office towers, occupied by businesses involved in inter-planetary and interstellar trade. Others were large apartment complexes, each housing thousands of residents. The buildings downtown housed about half of the population of the entire colony. They walked past these buildings; past the jumble of people going about their day. Most of them went by without noticing the kids. A few people smiled at them, perhaps curious at the sight of children in an area where few were ever seen. But mostly, people just went on with their own lives. What seemed strange about it all was that things seemed normal here, as if the attack from the previous day hadn't actually happened. Everything just seemed normal, except for the quiet: nobody was talking, not a single person. They were all going through the motions of their daily activities, but underneath the calm, hidden away, they must have been brutally scared about what might happen next.

They walked out of downtown, turned left, and started toward home. They were in a sort of "uptown" area. It was a mix of residential homes, retail, and small offices.

It was just about noon. They stopped for an early lunch at the Mars Diner. The inside was painted rusty-red. Adorning the walls were stylized paintings of imagined aliens, ancient film posters, and pictures of old Mars-related products. The whole place was a kitschy homage to an idea about Mars that had existed a thousand years ago. Bailey had a chocolate milkshake and some fries. Balraj had a mini-burger and onion rings. Shep had a sandwich with meat, cheese, and lettuce. They paid automatically as they left the restaurant.

They soon left the uptown area and walked straight into the center of Adriana Space Port. Large hangars flanked both sides of the street. The hangars had roofs that could open or close. Most of the roofs were closed, but a few were open. Some of the hangars appeared empty from their vantage point on the street, but a few had ships that were so tall that the tops were higher than the open roofs.

Every few minutes there would be a rumbling or humming sound and a ship would fly up out of one of the hangars or descend into one of them. As they walked along, they noticed a man standing by the door to one of the hangars. He was dressed all in black and had a black beard. His clothes were covered in dust or dirt, so the black outfit seemed more like a dark gray.

"Doesn't that guy look like the one we saw in the binoculars?" Shep asked.

Bailey and Balraj both agreed.

The man turned and walked into the hangar.

"Let's see what he's up to," Bailey said.

"I don't know if that's a good idea," Balraj suggested.

"Come on, he looks suspicious. We should check him out."

"Yeah, let's take a peek," Shep said.

They walked to the hangar doors. The doors were open and there was a pallet just inside. On the pallet was a large metal object. It was somewhat cylindrical and had a few seams, as if it were assembled in three or four large sections. There was a small circular clearing – a sort of doughnut hole – in the middle of it. They were standing in the doorway looking at it when they heard voices down the street. Two men walked around the corner and turned toward them.

The kids panicked. They hopped into the circular clearing in the object. The voices came closer. The men were standing inside the hangar doors, only a few meters away. The kids huddled down as low as they could, to keep out of sight.

"You sure it was a robot?" the first man said.

"Yeah, a small robot. It was spying on us or something," the second man said.

"And you didn't take it out?"

"That thing moved so fast nobody could catch it, unless you were on a bike or something."

"Well at least you managed to get it back here in one piece. You're sure nobody followed you?"

"We did a pretty good job of looking inconspicuous and taking the quiet roads. People probably thought we were with the emergency crews."

"Fine. Let's get out of here."

"Right."

The second man walked over to the pallet and pressed a button. The pallet floated a few centimeters off the ground and started moving toward a shuttle.

"Hold on," the first man said. "Did you secure this thing?"

"What do you mean?" the second man asked.

""What I mean is I heard what happened with the other one."

"Yeah don't worry. We disconnected the power."

"Good, let's keep it that way."

The pallet started to roll up a ramp. They could see the man with the black beard walk up to the other two men. They seemed to be passing something between them. Money maybe. Then the pallet went inside the shuttle and it settled down onto the floor. Shep jumped up.

"Let's get out of here!" He made a dash for the ramp, but the shuttle hatch closed before he could make it out. "Oh no! Guys this is bad!"

Balraj stood up and looked around.

"I'm in so much trouble now," he said.

Bailey was still huddled down. She was shaking.

"I'm scared guys, these are bed men. Really bad," she said.

The shuttle started vibrating. They could feel themselves get heavier. There was a small window on one side of the shuttle. Shep went over to look out the window. The ground of Adriana Colony was getting smaller beneath them. About thirty seconds later, they passed through a hatch in the colony dome. They were in space.

"My mom is really going to kill me now," Balraj said.

17

Aboard Horatio Station

Lauressa went back to the cafeteria for another coffee. It was just too hard to think without the help of caffeine, and besides, there was a persistent dull headache that felt better after having a coffee. She filled up her mug and she went on her way to the infirmary.

Dr. Poisson was leaning back in his desk chair, listening to some music.

"Good morning," he said when he noticed Lauressa come in.

"Hi there. You look relaxed," Lauressa remarked.

"Do I? Well I guess I am. And how are you?"

"Tired. Tired."

"How much sleep did you get?"

"Oh, I think five, maybe six hours. It wasn't enough."

"No, it's really not. It's an interesting thing, sleep. We've made so many improvements to health and longevity in the past five hundred years. Breakthroughs in every area. But sleep can't be bred out. It can't be fixed. Even though we shouldn't need it, we still need as much sleep as we did thousands of years ago."

"If there was a drug, or a treatment..." Lauressa said.

"There are. You can take drugs to keep you up for days. You'll be at peak cognitive ability for a few days. Then your brain will just shut down and go to sleep."

"You're talking about stims."

"Yes, and there's nothing new coming. No matter what you do, you have to sleep at some point. If you don't, you go insane, or you die. It's really quite interesting."

"Quite interesting. And a little morbid."

"That's what you get for spending time with the doctor. Oh, I guess I should ask if there was anything specific that you wanted to talk about? Or did you just come for a visit, which I always appreciate."

"I am here for something," Lauressa said. It took a few seconds to remember what she had come for. "Oh, that's right. The reason I came down here is because of Stellar Corp. I sent in my official report on the Bollox incident. I got a message back from them very quickly, and the strange thing is, well, they essentially said to drop it."

"What the hell," Dr. Poisson said. His face turned red. "Don't investigate drug smuggling and someone being drugged. Don't investigate a cargo ship blowing up. Don't investigate missing sensor logs. What the hell is going on with Stellar Corp?"

"I don't know. Something is wrong here. Stellar Corp can be bureaucratic, but it's usually bureaucratic in the direction of more investigation, and more paperwork. Not less."

"What are you going to do?"

"We're going to get a real-time radio discussion set up with Stellar Corp. Ask them directly what's going on."

"That's a great idea. But we're talking about almost a 6 hour round trip for each sentence."

"I know, but at least we can verify the integrity of the message using the radio network."

"You're worried our reports were tampered with?"

"Who knows. We write a report, hit send, and then a courier pod is supposed to launch and flash to Stellar Corp at superlight. But it's a physical object. We can't know for sure what's happening along the way."

"I suppose so. It's going to be a very slow conversation, so you might need some company."

"I think you're right. I'm going to have a shower, so why don't you meet me on the bridge in thirty minutes?"

"I thought I'd smelled something."

"Way to talk to your commanding officer."

"I suppose you don't need some company in the shower then."

"Ha ha, no. You know, you would have had a better chance if you hadn't just called me smelly," Lauressa said.

"True. I didn't think that through, did I?"

He laughed.

"Bye Doc. I'll meet you on the bridge."

Lauressa returned to her quarters and got in the shower. She turned the water temperature as hot as she could handle. She let the hot water fall on her chest and run down her breasts. It felt good. She rubbed her chest. There was a knot of tight muscle right in the middle where the ribs join together, which the heat was slowly relaxing. *It would feel good to have someone massage my chest. I know he wasn't being serious, but maybe I could have brought him along? We're both grown ups. Oh Lauressa, it doesn't matter how grown up you are. Twenty, thirty, a hundred and thirty. It's always complicated at any age. The Doc is a good friend, I'd better not mess it up.*

Lauressa made it up to the bridge a few minutes later than planned. Dr. Poisson was already there.

"Commander," Wayland Hauer said as Lauressa stepped onto the bridge. Doctor Poisson was standing beside Wayland, who was sitting at his operations/communications station. He was surrounded by a 180-degree curved monitor. This monitor displayed everything he needed in order to watch the area around Horatio Station and to perform functions like tracking ship trajectories, handling communications, and even maneuvering the station. He was also the only person on the bridge on most days.

"Mister Hauer. How are things?"

"Uh, fine Commander."

"Good. Say, Mister Hauer, we'd like to make a radio call to Stellar Corp."

"I don't understand, Commander," Wayland said.

"We want to communicate with Stellar Corp, on Earth."

"You mean a courier pod, right? Radio could take, uh, around 6 hours round-trip."

"No, I mean radio. Can you do it?"

"Of course I can do it. I mean, I'm sorry Commander, I just wasn't expecting... It's not a very efficient method of communication, but yes, I can do it."

"Whenever you're ready," Commander Tajiki said.

"Yes, Commander. Here we go," he said. Wayland brought up the radio system on his monitor. He selected the correct radio frequency and encryption method, so that Stellar Corp would receive the signal correctly. "You should record your first message now, otherwise you'll wait 6 hours just for the authentication round-trip. I'll tack your message on to the end of the authentication message."

"Good idea," Lauressa said. She leaned toward a Microphone on Wayland's station. "This is Commander Lauressa Tajiki, commanding officer of Horatio Station, Uranus Sector. We need to discuss the destruction of the cargo ship Bollox as well as the drugging of one of the crew on this station. We have received your initial responses that these do not warrant further investigation. However these situations are serious and need to be investigated thoroughly."

"Got it. Loading now," Wayland said. He brought up the interface for the long-range transmission antenna array. "The transmission array is powering on and will transmit our message in a few seconds."

Almost immediately, the station lurched. A vibration and a rumbling sound passed through the metal of the station walls.

"What's happening?" Lauressa asked.

"The transmission array blew out. I'm getting a camera on it now," Walyand said. A live image of the array appeared on his display. There was a hole where a cluster of antennas should have been. The hole was glowing red with heat, but cooling down rapidly.

"Hopefully nobody got hurt, but I'll be in the infirmary, just in case," Doctor Poisson said. He walked off the bridge.

"Thanks Doc," Commander Tajiki said. "Mr. Hauer, what the hell happened?"

"I have no idea. Everything was working fine."

"This makes no sense."

"No it doesn't. Oh great, we have no long range communications at all."

"What do you mean?"

"The courier pod bay was damaged too," Hauer said.

Lauressa Tajiki paced around.

"Can you get the S.C. Johnson on the line?" Tajiki asked.

"Let me see," Hauer said. He checked something at his station. "Short-range communication is still working. Bringing them up now."

A voice from the other ship spoke.

"S.C. Johnson here. Go ahead Horatio Station."

"S.C. Johnson. This is Commander Tajiki. We've lost long-range radio and our courier pods. What kind of communication capabilities do you have?"

"We've got medium-range radio."

"No courier pods?"

"No Commander, only interstellar ships have courier pods. We're dependent on the nearest station for long-range communication."

"Do you know if anybody else out here has long-range communications capability?"

"I don't, Commander. If an interstellar ship comes in then we could piggyback off of theirs."

"So, until then we're cut-off," Commander Tajiki said.

"It seems like it."

"S.C. Johnson, I want you to stay close to the station." Commander Tajiki said.

"Very good Commander. We're on our way. We're only about an hour out."

"Thank you. If you wouldn't mind, please come see me once you arrive."

"Will do."

"Thank you. Horatio Station out."

Wayland Hauer disconnected the call.

"Mr. Hauer, please let me know if you notice anything wrong. I'll be in my quarters. Or the infirmary," Commander Tajiki said.

"Yes, Commander."

Lauressa went back to her quarters. She began to pace. Bollox exploded. Ashley Chung drugged. Sensor logs deleted. Long-range communications lost.... Conspiracy? Or coincidence? She poured herself a shot of bourbon. It was too early to be drinking. Somewhere on earth it's evening. Not much of an excuse, but I'll take it. The drink burned on the way down. But it felt good. Relaxing. Okay, what next.... Wang.

Lauressa called Hamlet Customs Brokers. She looked at the three-hundred year old Chinese man on the screen. Not bad for three-hundred.

"Wang, we've lost long-range communication."

"What the hell is happening up there. Are you safe? I can send security," Wang said.

"How are your communications capabilities right now?"

"They're fine, but they're medium-range at best. I use Horatio Station for the long-range stuff."

"I was hoping you had something up your sleeve, something to help you contact your ships," Lauressa said.

"No, most of the time I only communicate with the ships when they're here, to give them payment and new itineraries. I get the occasional update via courier pod, but I rely on your station to reply to them."

"This isn't good."

"How long until Stellar Corp notices that you have no long-range capability?"

"Maybe a day, a week. I don't know for sure. Probably the next time they send orders and don't get a response. There are long stretches without communication sometimes."

"We're on our own out here then," Wang said.

"Yes."

"Look, I've got fifty security staff and shuttles at your disposal if you need them."

"What use do you have for a security team that large?" Lauressa asked.

"You'd be surprised at the kinds of things that happen. People trying to sneak things through. Trying to bypass my – the government's – share. Sometimes we have to deal with less than desirable cargo ship captains. I've got stories."

"I'm sure you probably shouldn't tell me about them."

"Maybe. But we're at your disposal."

"Thanks. I should go."

"Hold on. I did some checking in with some personal contacts at Adriana's spaceport on Titania. The Bollox only delivered half of the ore that was expected. They also unloaded a large crate that didn't look like an ore container. My contact just happened to see the crate as he was walking by the ship's hangar," Wang said.

"They delivered half the ore?"

"It appears so. They didn't have room to take the full quantity. They were definitely carrying something else."

"Why deliver any ore at all?"

"It's a front. You deliver the goods listed on the itinerary and use it as a cover for the real cargo. And if anybody checks you just say there was an error in the quantity that was written down."

"That's it."

"That's it, because nobody looks too deeply into these things," Wang said.

"Why not?"

"If you do, then eventually you'll run out of cargo ship captains willing to work for you."

"Wang, I'm going to let you go. Thanks for getting that info on the Bollox."

"I'll let you know if I find out more. Goodbye Lauressa."

"Bye Wang... Steven."

Lauressa went down to the infirmary. She walked into Dr. Poisson's office. Ashley Chung was sitting on the Doctor's lap.

"Oh, Commander!" Ashley cried as she jumped up.

"I guess this means you're all better?" Commander Tajiki asked.

"Yes, Commander."

"Good. I need to speak with Dr. Poisson."

"Oh, okay," Ashley said. She ran from the office.

"You really take good care of your patients, don't you."

"I try to. And, it's not what it looks like."

"She wasn't sitting on your lap just now."

"Oh no, she was definitely sitting on my lap. What I mean is there's something there. It's real, Lauressa."

"Oh, well that's good," Lauressa said. But what she thought was, *'I hate her'*. "Just try to not let it interfere with your investigation, okay?"

"Of course. And in case you were wondering, I'm not neglecting my duties. There were no injuries from the antenna explosion."

"That's good. No, it's not good. Doc, we've lost the courier pods too. We've got no long-range communication ability. We're on our own."

"This isn't good. This can't be a coincidence."

"No," she said.

"Okay, what have we got? Bollox exploding. Missing sensor logs. A drugged research archivist. And our communications array blew up."

"Oh, I talked to Wang. He thinks they were smuggling something."

"How does he know?"

"He said he has a contact on Adriana. They saw what got unloaded there."

"Okay, you figured the ship had to be carrying something volatile. Now it's confirmed."

"Yes, now I've got to figure out what to do. We're isolated. We don't even know if Stellar Corp got any of our reports."

"I think we can assume they didn't. Ashley's drugging points to someone on the station, but I haven't been able to find any evidence. If someone sabotaged the communications array, that could have been a last-resort. They could have been intercepting our messages for some time now," Dr. Poisson said.

"Okay. So I've got no long-range communications, and I've got someone on my ship, maybe more than one person. The good news is the S.C. Johnson is on its way, and their captain should be aboard within the hour."

"That's good. We could use some extra muscle."

"Also, Wang offered his security staff. He has fifty men down there. Can you imagine? He has his own private garrison."

"That's more than we've got. What do we have here, a dozen marines?"

"Maybe fifteen."

"This is interesting, Lauressa. Wang possibly has the largest armed force in the sector."

"S.C. Johnson has forty crew."

"But they're not all soldiers. They have at most twenty who have proper combat training. So I guess what I'm saying is it's a good thing Wang is on our side. I'm assuming that he's on our side?"

"He is," Lauressa said.

"You sound sure."

"I am."

"Okay, so we've got somebody on the station who's involved with the Bollox somehow. Someone who's going around drugging Ashley, erasing logs, and blowing up antennas. But in our corner we've got a ship with really big lasers, and Wang's men if we need them?" Doctor Poisson asked.

"Right."

"So we're in good shape."

"Are we? You said yourself that you haven't gotten anywhere with figuring out who drugged Ashley."

"True," Dr. Poisson said.

"I need to sit down. I think I need a hug."

Dr. Poisson sat next to her and put an arm around her.

Lauressa began to sob quietly.

"I'm not crying," she said.

"Of course not."

"Can I tell you something?" Lauressa asked.

"Go ahead."

"I've decided that I hate Ashley Chung."

"It's good to know that you care."

* * *

Wayland Hauer was at his station on the bridge. A message had just arrived from a ship orbiting Titania. It was from the S.C. Applegate. He hadn't heard from them in months, not that there was typically any reason for them to report in – patrol duty was usually quiet, and the Applegate was equipped to be self-sufficient for the better part of a year. Independence was one of the benefits of the old warships that were moved to local patrol duty. The newer, more powerful generation of frigates that replaced them were more dependent on local supply hubs to keep stocked with perishables.

"Commander Tajiki, it's Walyand Hauer," he said into the microphone at his station.

"*Go ahead,*" Commander Tajiki replied. Hauer heard what sounded like sniffling.

"Uh, Commander, I've received a message from the S.C. Applegate."

"*Applegate?*"

"Yes, Commander."

"*Okay, can you read it to me? I'm in the middle of something.*"

"The message says: This is Captain Jeremy Bach of the S.C. Applegate. Adriana colony has been attacked by a ship. We attempted to engage the ship but it flashed away. We've been unable to communicate with Stellar Corp. Can you please try to notify Stellar Corp for us? The situation on Adriana colony is stable. We've traced the attacker's superlight path back to Miranda. We are going there now to intercept them. S.C. Applegate out."

"*Thank you, Mister Hauer,*" Commander Tajiki said.

"Is there anything you want me to do?" Wayland asked.

"*Not right now. Just let me know when the captain of the S.C. Johnson gets here.*"

"Yes, Commander."

18

ABOARD S.C. APPLEGATE, IN ORBIT OVER MIRANDA

"Captain, the message to Stellar Corp failed in transit," Smitty said.

"What, Smitty? I don't understand."

"The ship's system reports that the message only got as far as the local communications hub. Then nothing after that."

"Communications hub? You mean Horatio Station."

"Yes sir. The Station reported that the message was lost."

"But the station is okay?"

"The station's computer is responding to message requests, but it reports that it can't actually deliver them. Apparently their long-range communications are off-line."

"We have to get this message to Stellar Corp. Somebody has to know what's going on."

"True, but we have to go after that ship, regardless."

"Alright Smitty, can you open a line with Horatio Station?"

"Sure thing... go ahead," Smitty said.

"This is Captain Jeremy Bach of the S.C. Applegate."

"*Go ahead Captain,*" Wayland Hauer said from Horatio Station.

"Adriana colony has been attacked by a ship. We attempted to engage the ship but it flashed away. We've been unable to communicate with Stellar Corp. Can you please try to notify Stellar Corp for us?"

"*Long-range communication is down currently, but we'll try.*"

"Thank you. The situation on Adriana colony is stable. We've traced the attacker's superlight path back to Miranda. We are going there now to intercept them. S.C. Applegate out."

"*Thank you, Captain Bach, good luck. Horatio Station out,*" Wayland said. The line disconnected.

"Are you ready, Captain?" Smitty asked.

"Let's do this," Captain Bach said. He buckled the safety belt in his command chair.

Smitty turned to the tactical console.

"All weapons are armed and standing by."

"Good. Let's go to Miranda."

"Mister Mulligan, enter coordinates to Miranda, and go to superlight."

"Yes, sir. Coordinates for Miranda entered, and flashing in 3... 2... 1. Flash."

In an instant, the S.C. Applegate lit up as if it were the filament of a lightbulb. The entire outside of the ship became obscured by a white-hot light. Then as quickly as it lit up, the light flashed even brighter, blinked out, and the ship was gone. A few seconds later it had arrived just outside the orbit of Miranda.

"We've arrived at the destination coordinates," the pilot said.

"Good. Keep an eye out for meteors. We're very close to the outer rings," Captain Bach said.

"Yes, Captain."

Smitty activated the sensors.

"I'm scanning for evidence of a ship. There are some remnants of previous flashes, but they're too old to trace now."

"Well, let's look around and see if we can find anything," Captain Bach said.

"The sensors show something metallic on Miranda. We need to get closer to see it," Smitty said.

"Go ahead Mister Mulligan," Captain Bach said.

"Yes, Captain," Jerry replied. He turned the S.C. Applegate toward Miranda and fired the forward thrusters. The Applegate accelerated toward the small moon. When it was within a few thousand kilometers, the pilot fired the front-facing engines to bring the ship to a stop. He then fired side-facing thrusters to start the ship moving in the direction of the moon's rotation. He had placed them directly above the metal object.

"I'm getting a good scan of the object now," Smitty said. "Great piloting as usual, by the way."

"Thank you, sir."

"I've got a hi-res camera on the object. I'll put it on screen."

A live image of Miranda appeared before them. Smitty zoomed in until the camera was focused on a small section of the moon's surface. The image was dark, but a distinctive rectangular shape was visible on the surface.

"Captain, that object is about one-hundred meters by seventy-five meters in size. It's about ten meters tall. According to the scan it is a mix of metals and plastics, painted with a dark low-observability coating. The estimated mass is low. It's hollow."

"A pirate base," Captain Bach said.

"The base of whoever is behind the attack, pirate or not," Smitty said.

"Get John Dvorak up here, I want his opinion."

Smitty sent a message to the head engineer, who arrived on the bridge in less than a minute.

"So what do you think?" Captain Bach asked.

"Definitely a base. It looks like one of the cheap prefab models that are sold to people who want to be off the beaten path," John Dvorak replied.

"How long would it take to build one of these?"

"You can build them fast. A week at most. It doesn't look like there are any meteor impacts, so it's pretty recent."

"Smitty, is there anybody home?"

"It doesn't look like it. The low-observability coating could be messing with the scans, but it looks unoccupied."

"Good. Let's go down to take a look. John Dvorak, I think I'll want you with me. And let's bring David too. Who knows what we'll find."

"Captain, bring a few marines with you. Just in case," Smitty said.

"Good idea. Send them down. You're in charge while I'm gone."

"Yes, Captain. Good luck," Smitty said.

They walked off the bridge and went to the shuttle hangar. Two marines were already there. David entered the hangar just a few seconds later. Crawler followed him as if it were a dog.

"Do you think we'll need it?" Captain Bach asked.

"I'm not sure, but it can't hurt. If something needs to be repaired, Crawler can do it," David said.

"Okay, bring him. Let's go," Captain Bach said. He walked into the shuttle and sat at the pilot's station.

"This is Applegate shuttle, requesting permission to disembark," Captain Bach said.

"*Shuttle, this is S.C. Applegate. Permission granted,*" Smitty said over the radio.

The hangar doors opened, and the shuttle lifted off and flew out of the hangar.

"*Good luck, Captain Bach,*" Smitty said.

"Good luck, Captain Smitty," Jeremy said. As soon as they had cleared the ship, Jeremy entered the coordinates to the small base. "We'll be there in a few minutes. Let's get in quick and get out."

The marines nodded. John Dvorak and David both said, "Okay."

The shuttle flew down to the surface of Miranda. Once they were within a few hundred meters of the base, the shuttle picked up an automated docking beacon.

"Why would they have their hangar automated?" Jeremy asked.

"Because there's nobody there to do it manually," John Dvorak said.

"Makes sense. Let's go in," Jeremy said. He flew the ship to the hangar. The doors parted and he maneuvered the ship in. The shuttle touched down and the hangar doors closed.

"There's air," said the marine in the co-pilot's seat.

"Good. I'm glad to be able to not wear a suit. Let's go," Jeremy said.

They stepped into the darkened hanger.

"Kind of dark," Jeremy said.

"A little bit," a marine said.

"Crawler, go in front of us and turn on your lights," David said. Crawler ran to the front of the group and turned on its lights. The area in front of them became dimly visible.

"Crawler, find the door," David said. Crawler looked around and then ran off to the right. "He found it."

"I'm glad you brought that little robot," Jeremy said. They went over to the door and Jeremy pressed a button on the door's panel. It unlocked and opened slightly. Jeremy pushed it open the rest of the way. "Let's go."

* * *

There were no ships in the area around the S.C. Applegate. Smitty was looking at the tactical display for any sign of activity, but the only thing in the area that the sensors detected was the shuttle. It was still visible to the Applegate's sensors even though it was parked inside the base. The presence of the shuttle overcame some of the effects of the low-observability coating. The outlines of multiple rooms became visible around the shuttle. Smitty checked his data. The Applegate had automatically combined its sensors with the shuttle's instruments to improve its ability to peer into the base interior.

"Captain Bach, this is Captain Smitty," Smitty said.

Jeremy received the message and spoke back. "Go ahead, Captain Smitty."

"I'm sending you new sensor information about the base. You should see it on your hand-held in a second."

"*Thank you Smitty,*" Jeremy said. The sensor data, showing the rooms immediately around the shuttle, appeared on Jeremy's hand-held. "*Got it.*"

"Good. Now, what you want to look at is this room here," Smitty said. He put a flashing icon over one of the rooms. "That's the –"

BANG! The ship shuddered violently and an extremely loud noise echoed through the walls. Alarms went off. Smitty turned to the tactical station.

"We're under attack! Come about, full thrusters!"

Jerry Mulligan used the thrusters to spin the ship so that its nose was pointing away from the planet instead of towards it. A trail of parts spread out around the Applegate as it turned. One of the rear-facing engines had been hit with a projectile and pieces were tearing away under the stress of acceleration.

"Shit, we've lost one of the engines," Jerry said.

"Accelerate, maximum Gs. I'm looking for that ship," Smitty said. He looked at the tactical display and switched between sensors until he found the attacker.

"There it is, that's the same ship. Keep our nose pointed at it," Smitty said.

"Yes, Captain," Jerry said. He continuously adjusted the ship's thrusters to keep them pointed at the attacker.

"I have a firing solution. Firing," Smitty said.

The Applegate's lasers shot out at the ship. They hit the attacker's ship for a second, but the enemy ship changed course and the lasers moved off target.

"Fuck!" Smitty said. He saw a small glowing dot on the screen. A missile was heading toward them.

"Firing chaff!" Smitty said.

A burst of metal bits flew from the Applegate. Jerry accelerated away from the chaff, to put as much distance between them as possible. A few seconds later the missile exploded on the patch of chaff.

"The ship is matching our moves now. They're keeping their nose pointed at us," the pilot said.

"Good, that'll get me another firing solution. Now!" Smitty yelled. He fired the lasers again. They hit the attacker, but the Applegate got hit with lasers at the same time. Layers of armor melted off.

"Evading," Jerry said. He rolled the ship to get it away from the lasers, which meant the attacking ship was also no longer under fire.

"Those lasers stung, but we'll get them back. Shit! The sensors are saying most of the lasers bounced off. They've got reflective armor," Smitty said.

"How's that possible?"

"I don't know, Jerry. Just get us closer, then show them our sides."

"Yes Captain." S.C. Applegate accelerated forward for a few seconds, then spun so that its side was facing the attacker. They were still moving toward them at high speed.

"Take that!" Smitty yelled. Four guns shot high-energy projectiles at the attacker. The projectiles were a cheap but effective weapon. Each was the size of an apple, very dense, and accelerated to a very high speed. Two of them hit. The other two passed by and would most likely hit Uranus in a few minutes. The two that had hit their target had impacted very hard. Two clouds of small particles and chunks of metal grew rapidly around the attacking ship.

"The guns are reloading," Smitty said. The attacker's ship started to glow. And then it flashed and it was gone.

"Fucking hell!" Smitty yelled. He punched in a command on the communications console. "Engineering, how does the damage look?"

"*We've lost one of the main engines and we've lost some armor around the nose.*"

"We'll have to set in to port to take care of that," Smitty said. He brought up a line to the team on the surface.

"Captain Bach, we've been attacked," Smitty said.

"*Was it the same ship?*" Jeremy asked.

"Yes it was."

"*But they're gone now?*"

"We hit them pretty hard, I don't think they have any interest in continuing the fight."

"*Good. We've found something down here,*" Jeremy said.

"What did you find?"

"*A box. A large box.*"

"Okay."

"*Smitty, the place is empty. We've been through eight rooms so far. Nothing. Except for the box.*"

"Let me guess. A Mars flag," Smitty said.

"*No. It's probably nothing. The box has no markings on it, except for some text etched into the wood on one corner.*"

"What does it say?" Smitty asked.

"Could be nothing Smitty. It could just be where the wood for the box was made."

"Go on, what does it say?" Smitty asked.

"Okay, don't jump to conclusions.... It says Gliese 832b," Jeremy said.

"On no. Jerry, get us back to that base now!" Smitty said. Jerry nodded and spun the ship around.

"Smitty, don't worry so much," Jeremy said.

"We'll be back in a few minutes, get ready to go," Smitty said.

"Smitty, we've got a few more rooms to check."

"Do it fast. We need to get out of here," Smitty said. He turned to Jerry. "Enter in coordinates for Horatio Station. We're flashing as soon as the shuttle is aboard."

"Smitty, calm down. We'll be quick, okay?"

"Okay," Smitty said. He took a deep breath but he was still visibly agitated.

* * *

There were several rooms left to explore on the surface. David knelt down to Crawler.

"Crawler, I want you to run through the rest of the rooms and let us know if any of them have anything in them. Okay?"

Crawler jumped up, spun around in the air and took off running. The display from its cameras appeared on David's handheld. It ran through all the rooms in under a minute. The view on the display was a blur, but it was a blur of nothing. The rooms were empty. Then, in the last room Crawler came across a computer console. Crawler stopped in front of it.

"That's a computer," David said.

"Let's go," Jeremy said. They ran through the empty rooms to the terminal.

Smitty came on the line.

"S.C. Applegate is ready for you now."

"Almost, Smitty. We found a computer. Stand by," Jeremy said.

John Dvorak connected his hand-held computer to the console.

"Let's see. Oh this is good. I can copy this, no problem," he said.

"You sure?" Jeremy asked.

"The security routines are non-military strength. Hold on. Done."

"That fast?"

"There wasn't much to grab."

"Okay, let's get back to the ship," Jeremy said.

* * *

The shuttle touched down in the hangar on S.C. Applegate.

"We're ready to go to superlight Captain," Smitty said.

"Not yet, Smitty," Captain Bach said.

"But Captain, we need to," Smitty said.

"We'll be on the bridge in a minute. Stand by," Jeremy said.

"Yes, Captain," Smitty said.

"What's going on with Smitty?" John Dvorak asked.

"He's worried," Jeremy replied.

They walked onto the bridge.

"Captain. Can we go now?" Smitty asked.

"Hold on, you can't be that worried."

"Gliese 832b!" Smitty yelled.

"We have no evidence that the – "

"But what if they are!" Smitty yelled.

"Do you really think, after all these years?" Jeremy asked.

"We can't afford to be wrong," Smitty said.

"Just because the box was made with wood from Gliese 832b doesn't mean that – "

"Three ships just flashed in!" the pilot yelled.

"What? Can you identify them?" Captain Bach asked.

"Flash now," Smitty said.

"They're too far away to identify, but they're heading straight for us," the pilot said.

"Flash now Mister Mulligan!" Smitty yelled. Jerry looked at the Captain and then at Smitty. "Now! Now!"

Without waiting for confirmation from the Captain, the pilot went to superlight and the ship flashed away.

A few seconds later the S.C. Applegate arrived at Oberon. Hamlet Station was nearby.

Jeremy Bach was stunned. Smitty had never spoken to him like this before. But he was glad that Smitty took the threat seriously – a threat that he didn't think was possible.

Smitty stared at the display of Horatio Station on the screen. The station was growing larger as the pilot brought the ship closer.

"They're back," Smitty said. He tightened his grip against his console until his hands turned white. "The Labians are back."

19

INSIDE A SPACESHIP

Bailey sat in the donut hole in the middle of the metal device. Her hands were wrapped around her knees. She rocked repetitively.

Shep leaned toward her and tugged at her shirt.

"Come on, we have to hide."

"Right here. Right here," she said.

"We need to find somewhere better. They'll come in here soon," Shep said.

Balraj looked out the window. The shuttle was heading toward a larger ship, but all he could see was a dark gray shape that blocked out the stars. The light from the sun reflected off the outside of the ship and scattered in all directions, so that the dark gray color would alternate with dull shimmers of red, blue, and purple that kept changing as the shuttle got closer.

"Guys, we're going to a ship," Balraj said.

"Let's go Bailey, we have to hide," Shep said. He pulled her arm hard until she stood up.

They searched the room for any place large enough to hold them. The walls were lined with storage compartments that were all locked shut. There was a vent on one wall, but the opening was too small to fit into. There was nothing else in the room that provided a hiding spot. Then Bailey – who had stood motionless while the others frantically looked for a place to hide – pointed at the floor.

"Guys, the floor," Bailey said.

"What?" Balraj asked. He came over to her and looked where she was pointing. A grate ran along the entire length of the room.

"We can go in there," Bailey said.

Balraj got down and took a look. There was an eighteen inch crawl space below the grate. The grate looked pretty easy to open – it was divided into multiple small sections with hinges.

The shuttle slowed down to a crawl so fast that they lurched forward. Balraj ran back to the window. The shuttle was maneuvering into the larger ship's hangar.

"It's landing."

The three of them went to the part of the grate that was as far away as they could get from the doors. Shep and Bailey lifted the grate. Balraj hopped in and got down on his knees and crawled away.

"You go next," Shep said.

"Okay," Bailey said. She hopped down and shimmied under the grate.

The shuttle shook as it touched down in the hanger.

"Hurry Shep," Bailey said.

"Coming," he said. Shep stepped down into the space under the grate. He sat in the crawlspace and slowly lowered the grate down on top of them. A few seconds later, the shuttle's ramp opened. They could hear footsteps come up the ramp.

A man walked over to the device.

"Boss, it's secure."

"Good news," said another man from just outside the shuttle. "Let's go see the Captain. I want to hear the latest news."

They heard the man's footsteps as he walked out of the shuttle and down the ramp. They could hear the two men's voices as they talked. Their voices got fainter until they couldn't hear them anymore.

It had become silent, and Bailey, Shep, and Balraj, who were laying under the grate, tried to think of what to do next. They laid there for ten or fifteen minutes before any of them said a word.

"Hey guys.... Maybe we should go look for a better hiding place," Shep whispered.

"Yeah, okay," Balraj said.

"But it's safe in here," Bailey said.

"How long can we lay down here? There's something poking in my back," Balraj said.

"Okay, fine, But we need to be careful," Bailey said.

"Fine," Shep said. He slowly pushed the grate open, as quietly as he could.

Shep climbed up out of the crawlspace, followed by Bailey and Balraj. Shep lowered the grate closed. It made a slight clanging sound when it touched the floor. Bailey jumped and gasped at the sound.

"God, Shep!" she yelled in a whisper.

"Sorry," Shep said.

Shep walked quietly toward the shuttle's ramp. The other two followed some distance behind him. He tried to walk as gently as possible so that his footsteps wouldn't make any noise. Once he got to the edge of the ramp he leaned out so that he could peek at the hangar.

"Nobody's around," Shep said.

"I'll go first," Balraj said. He walked down the ramp and stood in the hangar looking around. He waved at the others so that they would come down too. They all looked around. The hangar was more than twice the size of the shuttle. The shuttle was the only thing in the room.

"Okay, now what? We need to hurry," Bailey said.

"Yeah, I know," Shep said.

"Look at that door," Balraj said. He pointed to a door on the far side of the room. It wasn't the normal door to the hangar. The door was less than two meters tall, and had the word maintenance printed above it.

"Let's try it," Shep said.

The door had no security panel or obvious lock, just a regular knob. Shep turned the knob, and the door opened without difficulty. Behind the door was a hallway with a ceiling just slightly taller than the door. It was lit by bare lights hung irregularly along the length of the hall.

The three kids walked in. Shep turned around to close the door behind them, when he heard a mechanical sound come from the hangar. The other door in the hangar was opening. Shep quickly closed the door, but he left it open just slightly so that it wouldn't make any noise. Bailey started to feel faint, so Balraj put his arm around her and helped her to sit down.

A sliver of light made it through the gap in the door, so that Shep could just barely see what was going on. Two men went into the shuttle and came out a minute later with the large metal device. They hovered it down the ramp on its pallet, then guided it across the floor and out of the hangar. Shep heard the hangar doors open and close again. The men were gone. He let the door shut completely. The door clicked and made a slight hissing sound, as if it had some sort of seal around it.

"I think we're safe for now, Bailey," Shep said. She was sitting on the floor. Her face glistened with sweat.

"Okay, okay. We're okay," Bailey said.

"We're okay," Shep said.

Balraj still had his arm around Bailey. "I'll help you walk," he said.

"Thanks Balraj," Bailey said. She stood up. She was a little unsteady, but Balraj kept her from losing her balance.

Shep started to walk along the hallway. It appeared to be very long, or possibly just not lit well enough to see the other end. As he walked along the hall he could see other hallways branching off in different directions. There were also locked doors along the hallway. The locked doors had signs over them, such as: *reactor control*, or *missile storage*, or *waste elimination*. A sign on the wall read *sublevel zero*. Shep walked back to Bailey and Balraj.

"There's lots of locked doors and a bunch of hallways. But I saw a sign for sublevel zero," Shep said.

"What's that?" Balraj asked.

"I read about it in a spaceship textbook. It's the bottom of the whole ship. It's the guts."

"But why go there?"

"It's the guts. Nobody ever goes down there, unless something breaks," Shep said.

"Okay. Bailey, ready?" Balraj asked.

"I'm ready," Bailey said.

They walked along the hall. Shep pointed out the sign for sublevel zero and they followed it. They found another sign, which led them down another tunnel, until they came to a door. 'Stairs to sublevel zero' was printed above the door. This door wasn't locked, so Shep turned the knob and opened the door. They walked through and the door closed behind them. They passed a dozen doors to other hallways as they went down. Finally after a few minutes they reached the bottom of the stairs. The sign for the door at the bottom simply read *zero*.

Sublevel zero was a five-foot tall crawl space with cables and pipes criss-crossing the ceiling and more cables and pipes running up and down the walls. The lights were almost completely covered in some places by wires that drooped over them. The central hallway, which was where they were standing, ran along the entire length of the ship. Other halls branched out from it, so that the bowels of every part of the ship could be easily accessed.

"What's that smell?" Balraj asked.

"I don't know," Shep replied.

"Smells like eggs," Balraj said.

"Sulfur?" Bailey asked.

"Could be. I don't like eggs," Balraj said.

"Maybe it's just stuff building up down here. Let's look around, see if there's anything useful down here," Shep said.

They were starting to walk along the hall when the ship lurched slightly. A flash of light came from the far end of the hall.

"Did we just go to superlight?" Bailey asked.

"I don't know. I've never been outside of the colony," Balraj said.

"Me neither," Shep said.

"Well that's kind of how I imagined it would be. You feel the ship move under your feet, and there's a flash of light, and then you're gone," Bailey said.

"Why would there be light inside the ship?" Balraj asked.

"There wouldn't be, I don't think," Bailey said.

"I haven't read about light inside the ship, just on the outside," Shep said.

"You know what that means, right?" Balraj asked.
"What," Bailey said.
"What," Shep said.
"There's a window down that hall," Balraj said.
Shep and Balraj took off running down the hall.
"Guys, wait for me!" Bailey called. She ran after them. The sudden excitement made her forget about how afraid she was. So she ran, and for a moment she felt strong and wild and free.

They ran for a while. The ship was long. Some cables hung down and a few hit them in the head as they ran. Eventually they reached the end of the hallway. A large room lay before them. The far wall was dotted with multiple small windows, through which they could see the stars.

"This is amazing," Bailey said.

Light started beaming in through the windows. The light suddenly flashed brighter and then went away. The ship lurched beneath them. For a few seconds there was nothing but black outside. Then the stars reappeared. This time the blue disc of Uranus was visible off to the left. It was larger than they had ever seen.

"We flashed again," Bailey said.

"We're really close to Uranus," Balraj said.

They could feel the ship accelerate and turn away from Uranus. They could see a small moon very far away. A small shiny dot was sitting in front of the moon.

"Is that a ship? I can't make it out." Balraj said.

"Let's get a better look," Shep said. He pulled his binoculars from his shoulder bag.

"Good thinking."

Shep looked through the binoculars. The shiny dot was just large enough to make out. He couldn't see any detail but it was definitely a ship.

"It's a ship, for sure," Shep said.

Then the ship shuddered a little. There was a scraping sound and a missile flew out from their ship. They couldn't see the missile itself, but they could see the bright flare from its rocket as it accelerated forward.

"Oh no, there's a fight happening," Bailey said.

They could feel the ship start to turn and accelerate. The moon and the ship went quickly out of their view, so they didn't know whether the missile had hit its target.

A few seconds later the ship turned again. It was now heading straight for the distant ship, which was still so far away that it was nothing more than a spec. A spec that was growing. Something reached out from it and hit them, and the ship was bathed in a blue glow.

"Lasers!" Balraj yelled.

"We're gonna die!" Bailey screamed. She turned white and began to tremble.

But nothing happened to them. The ship didn't seem to be damaged. Maneuvering thrusters fired and the ship slid out of the path of the lasers. Then a bright flare passed overhead. Another missile was on its way to its distant target. A few seconds later the missile exploded, but it wasn't close enough to the target to do any damage.

"Did it malfunction or something?" Balraj asked.

"Maybe they have some kind of jammers," Shep said.

Suddenly their ship was awash in a dull blue glow again. They were being bombarded with lasers once more. This time instead of sliding away, their ship fired its own beam back at the enemy ship. Almost immediately the blue glow they had been bathed in vanished.

The enemy ship started growing rapidly. They were getting closer to it, or it was getting closer to them. Its shape was recognizable in the binoculars now. Suddenly the ship turned sideways, so it now appeared several times larger. There were a few small flashes of light from the side of the ship, and four small glowing specs were now hurtling toward them.

Their ship started to move away, but it was jolted twice at almost the same time. Two of the glowing specs had hit them. Bailey was knocked off her feet. The whole ship began to spin in space. All sorts of small bits of the ship were now floating around outside the window. They could hear strange sounds coming from other parts of the ship.

The skin of their ship started to glow, and then it flashed and the stars were replaced with black. A few seconds later the stars reappeared. Some more ship-bits floated out in front of the windows. Four other ships – ships that looked similar to the one that they were on – were now very close to them. A shuttle came out of one of them and was headed toward them.

"Repair team maybe," Shep said.

Three of those ships glowed and then flashed away. The ship that had sent the shuttle remained.

"I wonder where they went," Balraj said.

"Payback," Shep said.

"Payback."

20

Aboard Horatio Station

ARCHIVIST'S NOTE: *This section contains material that may be stressful to some researchers, specifically a depiction of sexual violence between two Stellar Corp officers. This is presented exactly as it was reported to the Archivist, and is included (a) for completeness of the historical records, (b) to note the sexual mores of the era, and (c) to provide testament to the mental state of the subjects under extreme circumstances.*

    -- Ashley Chung, Archivist

Lauressa Tajiki paced about her cabin. The coffee she held risked splashing out of the mug every time she turned around to move in the other direction. Her coffee was stronger than usual. She had gone to the cafeteria and got herself a double shot of espresso with lots of milk. Then, once back in her cabin, she poured in a good helping of Irish whiskey. The combination was pungent and warming. She continued to pace, sipping the drink as she tried to think about what to do next.

Wayland Hauer interrupted her thoughts via the intercom.

"*Commander, the Captain of the S.C. Johnson is here,*" he said.

Lauressa went over to an intercom panel on her desk, then pressed a button and spoke. "Thanks Wayland. I'll meet him on the bridge."

"*Thank you Commander.*"

Lauressa walked over to the bed and put on her jacket. She buttoned it up and smoothed out the pink fabric. Stellar Corp uniforms were supposed to be crisp, but hers was rather wrinkled and rumpled. It seemed to show the stress that she was feeling. She checked her appearance in the mirror. Her hair was wild and disheveled. Her face was red. *Shit, you look like an alcoholic wreck.* A single grey hair poked out near her forehead. *Great, on top of everything else....* She pulled out the grey hair, pulled her hair up into a bun, and stuck a large hairpin through it. She looked herself up and down, straightened her jacket, and left.

Lauressa arrived on the bridge without being noticed. Wayland Hauer and the Captain of the S.C. Johnson were busy having an intense conversation. Mr. Hauer was showing the Captain photos of the underside of the station, specifically the blown-out section where the transmission array had been.

Lauressa walked up behind them.

"But how does someone just walk onto your station and do this without you knowing –"

"We're trying to figure it – you know, I don't like the tone of –"

"Who's in charge of security here anyways."

The conversation was getting heated.

"I'm in charge," Lauressa said. The two men turned, startled by her voice.

"Well you've got some explaining..." the Captain said. He stopped when he realized who we was talking to. "Oh, Commander Tajiki. Of course, my apologies."

"Thank you, Captain, uhh...."

"Thomas. Captain Randy Thomas."

"Thank you, Captain Thomas. I see you've met Mister Hauer."

"I have. We were just having an animated conversation, that's all."

"Wayland Hauer is the station's sensor and communications technician. He also oversees general operations."

"Very good," Captain Thomas said.

"Mister Hauer, I'll see you later. I'll debrief Captain Thomas in my office."

"Thank you, Commander," Wayland said. Lauressa looked back as they were leaving the bridge. She noticed that Wayland Hauer was watching Captain Thomas with narrowed eyes. Wayland caught her eye, looked away immediately, and went back to his work.

Lauressa took the Captain to her office. It wasn't a real office. It was just the sitting room of her quarters. There was a desk and a few chairs. A computer terminal sat on the desk.

"Please come in, Captain Thomas," Lauressa said. She opened the door and waved him in.

"Thank you, Commander." He walked in and Lauressa followed. The door closed behind her.

"The situation is dire, Captain," Lauressa said.

"Apparently so. Mister Hauer showed me the damage to your communications equipment. That doesn't look repairable."

"You're right. It's beyond any chance of repair," Lauressa said.

"What can I do?" Captain Thomas asked.

"I'm not sure, Captain," Lauressa said.

"You're not sure?"

"As you know, a ship, Bollox, has blown up in orbit, which we suspect was caused by some volatile smuggled goods. Sensor logs of that explosion were deleted, but we were able to restore a backup. What does this suggest?"

"Hmm, sounds like there's someone on the station covering a smugglers tracks," Captain Thomas said.

"Oh, one of my staff was knocked out by a drug. And when the Doctor reported it to Stellar Corp, they said to not investigate. And when we tried to open a direct line to Stellar Corp our communications array exploded."

"You tried to open a direct line?" Captain Thomas asked.

"Yes, both the Doctor and I received replies to our initial reports that instructed us to not investigate further. That just seemed wrong, so we decided to open a radio link."

"With the time delay, that would be a very slow conversation."

"We knew that. The goal was to verify it was really Stellar Corp we were talking with. Then, boom, the whole thing blows up."

"Somebody here really wants to stop you from discovering whatever it is they are doing."

"Yes. Oh, I forgot the best part," Lauressa said.

"What's that?"

"A patrol ship, the S.C. Applegate, is going after a pirate ship. That ship launched a missile into the center of the Adriana colony on Titania, and then fled."

"A missile?"

"And so, with communications down, the entire Uranus system is on its own.... Do you think it's related?"

"The attack on Adriana and your exploding smuggler's ship? And your communications array, which 'self destructed'?"

"All of that, yes."

"It looks like somebody is putting in a lot of effort to cover up something. But with that attack on Adriana, it looks like... Oh great. It looks like a conspiracy, Commander Tajiki."

"So, I said I'm not sure what to do, and I meant it," Lauressa said.

"I understand," Commander Thomas said.

"Good. I'm open to suggestions."

"Alright, here's a suggestion. I'm relieving you of command."

"Excuse me?"

"That's how I'm helping you. You're unfit for command. You've let your station get overrun by one or more conspirators and you haven't really done anything. Why aren't you going room to room with your marines? Why aren't you applying pressure?"

"I don't want to tip our hand. If we push too hard, if they feel cornered, they might do something drastic."

"More drastic than what's already happened? Your long-range communications have already been destroyed. What has to happen next before you act?"

"I won't be talked to like this on my station."

Lauressa felt her face turning red.

"Your station? You mean my station. Look at you, your uniform is a mess, and you smell like coffee and booze."

"It's been a long couple of days, I don't owe you an explanation for my dress, and I certainly didn't invite you to smell me!"

"You're failing, Commander. You need to act now and secure this station. You don't seem to be able to do it, so I'll do it for you. I'm in charge now," Captain Thomas said.

Captain Thomas moved closer to Lauressa, grabbed her upper arm tightly, and said, "I'm locking this station down."

"Take your hand off me!"

She punched him with her free hand. Captain Thomas stumbled backward and landed on the floor.

"That's it!" Captain Thomas yelled. He hurled himself at her and pushed her to the floor. He sat on top of her.

"You're finished. God, you smell."

Lauressa struggled beneath him. She yelled. Captain Thomas seemed to be enjoying the struggle. Lauressa was not. Finally she slapped his ear and he fell sideways.

Lauressa got on top of the Captain.

"This is my station!" she yelled. She ripped open his jacket. "I'm in charge!" she yelled. She punched him in the stomach. She tore at his shirt.

Captain Thomas reached up and pulled Lauressa down by her hair. He kissed her hard and kept pulling at her hair. She started grinding her pelvis against him. She put her hand over his mouth.

"This is my station!" she yelled as she pressed her body against his. She slapped him. He slapped her back and ripped open her top.

"On my station I am sovereign. What I say goes," Lauressa said as she pushed his face into her breasts.

Captain Thomas pushed Lauressa down and got on top of her.

"Yes Commander," he said. "You're in charge."

He pulled her pants off and ripped at her underwear.

"Stop Captain," Lauressa said.

"Not on your life," Captain Thomas said.

"Captain stop," Lauressa said.

"You want this," Captain Thomas said.

"You can't just take what you want."

"Watch me."

He removed his pants and got ready to lunge at her. Lauressa grabbed his head and pushed it down below her belly button.

"You can't just take what you want!" she yelled as she forced her pelvis against his face. She kept a tight grip on his hair. Yes! God yes!

The battle for dominance was over, and Lauressa Tajiki had thoroughly and completely won for a good half hour. They lay in bed with their legs intertwined. Captain Randy Thomas had fallen asleep still inside her. A stream of drool ran from his lips and onto her shoulder. He was snoring faintly. Lauressa looked at his body. He wasn't in very good shape, and that was probably a good thing. It seemed like he really would have forced himself upon her had he been strong enough to do so. Instead, she had gotten the upper hand and turned an impetuous prick into a good time.

Lauressa slipped out of the Captain's embrace and walked over to her mirror. He mumbled something and rolled over and resumed snoring. She looked at herself in the mirror. She had a bruise on her face and claw marks on her breasts. She went into the shower and washed everywhere. She rinsed away the remnants of Captain Thomas.

Lauressa dried herself and put on fresh clothes. She sprayed a bit of perfume. She put on her dress uniform. It was clean and sharp. The dress uniform was a darker shade and had silver details that the regular uniform lacked. Finally, she put her hair in a bun. It looked silky and clean rather than tangled and matted.

Captain Thomas woke up and sat up in bed.

"Oh, Commander Tajiki, you clean up well," he said.

"Go ahead and take a shower. We're going to see Doctor Poisson. I know how you can help me," Lauressa said.

"Good idea. Okay," Captain Thomas said. He disappeared into the shower and was back only a minute or two later. He was quickly dressed and ready to go.

They arrived at the infirmary and Doctor Poisson was busy in research.

"Good afternoon Doctor," Lauressa said.

"Ah, hi there Lauressa," he said without looking up from his work.

"Doctor, this is Captain Randy Thomas, from the S.C. Johnson."

The Doctor paused for a second and looked at the two of them. He noticed the bruises on Lauressa's face. He also noticed that Captain Thomas had a swollen ear and a cut on his lip.

"What happened to the two of you?" the Doctor asked.

"We had a disagreement," Lauressa said.

Doctor Poisson looked at Captain Thomas. His face flushed.

"You bastard," Doctor Poisson said. He took a step toward Captain Thomas.

"Relax Doc. I give as good as I get. Very good," Lauressa said, stepping forward to block the doctor's way.

"Oh... Oh. I see. Whatever floats your boat," Doctor Poisson said. He turned back to Captain Thomas. "You're lucky she's on your side right now."

"I'm not sure she's on my side," Captain Thomas said.

"We've come to an understanding," Lauressa said.

Doctor Poisson shook his head and sat down.

"So did you come down here just to show off your battle scars?"

"Oh no, I came down here because I have an idea," Lauressa said. "The S.C. Johnson has decent range. They could use their superlight drive to go to the next nearest long-range communications center."

"Where is that?" Doctor Poisson asked.

"Pluto," Lauressa said.

"Pluto? There's nothing out there."

"Nothing except the old base. But it's too far." Captain Thomas said. "We have enough fuel for superlight for 15 AU max. More than enough for paddling around Uranus and the area. But we can't make it past Jupiter."

"I should pay more attention to astronomy," Lauressa said.

"Lauressa, I'm glad you came to me with this plan, but you really don't need my opinion," Doctor Poisson said.

"But I respect your opinion. And I'm at a loss about what to do next."

"You could help me search through the staff files and logs. I'm trying to find anything that looks like a red flag."

"Okay," Lauressa said. She sat down on the couch. Captain Thomas backed up toward the door.

"Look, I think I'll get back to my ship. The least we can do is stay vigilant."

"I'll walk you to your shuttle," Lauressa said. "I'll be back soon, Doctor."

Lauressa escorted the Captain back to his shuttle. He turned to walk up the ramp. Lauressa grabbed his arm and leaned in close.

"The next time you're on my station, you'll do as I tell you. And you'd better bring chocolate with you. Now get your shuttle out of my hangar."

She rapped her hand against his pants.

"Thank you, Commander Tajiki. Until we meet again," Captain Thomas said. He walked up the ramp and closed the shuttle hatch behind him.

Lauressa walked out of the hangar. *I own him.*

21: Educational Material

A Brief History of the Earth-Mars Conflict: 2550 – 2625

The Grand Council of Mars declared independence from Earth in March 2550. Each colony on Mars contributed four representatives: one religious, one merchant, one scientist, and one laborer. The Council had originally been established to promote Martian inter-colony cooperation and allow for the settling of disputes which otherwise would have had no unbiased adjudication process.

Over a period of around one hundred years, from 2450-2550 the council increased in importance until the colonists began to see the council as their de-facto government. This occurred because of a number of factors, primarily being the growing prosperity gap between Earth and Mars.

Earth was at that time undergoing a new Renaissance. By 2450, a strengthened United Nations had finally consolidated all nations into one world government, ending armed conflict and easing economic disparity. Centuries of environmental remediation meant a stable and healthy ecosystem. Advances in genetic medicine meant the near-elimination of disease and aging for those who could afford it (these weren't officially cured until 2605). And because of the rapid political and environmental improvements, almost everyone could afford some level of treatment.

Mars did not benefit from these changes. Life on Mars was still a life of struggle. The ecosystem, while terraformed, primarily resembled the arctic tundra – moss, lichen, grass, and the occasional shrub. The official plan had called for the development of a temperate-zone climate. However, Earth lost interest in Mars once the environmental conditions on Earth had been stabilized. The flow of supplies had nearly stopped, leaving the colonists to live in a cold and harsh environment.

The economy of Mars was also rather undeveloped. Most of the trade was inter-colony, with only a small percentage of overall trade being conducted with Earth. This meant that there wasn't much Earth currency available, and Earth currency was the only way to purchase the new anti-aging, anti-disease treatments. Most colonists looked at the new reality on Earth with jealousy.

Another factor leading to the declaration of Martian independence was religious practice. The unified government of Earth was officially secular, and public religious display of any kind was outlawed. Religions were a matter for private practice only and were viewed as an anachronism. This meant that religious conflicts were almost entirely eliminated on Earth, but it also meant that the staunchly religious felt persecuted and fled the planet.

Religious refugees either went to Mars, or volunteered to take colony ships to new stars, beginning with the first wave of generational ships in 2500. Those who went to Mars fit in well with the existing colonists, who had retained much of their religious predisposition over the centuries.

The seat of government on Earth was still officially sovereign over the Martian colonies, despite their distance and their neglect. By 2550 the colonists considered the Grand Council to be their true government for all practical matters and there was little loyalty to Earth. These issues finally became a crisis when the supreme court on Earth issued a ruling that Earth's secular anti-religion laws applied to Mars, even though they had not specifically included Mars in the original text. The Grand Council, which was by then dominated by its religious members, saw this as a threat to their religious freedom and so declared independence from Earth.

Earth's initial response to the declaration was silence. In fact, the period of 2550 – 2600 was marked by no official communication of any sort. Mars used this period of time to build up its own technological and military capabilities. The entire infrastructure of Mars was transformed to serve the purpose of securing their independence.

In 2600 the Grand Council imposed a tax on all Earth corporations operating on Mars. Earth's government responded with a notice that this tax was illegal and unenforceable. Mars responded by placing an embargo on ships until the tax had been paid.

Corporations complained to the Earth government, and Earth launched a small police action against Mars. The force was met in orbit by the new fleet of the Free Martian States. The Martian ships outnumbered the Earth ships ten to one and so the initial battle was short. There were high casualties among the Earth ships. This victory was celebrated across Mars.

On Earth, the battle was considered an out-right act of war, and so a military fleet was launched. These ships were larger and more powerful than the police ships that had been previously sent. The space war was over within a week and the Free Martian States were now without viable space capabilities.

Although the space war was lost almost immediately, the war continued on the ground for twenty-five years. The Free Martian States had built up a large and dedicated volunteer army. Their weaponry and defenses were formidable. Over the course of twenty-five years Earth slowly laid siege to Mars. The battles were drawn-out and bloody. Territory changed hands at a rate of meters per day.

By 2625, Earth had managed to occupy most of the Southern Hemisphere, although they were subject to frequent guerrilla attacks within the occupied cities. The more highly populated Northern Hemisphere was very well defended, especially in the region around the Grand Council at Kasei Valles. Earth's military planners had only two scenarios in front of them: a hundred more years of ground war, with the outcome uncertain, or to bombard Mars from space until the Free Martian States surrendered. The war had become politically unpopular on Earth, and a new global leadership was elected with a mandate to seek peace with Mars.

The peace deal with Mars involved compromise on both sides. First, Mars accepted Earth rule. Earth's government and legal system superseded those of Mars. Mars would not be allowed to have its own standing army or space fleet. In exchange, Mars was granted significant independence over most local decisions – issues like religion and the local economy were under the jurisdiction of the Grand Council. Finally, Mars was given subsidized access to anti-aging and anti-disease treatments.

Mars accepted the terms of the peace deal in a referendum, where it was approved by more than 90% of the population. Analysis of voter intentions indicated that access to the new medications was the primary factor in colonists' decision to vote for peace.

- From the Files of Ashley Chung, Archivist

22

Labia Minor, on Gliese 832c

Shauna Lone stood below the proscenium arch in the Imperial Hall. Technicians were working all around her, putting up decorations and testing lights in preparation for the coming coronation ceremony.

"Do you know why we're moving the government to Labia Minor?" Shauna asked.

"No, I have no idea," said the wrinkled old man.

"Labia Minor was the seat of power at the height of the Empire. The Imperatrix ruled from the Senate building next door. She gave her public speeches from this stage."

"That's great. Great news. Congratulations," the man said.

"You don't really care, do you," Shauna said.

"Not in the least. I figure how you run your government is your own business, as long as you come through with your side of the deal."

"The Labian Empire has always honored its word," Shauna said.

"So does the Free Martian States," he said.

"And how's that working out so far, Mandala?" Shauna asked.

"It's working fine. We've got people placed at critical locations in the infrastructure on Mars and in Stellar Corp."

"Oh?"

"We're ready. By the time Stellar Corp realizes what happened, we'll have Mars back under our sovereign control and Stellar Corp will be paralyzed."

"And then what?" Shauna asked.

"And then we wipe them out, or at least punish them until they give in to our demands," Mandala said.

"Earth," Shauna said.

"Earth. They stay grounded on their own planet. The solar system is ours. Stellar Corp is ours. Never again will the godless bureaucracy of Earth threaten the religious freedom of.... Of anybody, anywhere."

"What about the Labians?" Shauna asked.

"As we agreed, you help us, and you stay out of our solar system. You restore the Empire to its former holdings in the Near Cluster."

"And our future growth?"

"As we've already agreed, the systems within the Labian Empire and those of the Lower Reach are yours to colonize. The Upper Reach is ours," Mandala said.

"Peace in the Galaxy," Shauna said.

"Of course. Peace, and the freedom for us to live as we desire. Our ends are quite compatible. But we've discussed all of this before," Mandala said.

"With the loss of one of your transport ships, there are some who are questioning the ability of your people to complete your mission."

"The Bollox was a great loss. The captain was a veteran of the War of Independence. But we will succeed. We have another force-field generator, and it has been successfully delivered to our frigate," Mandala said.

"Our frigate. Which arrived at the rendezvous point with two large projectile holes in its side. But I suppose it's your choice if you want to risk the mission by engaging in firefights."

"We're warriors too, we fight when we choose to. But that's not the problem. The problem is we had no intelligence about a ship protecting Titania. The only Stellar Corp frigate that was near Uranus at the time was the S.C. Johnson, stationed at Oberon. The sabotage of the weather station on Adriana was timed to be sure that there would be no other ships around. We were wrong, unfortunately. But our contacts have reconfirmed that no other Stellar Corp vessels are scheduled to arrive in the Uranus system for at least a week. Their communications are down, so they are isolated until then. We have all the time we need to finish what we've started."

"And what do I say to those among us who want additional assurances? I may be Imperatrix, but I don't rule by my will alone."

"What assurances can I give? We're committed. The foundation has been laid. Now we need to finish the job," Mandala said.

"And if you fail?"

"If we fail, most likely Stellar Corp will find us out. So I'll give you this to tell the doubters among your ranks: if we fail, you can go ahead and shoot me yourself. That should satisfy your compatriots of our commitment. Though to me it doesn't matter. Because if we fail, we're all dead men anyways."

"Well put, Mandala. Your conviction has obviously not wavered. You truly do have a warrior's spirit, if not his body," Shauna said.

Mandala patted his stomach.

"My body has been failing me for some time. But my dedication to the Free Martian States has never faltered."

"Good, good. Continue your mission, once the repairs to our frigate are complete. It will flash to Uranus and deliver the force-field unit to your technicians. Our remaining ships will stay at the rendezvous point until they are needed."

"And then we begin the liberation of Mars. To the future, Imperatrix. I'll leave now. I intend to be there when the liberation begins," Mandala said. He saluted Shauna in the traditional Martian way and walked away.

Standing beneath the proscenium arch, Shauna Lone rehearsed the lines of her coronation speech:

"I pledge my life to the Empire. I pledge my soul to the Empire. I pledge my blood to the Empire. I am Imperatrix. The Glory of the Empire comes first. I lay my life down for the Empire, just as my subjects lay their lives down for their Imperatrix. May the Labian Empire never fall."

23

Aboard Horatio Station

Captain Jeremy Bach stood on the bridge of the Applegate. Horatio Station was only a few kilometers away. A large black scar was visible on the underside of the station. That wasn't a good sign.

"Smitty, I'm going for a visit," Jeremy said.

"Anyone you want to bring with you?" Smitty asked.

"Nobody. Just me."

"That's good, we'll work on the ships' systems. We'll repair the battle damage."

"Call me if anything comes up."

"Will do."

"You're in charge, Smitty," Jeremy said. He left the bridge and went straight to the hangar.

The shuttle touched down in Horatio Station's hangar. Jeremy lowered the shuttle side hatch and stepped out onto the hangar deck.

"*Would you please come to the bridge?*" Wayland Hauer asked over the intercom. "*Once you leave the hangar, turn right. Follow the corridor until you reach the elevator. I'll program it to allow you onto the bridge.*"

Jeremy followed his directions. The elevator door opened right away and he stepped in. There was a button labeled "bridge" on a panel on the wall. The button lit up on its own and the elevator started moving. A few seconds later the doors opened. Jeremy stepped onto the bridge.

"Captain Bach, I'm Wayland Hauer. I've told Commander Tajiki that you're here. She'll be here in a minute. Can I get you anything?"

"No, I'm fine. Well, actually, I could use a drink," Captain Bach said.

"What would you like?"

"Anything. Water is fine."

Wayland walked over to a corner of the bridge. He slid open a panel on the wall, to reveal shelves lined with an assortment of bottles.

"This is the bridge's convenience bar. Here you go," he said. He handed Jeremy a bottle of water. "Sorry it's not chilled. The cafeteria has a better selection, and refrigeration. But this is convenient."

"This is fine. Miigwech."

Jeremy took a drink and looked around the bridge. Horatio Station seemed to have a more recent design than that of his ship, not that it was always possible to tell by stylistic features. Styles came and went, so some newer ships and structures looked old-fashioned compared to some older ones.

Commander Tajiki arrived on the bridge. Jeremy smiled broadly. She was tall and lean. Her hair was shiny and her skin was flush.

"Captain Bach, good to meet you," Tajiki said. She extended her hand.

"Thank you Commander, good to meet you too."

"Captain, how was your trip? A success?" Commander Tajiki asked.

"Not exactly. We need to talk. Can we speak in private?" Captain Bach asked.

"Of course. Let's go to my office," Tajiki said. She led Jeremy off of the bridge and they went to her quarters.

"Have a seat Captain Bach," Commander Tajiki said.

"Thanks. You can call me Jeremy. Jeremy is fine."

"Oh, okay, Jeremy. I'm Lauressa."

Jeremy sighed.

"Things are not good, Lauressa."

"What happened?"

"We tracked the ship to Miranda. When we got there we found a small base."

"Oh, really? What did you find?" Lauressa asked.

"Nothing. It was entirely empty. We found a computer and we managed to copy some data from it. Our engineers are reviewing the data to see if anything valuable was found."

"So the base was abandoned?"

"That's what we thought. But while I was down on the base, a ship attacked the Applegate. It was a surprise hit and they blew out one of our engines."

"Oh that's not good. Is everyone okay?"

"Oh we're fine. Smitty is a fine Captain. He handled the Applegate better in combat than I could have. The ship that attacked us was the same ship that attacked Adriana colony."

"Did you destroy it?"

"No, it retreated. They had reflective armor. It made our lasers almost useless. But Smitty did manage to put two slugs through their hull. They flashed away, but hopefully they'll be out of commission for a while. If we're lucky they're drifting somewhere in deep space."

"Reflective armor?" Lauressa asked.

"Yes," Jeremy said.

"That's expensive stuff. Not many ships have it."

"That's true. But I'm not really surprised, now that we know who they are."

"Who are they?"

"I really didn't want to believe it. I thought it was one rogue ship, a pirate. But a few minutes after that ship flashed away, three more just like it flashed in and raced toward us. We ran."

"So it's some kind of organized group. Not a lone pirate."

"No."

"Then who are they?"

"They're the Labians."

"I need to lay down. This is not good. Not good," Lauressa said. Her face turned white. She got out of her chair and dragged herself over to the bed and fell onto it.

"Do you know what we've been dealing with over here?" Lauressa asked.

"Well, your antenna blew out," Jeremy said.

"Here's my list so far: blown antenna, erased sensor logs, drugged crew, exploding ship."

"My list is: Adriana colony attacked with an old nuclear weapon and somehow an old forcefield was involved. We thought it was the Martians, but then we found the base on Miranda. Empty except for a box from Gliese 832b. Did I mention the box before? Well there it was. The only thing in the base. A box from the Labian homeworld. And then we get attacked and find out that it's not one ship, it's four. And they're Labians."

"We're under attack, Jeremy. It's not an all-out military action, but it's an attack just the same," Lauressa said.

"You think the Labians are attacking your station?"

"It could be. There's someone on the station. We're trying to figure it out. Doctor Poisson is reviewing personnel files right now to see if he can spot anything out of place. Labians are as likely behind it as anybody else. They're softening us up."

"I don't like the sound of that," Jeremy said.

"Because it means this is just the opening act."

Lauressa sat up in bed.

"Could you come over here?" she asked.

Jeremy walked over to the bed and looked down at Lauressa.

"Sit down. I won't bite."

Jeremy sat beside Lauressa. He looked away from her.

"I'm just, I'm just scared. We're all alone out here without our long-range communications," she said.

"So Stellar Corp really doesn't know," Jeremy said. He stared off at the wall. Lauressa was watching him intently.

"They don't know anything. We have to assume that our earlier messages were intercepted somehow."

"So we're on our own."

"We're on our own. A torrent is heading our way and there's no higher ground to go to," Lauressa said. She reached out and touched the back of his head and stroked his hair. Jeremy shuddered.

"Commander. Lauressa. I don't know if you should be –"

"What does it matter? We could be dead in an hour, or in a day."

"I'm not counting on that. I've got a lot to live for," Jeremy said.

"Let me give you something else to live for," she said. She leaned in to kiss him.

"Stop," Jeremy said. He pulled back. "Just stop a second, just hold on a minute."

"What's wrong?"

"You're a higher ranking officer for one thing. Not that it matters really. But I barely know you."

"So? I'm a hundred and eighty-three years old. I'm going to keep on going for at least another hundred and eighty-three years, if not more. Unless I get pushed out an airlock or vaporized by a laser. So what does it matter if we barely know each-other — we're demi-gods, and we might as well enjoy the benefits that divinity has to offer us."

"You're a lot older than I am," Jeremy said.

"How old are you?"

"I'm sixty-five," he said.

"You're a kid. It's okay, I won't hold it against you. How many women have you had?"

"Two.... Three."

"That's not a lot, Jeremy."

"I know, I guess I'm just shy about these things."

"You've got time I suppose. Or maybe not."

"You know Lauressa, I think we will have time."

"Why is that?"

"Because we might not be as isolated as we think," Jeremy said.

"What do you mean?"

"My ship might be able to make it all the way to Earth and warn Stellar Corp."

"There's no way. The S.C. Johnson only has a range of 15 AU. And that ship is only ten years old, with top of the line technology. There's no way your old ship can make it all the way to Earth if they can't."

"We might. I'll tell you a secret. My ship is over three-hundred years old."

"It's antiquated."

"Not so much. The Applegate was one of the last Stellar Corp ships built to war-time specifications. It's armed to the teeth for a ship of its size. In terms of firepower we're probably almost a match for the S.C. Johnson. After all, Stellar Corp has been building ships for peace-time duty for the last three-hundred years, which means that each new ship is built as frugally as possible."

"Okay, so your ship is tough and it cost a lot."

"That's not all."

"What else?"

"The S.C. Applegate has something none of the new frigates have these days. I've got an interstellar superlight drive."

"WHAT!?"

"My ship has an interstellar superlight drive. They cost a fortune to manufacture, but when you're building ships during war-time, you build them for superiority, not for cost-effectiveness."

"Oh my god, Jeremy. This is incredible. I hadn't even thought of that. I would have assumed it was removed and put on a different ship years ago."

"No, it's still there and in one piece. Now it hasn't been used in – who knows – almost two-hundred years. So we'll need to do some restoration work, but I don't see why it wouldn't work."

"Jeremy, I'm stunned. If you can get to Earth –"

"Then we might be able to stop this before it starts."

"This is great news. Go and save us."

"Absolutely, Lauressa," Jeremy said.

"But first, I have something for you."

Lauressa grabbed Jeremy and pulled him close. She kissed his neck and ran her hands down his back.

"I'm not sure...."

Lauressa kissed him on the lips and brushed her hands across his thighs. Jeremy let out a sigh and melted into her arms.

"That's it. Just relax," Lauressa said.

She removed his pants and began to massage his thighs.

"Lauressa..."

She got on top of him and they became, for a time, one creature. Moving as one. Breathing as one. Moaning as one.

Jeremy looked up at Lauressa. Her eyes were closed and her lips were parted. She moved up and down on him slowly. He closed his eyes and floated away to some other world, some other place. Then he almost passed out beneath her.

Lauressa stopped and lay beside him.

"That's a proper send-off for the Captain who will go get the cavalry," she said.

"I'll do my best."

Lauressa stood up and took his hand.

"I'll walk you to your shuttle. Actually, let me introduce you to the station's doctor first."

* * *

Doctor Poisson was still studying personnel files when Lauressa walked into his office.

"Oh, hi Lauressa," Doctor Poisson said.

"Hi Doc. I wanted to introduce you to Captain Bach of the S.C. Applegate," Lauressa said.

"Pleased to meet you Captain Bach," the Doctor said. He realized that Lauressa was holding Jeremy's hand.

"Pleased to meet you as well. Just call me Jeremy."

"So what have the two of you been up to?" the Doctor asked. He looked at Lauressa and smirked.

"Talking about our situation. Jeremy has some good news and some bad news."

"Bad news first," Doctor Poisson said.

"The bad news is his ship was attacked by the Labians."

"Oh no. Are you sure?"

"We're sure," Jeremy said.

"The good news is that Jeremy's ship has an interstellar superlight drive."

"Amazing! That's amazing!"

"It's old and we have to get it running again. There's no guarantee that it will work," Jeremy said.

"Maybe not, but this sounds like the best break we've had so far," the Doctor said.

"Lauressa said that you're trying to figure out who the saboteur is," Jeremy said.

"Yes, but I've had no luck yet. That pile over there are the candidates so far. I've got to look further to narrow them down. I'm not sure how I'll do that."

Jeremy was about to speak when Lauressa said, "Jeremy, did you know that Doctor Poisson here is an engineer?"

"Really?" Jeremy asked.

"He is."

"That was another lifetime ago. I'm a doctor now," Doctor Poisson said.

"Lauressa, do you think I could borrow Doctor Poisson for a few hours?" Jeremy asked.

"I suppose so. What for?"

"Well, he could meet our Doctor and they could help prepare our infirmary for battle. And I also think my interstellar superlight drive might be interesting to you, as a former engineer."

"Your friend makes some good points Lauressa," Doctor Poisson said.

"Okay, go ahead, but only for a few hours. I really feel safer when I have a Doctor on my station."

"I'll have him back by dinner time," Jeremy said.

* * *

"Thank you for agreeing to visit the Applegate," Jeremy said.

"It's my pleasure. I haven't been off the station for a few months now, so this will be fun," Doctor Poisson said.

They entered the hangar and walked to the shuttle. Jeremy pressed a button on the side of the shuttle and the hatch lowered.

"This is an old shuttle," Doctor Poisson said.

"It belongs to an old ship."

Doctor Poisson looked at the shuttle's outer skin.

"The armor on this thing looks like it's at least a foot thick," the Doctor said.

"It was built to take a hit and stay in one piece," Jeremy said.

"To take a hit?"

"Oh, I explained it to Lauressa already. The Applegate was one of the last ships built to war-time specifications. It was designed to operate in the hostile conditions of the last Labian war."

"Everything old is new again. This is going to be a real asset under the circumstances," the Doctor said.

"I hope so. Labian ships are tough. Our last tangle was a hard fight. I think their technology has advanced in the past few hundred years. That's why I want our infirmary to be ready for anything."

"I'll do everything I can to help."

They sat down in the shuttle's cockpit. Jeremy sealed the hatch and powered up the engines. He activated the radio.

"Horatio Station, this is Applegate shuttle. We're ready to depart when you've cleared us," Jeremy said.

"*This is Horatio Station. I'm opening the hangar doors now*," Wayland Hauer said.

The air inside the hangar was sucked out into the air vents. The hangar door unlocked with a clang, and the door started lifting up into the ceiling. The dark expanse of space was visible ahead, a black void dotted with points of light.

"*You're cleared to depart, Applegate shuttle,*" Mister Hauer said.

Jeremy gently maneuvered the shuttle up a few feet from the hangar deck and then forward toward the door. The shuttle began to exit the hangar. They were about a quarter of the way out when the shuttle was rocked with an incredibly loud jolt. The hangar door had rapidly and forcefully closed, violently pinning the shuttle to the hangar deck. Warning sirens went off in the shuttle.

"What the fuck!" Doctor Poisson yelled.

"Horatio Station, emergency!" Jeremy yelled into the communications console.

"This is Horatio Station. There's a mechanical failure in the doors," Wayland Hauer said.

"Can you open them?"

"I can't control the doors at all. It's like the system's burnt out. What's your status?"

Jeremy looked at the cockpit displays.

"Red across the board... but we're still in one piece. We're going to do a manual inspection."

Doctor Poisson got up from his seat and walked back a few meters. He looked around.

"Everything looks fine back here," he said.

"I have a camera view of your shuttle. I'll stream it to you now," Wayland Hauer said.

Jeremy could now see his shuttle via a camera mounted inside the hangar.

"Doc, come take a look at this."

The Doctor looked at the video display and gasped.

"All that armor just saved our lives," he said. On the screen they could see that the hangar doors had gouged deeply into the shuttle's skin. The armor had stretched and deformed, but it was still air-tight.

"Horatio Station, the shuttle is damaged but the hull is intact," Jeremy said.

"That's good news. But I can't get the door open. There's no power. I've put a call out for the station's engineer," Wayland Hauer said.

"How long will this take?"

"I don't know," Mister Hauer said.

"That's a problem," Jeremy said.

"What do you mean?" Doctor Poisson asked.

"We have a war to stop, and I don't plan on sitting here for who knows how long."

"Good point."

"We also don't have water, so if it takes too long we'll get very thirsty."

"Another good point."

"Screw this," Jeremy said. He hit the thrusters and the shuttle started to lift off the hangar deck. The shuttle began to push the hangar door. Its armor creaked, but it held fast.

"Shit! You could have warned me," Doctor Poisson said.

"Sorry! I just had a feeling it would work."

Once the shuttle was close to the hangar ceiling, Jeremy reversed the thrusters. He pulled away from the door and bits of armor tore away from the hull. The door started descending slowly. The shuttle moved forward and they made it into open space. The hangar door closed behind them.

Doctor Poisson got up and walked back. He could hear a gentle hissing sound coming from the ceiling.

"We've sprung a small leak," he said.

"Our ETA is five minutes. Think we'll make it?" Jeremy asked.

"It sounds really small, I think we should be okay," Doctor Poisson said.

"Good. Next stop, S.C. Applegate."

"You're a menace, by the way."

24

Aboard S.C. Applegate

"Smitty, meet Doctor Poisson."

"Hi there Doctor," Smitty said. The window of the Applegate's bridge was behind Smitty.

"Doctor Poisson is going to help Doctor Smith prepare the infirmary for battle," Jeremy said.

"Battle? You're looking to get us into more fights?" Smitty asked.

"Commander Tajiki confirmed that their long-range communication has been sabotaged. Nobody at Stellar Corp knows what's going on here. We have to warn Stellar Corp about the Labians."

"What can we do about it?"

"We're going to visit Earth."

"Oh, so I suppose you'll want me to get the interstellar superlight drive up and running."

"You've got it."

Smitty sighed.

"Fine. Just don't expect any miracles. I'm not sure how long it's been since it was shut down."

"Make it rain, Smitty."

Smitty shook his head.

"I'll get on it," he said. He left the bridge.

"Smitty's a little annoyed. About the Labians I suppose. Anyways, I'll take you down to see Doctor Smith," Jeremy said. He led Doctor Poisson off the bridge. They took the elevator down several levels until they'd reached the level where the infirmary was situated.

Doctor Smith was inventorying supplies when Jeremy walked in with Doctor Poisson in tow.

"Oh, Captain Bach, everything okay?" Doctor Smith asked.

"We're alright. I'd like you to meet Doctor Poisson from Horatio Station."

"Doctor," Doctor Smith said as he extended his hand.

"Doctor," Doctor Poisson said.

"I was hoping that Doctor Poisson would be able to assist you with preparing the infirmary for battle," Jeremy said.

"I'm always happy for extra help, although what I really need are supplies," Doctor Smith said.

"I can help you with that. I've got a decently stocked store on the station. Nothing too exotic, but all the staples are there."

"That's good news. Do you have blood units?" Doctor Smith asked.

"I don't have any real blood, but I do have a large quantity of synthetics."

"That will do fine."

"I'm off to engineering, so I'll just leave you two to get to it," Jeremy said,

"See you later, Captain... Doctor Poisson, would you mind helping me complete my inventory?"

"I'd be happy to," Doctor Poisson said.

Jeremy left the infirmary while the two doctors got to work. He headed to the elevator and went down a few levels to engineering.

In engineering, Smitty was working with John Dvorak and David the Mechanic.

Parts were strewn about the floor and on work benches.

"It's burned out, we'll need to build another," David said.

"It looked fine. How did it burn out?" Smitty asked.

"It's three-hundred year old electronics. Some of it was bound to have degraded," David said.

"So what do we do now?"

"We need to build a replacement part," David said.

"I don't think the workshop has the right tools," John Dvorak said.

"You might be right. I wonder if we can repurpose something that we already have," David said.

John was about to answer when he noticed Jeremy standing in the doorway.

"Oh, Captain, sorry about the mess."

"It doesn't bother me, but I'm a little worried about stepping on something."

"We're inspecting the interstellar superlight drive piece by piece. It's on the workbench over there."

"So what are all these pieces on the floor?" Jeremy asked.

"That's our running inventory of all the spare parts," John said.

"Spare?"

"There was an entire inventory of spare parts for the superlight drive left sealed up in a closet. Lucky for us."

"That is pretty lucky. What were you two just talking about? Something burned out?"

"One of the parts of the drive is burned out," John said. He held up a small cube.

"What is it?" Jeremy asked.

"It's a very specific kind of capacitor, and there's no working spare. Every other part has a spare in the inventory. So this is the only thing holding us back right now."

"We still have to test all the spares. But so far this is the only thing stopping us from testing the superlight drive," Smitty said.

"Well let's hope you find a way to replace that capacitor," Jeremy said.

"You know, I'm pretty sure we have a capacitor with almost identical specifications on our short-range superlight drive," John said.

Smitty put his hands up.

"Woah. Are you sure you want to take the short-range offline? We'll be sitting ducks if we're attacked," Smitty said.

David and John Dvorak looked at the Captain.

Jeremy looked at the three of them. *The burdens of command, why can't they just figure it out themselves. Oh here goes....* "Do it. We need to take the risk."

"Okay, let's get to it," Smitty said.

They went over to the engine room, which was only a few dozen meters away. The short-range superlight drive was installed on one side of the room. Computers and displays lined the walls.

"I'm entering the command to shut down the superlight drive now," Smitty said. He typed in a few commands at a console. The diagnostic lights on the superlight drive turned off.

"Alright, it's off," Smitty said. "Go ahead and trip the breakers."

John Dvorak and David were standing on each side of the superlight drive. Each of them grasped a large circuit breaker and pulled down with their entire weight. The circuits disconnected with a loud thud, which meant that the superlight drive could now be safely removed from its housing.

"Careful guys, let's get it over to the table," John Dvorkak said. They carried the superlight drive to a workbench. John carefully removed the cube-shaped capacitor from it.

"Does this look familiar?" John asked.

David took the cube from John and looked at it closely. "This looks identical."

"As in, one-hundred percent identical?" John asked.

"I think so," David said.

"We just got really lucky," John said.

Smitty smiled. "This is really good. Really good."

"How does a new short-range superlight drive have the same parts as our old interstellar unit?" Jeremy asked.

"It looks like some of the parts are the same," David said. "The two drives were probably made using shared specifications to maximize the ease of maintenance."

"That makes sense," Smitty said. "It's an old ship with old guts. Anything you put in it would have to be able to work with those guts. So we have an old superlight drive that got taken offline and replaced with a new-ish one that's almost identical. Which you'd have to do because everything on this bird is so ancient."

"You know what this means?" John asked.

"What?"

"We might be able to put the interstellar superlight in the housing without making any other changes. Just swap the units out. With everything so similar between the two units, that's the logical conclusion."

"Make sure you test that theory first," Smitty said. "You don't want to push too many amps through it and blow the drive out."

"We'll test carefully before we actually plug it in," John Dvorak said.

"When do you want to do the test?" Smitty asked.

"How about now," David replied.

"Works for me," John said.

John and David walked out of the engine room and returned with the interstellar superlight drive unit. David plugged the cube-shaped capacitor into it.

John connected some diagnostic cables to the unit. A readout began to appear on one of the console screens.

"The interstellar drive's diagnostic system is functioning correctly. It's waiting for us to apply power to the drive so that it can diagnose all of the components," John said.

"I'll bring over a power conduit. How much power do we need to test?" David asked.

"One second, let me check... The diagnostics system says we need to supply one hundred amps for testing."

David went to the wall and opened up a panel. Inside there were spare wires ready for use. He took one of the wires and connected it to an electrical socket. He brought the other end of the wire to the workbench.

"I plugged it into a hundred amp circuit," David said.

"Okay, go ahead," John said.

David plugged the wire into the interstellar superlight drive. Lights blinked on around the unit.

"Diagnostics are starting now," John said.

The diagnostics system sent power to one component of the drive after another, and reported the results. It tested the capacitors – including the one they had replaced. It tested the electro-magnet system, and then it tested the force-field generator. Finally it did a simulated flash to superlight. With each test, it signalled OK on the display console that John was observing.

"It's good. Everything passed," John said.

"Amazing," Smitty said.

"John, what do the diagnostics tell you about the main power feeds?" David asked.

"Let me check. Sixty hertz, one-hundred-thousand volts, ten-thousand amps." John said.

"Okay, I'll check the schematics for the short-range superlight," David said. He brought up the schematics on one of the console displays. The power levels were the same.

"So, it's identical? That's good. We're lucky. The short-range superlight drive must have been built to be drop-in compatible with the ship's original systems," John said.

"So nothing was changed, other than ripping out the old drive?" Smitty asked.

"Exactly," John said.

"Whenever you're ready. Drop it in," Smitty said.

John and David picked up the interstellar superlight unit and walked it over to the housing. They lowered it in.

"Oh, that was it? You're ready now? Okay, we'll head up to the bridge," Smitty said.

* * *

Jeremy was on the bridge of the Applegate with Smitty. The pilot and other bridge crew were around them.

"Engineering, this is the bridge," Smitty said.

"*Go ahead*," John Dvorak said from engineering.

"We're ready up here, we'll jump to superlight when you're ready."

"*We're connecting the drive to the main power now.*"

John and David went to the two large circuit breakers. They pushed up at the same time and the circuits closed. Power flowed to the superlight drive. The lights dimmed for a second and then recovered.

"*The superlight drive is online. Diagnostic status shows that everything is running normally.*"

"Thank you," Smitty said.

Jeremy activated a communications console and addressed the ship.

"This is Captain Bach. We're going to flash to superlight in one minute. All personnel report anything out of the ordinary to the bridge. Stand-by to flash."

"Mister Mulligan, put in superlight destination coordinates of one million kilometers. Pick any location away from Uranus," Smitty said. The pilot found an empty patch of space and entered the coordinates.

"Bring the superlight drive to full power," Smitty said.

The pilot entered the command to charge the superlight drive.

"*Bridge, this is engineering. The superlight drive has fully charged and is holding steady,*" John said.

Smitty held on to the safety bar beside his seat.

"Pilot, prepare to flash in ten, nine, eight..."

"*Engine room standing by,*" John said.

"Seven, six, five, four..."

"*Initiating pre-flash surge,*" John Dvorak said. The hull of the Applegate began to glow and quickly got brighter.

"Three, two, one. Flash."

The pilot entered the command to flash.

"*Here we go!*" John yelled in Engineering.

The Applegate was enveloped in a white ball of light and then vanished. One second later, it appeared one million kilometers away.

"Engineering, status?" Smitty asked.

"*No issues at all down here,*" John said.

Jeremy stood up, and slapped Smitty on the back.

"Way to go!"

"Any reports from the rest of the ship?" Jeremy asked.

Smitty looked at his console.

"Nothing. No reports."

The captain smiled.

"Okay, we made it this far. Mister Mulligan, take us back to Horatio Station at normal speed."

The pilot started the ship back toward Horatio Station, which would take around five minutes at sub-light speeds.

* * *

Doctor Poisson felt the floor shake beneath his feat.

"Did you feel that?" he asked.

"We just went to superlight," Doctor Smith said.

"Oh, that's all. Once we get back to Horatio Station I'll have all the supplies you need loaded onto the shuttle for you.

"I appreciate it. I don't know what to expect, but I want to be prepared for anything," Doctor Smith said.

"You will be, or at least as close as you can be without a full hospital and staff to help you."

"You sure I can't convince you to come along for the ride?"

"Exciting as it would be, I'm needed on Horatio Station. I couldn't leave Lauressa alone," Doctor Poisson said.

"You two have something?"

"We're friends. And we take care of each other."

"It's good to know who your friends are, doc."

"Especially now, especially today. I have to say I'm scared," Doctor Poisson said.

"I agree. But don't you go telling anybody that I'm worried. I have an *image* to maintain," Doctor Smith said.

"Your secret is safe with me."

"*Doctors, are you all ready? We'll be back at Horatio Station in a minute, and as soon as you're done we'll head out,*" Captain Bach said over the intercom.

"Doctor Poisson is going to send a shipment of supplies back with the shuttle. Then we'll be ready to go."

"*That's great news. I knew you two would hit it off.*"

* * *

The shuttle took Doctor Poisson back to Horatio Station. It landed in one of the hangars that still had functioning doors. Fifteen minutes later, the shuttle returned to the Applegate loaded with medical supplies. Doctor Smith took the supplies to the infirmary.

"*Captain Bach, the infirmary is ready,*" Doctor Smith reported via the intercom.

Captain Bach turned to Smitty.

"Let's go," he said.

"Where to?" Smitty asked.

"Let's head to the nearest long-range communications facility."

"Callisto?" Smitty asked.

"That's the one."

"Mister Mulligan, enter in superlight coordinates for Callisto," Smitty said.

The pilot entered the coordinates.

"Hold on, let's let Commander Tajiki know where we're off to," Jeremy said.

He connected his intercom to Horatio Station.

"*Horatio Station here,*" Wayland Hauer said.

"Wayland, we're going to Callisto. That's the nearest long-range communications facility."

"*Understood Applegate, I'll let Commander Tajiki know.*"

"Thank you, Applegate out. Smitty, at your leisure."

"Mister Mulligan, prepare to flash," Smitty said.

The pilot entered the command to flash. The superlight drive built its charge and the pre-flash surge began. The skin of the ship began to glow. The ship glowed brightly for an instant and then was gone. Without a manual countdown the entire procedure took only a second.

A few seconds later they appeared in orbit around Callisto. Jupiter loomed large in the distance.

"Let's get Valhalla base on the line," Jeremy said.

"Let's see... I've got a line opened now," Smitty said.

"Valhalla base, this is Captain Jeremy Bach of the S.C. Applegate," Jeremy said.

After a few seconds of silence he heard a response.

"This is Valhalla base. I'm Commander Waterston. Where did you come from? We're all alone down here."

"We came from the Uranus system. What do you mean you're all alone?"

"Our patrol ship in orbit hasn't responded to us in days. And our long-range communications are down. Do you know what's happening?" Commander Waterston asked.

"You might have been sabotaged, Commander. Long-range communications were destroyed in the Uranus system too," Jeremy said.

"Destroyed? By who?"

"You won't like the answer. We think it's the Labians," Jeremy said.

"The Labians? Oh no, we're not prepared for battle. We have pistols down here. That's it."

"Just hold tight, Commander," Jeremy said.

Suddenly, Jerry Mulligan gasped.

"What is it?" Smitty asked.

"Look," the pilot said. He brought up a camera feed on the main display. A patrol ship floated in Callisto's orbit. The ship was dark. No lights were visible. The bow of the ship was a mess of melted and twisted metal. The body was riddled with dozens of holes.

Jeremy walked toward the display.

"This is unforgivable," Jeremy said.

"This is war," Smitty said.

"What? What's happening?" Commander Waterston asked from the surface.

"I'm sorry Commander. We found your patrol ship. It's been attacked," Jeremy said.

"Are they.... are there any survivors?"

"No. I'm sorry."

"What can we do? We can't defend ourselves," the Commander said.

"If they come down there, just surrender. Stay alive."

Silence.

"Commander Waterston, we have to go. We need to try to find help. Stay alive."

Silence.

"Valhalla base? Are you there," Jeremy said.

"*We're here.... Thank you. We'll manage down here. Good luck.*"

"Thank you Commander Waterston. S.C Applegate out."

Smitty disconnected the line.

"Now what, Captain?" Smitty asked.

"Let's go directly to Stellar Corp," Jeremy said.

"Mister Mulligan, enter superlight coordinates for Earth," Smitty said.

The pilot entered the coordinates.

"Flash now," Smitty said.

25

Aboard Horatio Station

"Has the Engineer started repair work on the hangar door yet?" Commander Tajiki asked.

"No, Commander. He hasn't responded to any of my messages," Wayland Hauer said.

"How many times have you tried to reach him?"

"Ten times in the last hour."

"Petty Officer, uhh, Davis. Right?"

"That's right."

"Can you use the computer to locate Petty Officer Davis please."

"One second," Walyand said. He entered some commands into his console. The computer began using its internal sensor system to look for Petty Officer Davis.

"This is odd. The computer can't find him."

"Are you sure?"

"The computer's sure. It searched the entire station. No sign of him."

"So, where did he go? Pushed out an airlock or something?" Commander Tajiki asked.

Wayland looked at Commander Tajiki, and then deciding that she wasn't serious, said, "We can look through the sensor logs to determine last time that he was detected by the system."

"Okay, let's do that," she said.

Wayland brought up the log history on his console. He started searching through it for the last signs of Petty Officer Davis.

"Found something. Here we go. A few hours ago Petty Officer Davis was in hangar number four," Wayland said.

"And then what?" Commander Tajiki asked.

"Then nothing. That's the last time he appears in the sensor logs. Hold on. This is odd."

"What is it?"

"The doors in hangar four opened and closed at almost exactly the same time that the Applegate shuttle had a run in with hangar one's doors."

"Malfunction? Did Davis actually get sucked into space?"

Wayland brought up some security camera feeds.

"This camera always points at hangar four from the outside. I'll reverse the video until we see the door open."

The video ran backwards rapidly. The time code on the bottom of the screen showed that the video was running backwards, but it wasn't evident on the video since nothing changed on screen.

Suddenly hangar four's door opened, and a small shuttle appeared on screen.

"Woah!" Commander Tajiki said.

"I saw it, I'll play it back. One second."

Wayland stopped the feed and then started playing it forward.

The hangar doors opened. A small shuttle exited the hangar and the hangar doors closed.

"Davis took off in a shuttle?"

"It looks like it. But the shuttle doesn't show up in any of the logs. He must have concealed it from the sensors somehow," Wayland said.

"But he didn't realize that the sensors also record all hangar door activity."

"Maybe, or maybe he was only worried about activities that would set off an alarm on the bridge. Hangar doors don't automatically notify the bridge, but a shuttle leaving without clearance would set off all kinds of alarms."

"He could be anywhere by now," Commander Tajiki said.

"He's probably on Hamlet somewhere," Wayland said.

"Why do you say that?"

"Look at that shuttle," Wayland replied. He reversed the video until the shuttle was on screen and then froze the image. "That's a very short-range shuttle."

"You're right. That would maybe get him to the next moon if he's lucky. So he had to have gone to Hamlet, or at least to another nearby ship."

"I'll take a quick look at the logs, to see if I can verify where he went to."

"Okay, thanks. I'm going back to my cabin. Just send me a message as soon as you've figured that out."

* * *

Lauressa threw herself down on her bed. The console at her desk rang within a second of her head touching the pillow. She walked over and turned on the screen.

"Oh, that was fast, Mister Hauer," she said.

"It was easy because we knew exactly what we were looking for."

"So what did you find?"

"The shuttle definitely went to Hamlet. The radar logs show it heading straight to Hamlet, until it disappears from the radar."

"Disappears?"

"We can't track a ship once it gets inside the colony dome."

"Oh, that's right, of course. Well thank you, Mister Hauer, I'll let you know if I need anything. Oh, Wayland, one second."

"Yes?"

"Do you think you can figure out how he got that shuttle onto the station? I mean, it didn't look like one of ours, did it?"

"I'll look into it."

"Thanks."

Lauressa turned off the display and crawled back onto her bed.

She pulled off her pants. She brought them to her face and smelled them. *I need to have a shower.* She ran her hand down between her legs and pushed against her pelvis. *Come on girl. That's right.* She threw her head back and breathed hard. *God dammit. If I'm going to die in this war I'm going to enjoy every minute that I can.* She made a moaning, wheezing sound, and collapsed onto the bed. *Okay, that's what I'm talking about.... Oh... I really need a shower now.*

Lauressa headed for the shower and washed away the evidence of her most recent adventures with herself and with Jeremy Bach. She smiled when she thought of him. So young. Only sixty-five. She was almost three times his age. But despite his youth, she had faith that he would succeed, or die trying. At least she was able to send him away satisfied, and a bit more of a man than he was before. When he made it to her age – if he made it to her age – then he'd understand how easy it was for her to have sex with whoever she liked. Just for the fun of it. Just another distraction to help pass the time until you either got electrocuted, exposed to the vacuum of space, or shot up with a laser or met some other hideous end. Or until you did yourself in. Other than that, life was just a bowl of cherries, with no real limit yet discovered to how long medical science could keep the cherries coming. The only problems were the complications – some people just got too attached and would haunt you for decades, if not centuries. People like Steven Wang. Wang.

Lauressa got out of the shower and went to her console. She connected to Wang's office, and activated the video feed. Carol Answered.

"Hello Commander Tajiki. Oh my. You're..."

Carol turned away from the display, which had a view of Lauressa's bare breasts and hips.

"Can I speak to Steven Wang please?" Lauressa asked.

"*Okay, one second,*" Carol said. She put Lauressa through to Wang.

"Oh wow, hi Lauressa," Steven said.

"Hi Wang. Steven."

"*You look different.*"

"I'm naked," Lauressa said.

"*I noticed. I haven't seen you, uh, shirtless, in a long time. I'm a little confused.*"

"I'm losing it, Steven, I'm just losing it. I need your help," she said.

"I'm here for you. What do you need?"

"I need to find my Engineer. He disappeared from the station at the same time that one of our hangar doors malfunctioned."

"You think he did it?"

"I think I need to find him and ask him a lot of questions."

"What can I do to help?"

"He took a shuttle down to Hamlet. I'm coming down there. I want you to help me catch him."

"Okay, just you and me?" Steven asked.

"You, me, and your garrison. We can't take any chances."

"Really? Is it that bad?"

"Yes."

"What's happening, Lauressa?"

"Labians."

"I'm sorry, I thought I heard you say Labians."

"That's what I said."

"Oh. Fuck. Are you sure?"

"Pretty sure. So I need to talk with my Engineer. Maybe he knows something that can help us. Because so far things are not looking good."

"Okay, I'll get the garrison ready. You come down here as soon as you can. Uh, dressed maybe? Some of the men can be a little unruly."

"I can handle them. All of them at once if I need to," Lauressa said.

"I know that, just.... just get dressed and come down here."

"Okay, okay, fine. I'll put on my clothes, but I don't have to be happy about it. I'll see you soon, Wang."

"See you soon."

26

LABIA MINOR, ON GLIESE 832C

Imperatrix Shauna Lone smiled. Her regional commanders had been assembled before her to give her the latest news from the front. She knew the news would be good.

"Jessica Jameson, Commander for the Far Cluster, what is the latest news?"

"Imperatrix, the news is good. We have operatives in place at all the major colonies: Epsilon Eridani, Luyten's Star, and Planet Fabulous. They confirm they are ready to act when required. So far the colonies are unaware of our actions."

"Excellent. Thank you Commander Jameson. And now, what about the Near Cluster? Anna Kuresha, what do you have to report?"

"Imperatrix, all of our assets are in place in the Near Cluster," Commander Kuresha said. "The governments of Alpha Centauri and Mount Sinai II have been infiltrated. We are ready to seize control, or continue to monitor communications and ship movement, at the will of the Imperatrix."

"Excellent, Commander Kuresha, thank you. Davida Jelenov, Commander for the Lower Reach, what news do you bring?"

"The Lower Reach is ours, Imperatrix," Commander Jelenov said.

"Excuse me, Commander? Ours?" the Imperatrix asked.

"Imperatrix, our operatives on Delta Pavonis have control of the government."

"There was no order to seize control," Imperatrix Shauna Lone said.

"Imperatrix, the operatives there were already embedded in the government. The colony governor died in an accident – not of our doing – and power fell to the next in line, who is allied to us."

"A fortunate event then."

"Yes Imperatrix. Now since Delta Pavonis is the gateway to the Lower Reach, this meant we were able to fully utilize the colony's ships and resources to cement our presence in the other star systems. We now have operatives and ships in the following systems: Beta Hydri, Zeta Tucanae, GL 693 and 588, 61 Virginis, and GL 480 and 433. The existing colonies are small and incapable of offering us a challenge. The Lower Reach is ready to be colonized and subjugated, at your will, Imperatrix."

"Very good Commander Jelenov. Your initiative is impressive," the Imperatrix said. "Now, Commander for the Upper Reach, Apple Kaur, what is the status of the systems reserved for the Martians?"

"Imperatrix, I have all ships under my command waiting at GL 884. From there they can suppress the rest of the Upper Reach. As you know, the few colonies in the region are in their infancy. They will provide no viable opposition to Martian rule. If the Imperatrix requires my ships to move further into the Upper Reach, or to return to the Empire, we are situated to do both easily."

Shauna Lone nodded. "Sensible. But what about the Martians themselves?"

"They have a small team preparing to take over communications and government on the colonies. We will help them when the time comes, at the pleasure of the Imperatrix."

"Thank you Commander Kaur. Now, Supreme Commander of the Core Fleet, Mei Lun, please update us on your status," the Imperatrix said.

"The fleet is deployed to Epsilon Indi, Lacaille 8760, GL 682, and GL 784. We have taken control of the government and communications on all colonies. We moved quickly and simultaneously on all colonies. The core worlds of the Labian Empire are ours once more."

"Well done, well done."

"As soon as we were certain that the colonies were unable to send any kind of warning to Earth, we deployed the Advance Fleet to the Earth system."

"And where are they now?"

"The Advance Fleet is deployed around Saturn and Jupiter. They quickly cut off long-range communications and eliminated what little resistance we found."

"And the Martians?"

"They have accomplished their tasks expertly. Their resources on Mars and Earth tell us that Stellar Corp is unaware of what is happening."

"So the noose is tightening as planned, and they don't even know it," the Imperatrix said.

"Yes Imperatrix. When the order is given we will be able to act, unhindered by Stellar Corp," Mei Lun said.

"Perfect. The Labian Empire is rising again. We are all a part of history now. In the next few days we will find out if we will succeed at this task, or die trying."

Imperatrix Shauna Lone stood and reached out her arms toward the women around her.

"Commanders, Stellar Corp has numerical superiority, and they are a technological match for us. But they are not Labians. We will use our intellects, our intuition, and our mastery of strategy to outmaneuver them and to defeat them. Go in the name of the Empire and bring victory for your Imperatrix."

The Commanders saluted and left for their ships. Shauna Lone was left standing alone. She began to shake slightly. Jensen Mandala came in from his hiding spot in another room.

"I'm impressed by your mettle under pressure," the old Martian said.

"But look at me now."

"You're taking your people to war. Isn't it understandable that your nerves might be a little worn?"

"Not for someone – a Labian like me – who fancies herself a warrior."

"We're almost there. The hard parts – the coup of parliament, convincing the Commanders to support you as Imperatrix, placing spies and co-opting the colonies – those are done. Now we just need a few days to complete our plan. Mars and the Labian Empire will be free from the heavy boot of Earth."

"You've been fighting this war a long time."

"Five-hundred years, Shauna. And I haven't found an ally as strong as you in all that time."

"Does that speak to my greatness, or to your inability to pick strong allies?"

"We'll know soon enough. I'm heading back to Uranus now, to oversee things personally. It was good to be here in person to learn about your progress, but I need to get back."

"Good, good. I must stay here until I feel confident that I've consolidated my rule. I'm afraid that if I leave there could be a counter-coup against me."

"This game we're playing is dangerous. You knew that when you first agreed to work with me."

"I know that. And don't talk down to me. Don't forget who I am."

"I know who you are now. You're the Imperatrix. Show them only confidence and strength."

"That's all they'll see," Shauna said.

"I'll send you a message when we're in place. Good bye, my Imperatrix."

"Good bye, Jensen."

27

INSIDE A SPACESHIP

Bailey, Shep, and Balraj sat at the window, staring out at the stars. They watched as the shadowy figures of the repair crew moved past the window. It was dark in sublevel zero, so there was little risk of being seen from the outside. Time elapsed slowly for the children, and it seemed to them that hours had passed while sitting at the window.

"This is getting boring," Shep said.

"Well at least we're alive. I just wish we hadn't even gone near that shuttle. We're paying for our nosiness now," Bailey said.

"I hope I get to go home, to see my mom," Balraj said.

"Aren't you worried she's going to kill you?" Shep asked.

"I don't care anymore. I just want to go home. She can kill me all she wants, as long as I get to go home."

"We'll figure out a way, somehow. But for now we just have to sit tight," Shep said.

The ship started turning. They could see the stars move from right to left across the windows.

"Something's happening," Bailey said.

"Maybe the ship is fixed," Balraj said.

The outside of the ship started to glow, first dully, then brightly. Then it flashed incredibly brightly, and went dark. There was nothing outside but black for a few seconds. Then the stars appeared. Sunlight peeked in through a corner of the window.

"I guess they fixed the ship," Balraj said.

"Do you see the sun? Look how big it is! Look!" Shep said.

The sun was much bigger than they had ever seen it in their entire lives. It bathed a sliver of the room in a soft yellow glow.

"We're closer to the sun. I wonder where we are," Shep said.

The ship started to turn, and the sun moved toward the center of the windows.

"Do you see that? What is that?" Balraj asked.

"The sun," Shep said.

"No, not that. Look. There's something else there."

Shep looked out into space, looking for something that he just couldn't see. Then, after a while of searching, he saw a dark object silhouetted against the sun. It was growing larger.

"What is that?" Shep asked.

"I don't know," Balraj said.

"Obviously it's some sort of ship or satellite," Bailey said.

"How do you know?"

"What else would it be? If it was just a rock they wouldn't be heading toward it."

"You're smart. I didn't even think of that," Balraj said.

"I wonder what they're going to do," Bailey said.

The object grew larger and larger, until it was clearly visible and they could make out some features.

"Do those look like antennas?" Balraj asked.

"Kinda looks like that, doesn't it," Shep said.

"So it's a satellite. Wait, do you hear that?" Bailey asked.

"What? Hear what?"

"It sounds like people talking. Listen."

They could hear voices talking, off in the distance. It was coming from the far corner of the room.

"They're coming for us," Bailey said. She started to feel sick again.

"I don't think so. Hold on," Shep said.

He walked across the room. A few seconds later the voices got louder.

Shep came back, smiling. "It's a speaker. I turned it up."

"So we can hear people on the ship?" Bailey asked.

"That's what it seems like. Kinda makes sense that you'd want a way to communicate if you're down here."

"Weapons armed. Ready to fire on the satellite...."

"Go ahead...."

The satellite became awash in a dull glow. It rapidly began to glow red, then white, and then split apart into thousands of pieces.

"Oh wow! They blew it up!" yelled Shep.

"Good work. Prepare to flash."

"Oh, where are we going now?" Shep asked.

"*Set destination to the Rhea communications platform. Flash.*"

The outside of the ship glowed brightly, the ship lurched slightly beneath them, and the stars vanished. Less than ten seconds later the stars reappeared, this time with Saturn looming in front of them.

"Look, there's Rhea," Balraj said. The moon sat just off to the right. There were multiple scraping sounds, and the bright lights of rockets streamed toward the moon.

"Oh, no. This is horrible! Is there anybody down there?" Bailey asked.

"I don't think so. I think Rhea just has an automated communications platform. I don't think there's anyone down there at all, usually," Shep said.

A few seconds later the rockets slammed into the surface of Rhea. Dark clouds spread across the surface. They soon dissipated, revealing a mass of smouldering wreckage.

"*Good work. The Saturn system is blind now. Jupiter and the inner planets will be handled by the other teams. Let's flash before anyone spots us. Set coordinates for the Uranus system.*"

They could hear some other voices, but not clearly.

"Flash."

"Here we go," Shep said.

The hull of the ship glowed, the floor lurched, and the stars turned black. The sequence was now becoming familiar to the three of them. The blue orb of Uranus appeared outside the window a second later. Bailey smiled at the sight of it.

"We're almost home," she said.

"Almost, if we can figure out a way to get out of here. Steal a ship maybe?" Balraj asked.

"I don't know. It's hopeless."

"*Set coordinates for Labia Minor. Flash.*"

The ship flashed away. This time the stars stayed black – they were on a long-distance trip.

"Labia Minor?" Shep asked.

"No idea. I guess it's not even in the solar system," Balraj said.

"So we're going far, really far."

"Well this sucks, one hundred percent sucks. We were almost home," Bailey said.

"I know," Shep said.

"I'm getting hungry now."

"Me too. Maybe we can look around for food."

"Think we'll find any?"

"I don't know. Maybe they store stuff down here."

"Okay, let's look around."

"Guys, I'll hang out here. I need to have a nap," Balraj said.

"Okay, me and Bailey will go look. See ya."

Shep and Bailey walked out of the large room at the front of the ship. They headed down the long corridor. Passages branched out from both sides of the corridor. The sound of the intercom faded away once they'd gotten a few paces down the corridor.

"So, I hope we find food," Bailey said.

"So do I. A burger maybe? Or some pizza," Shep said.

"Haha. Down here? I don't think so."

"You never know. So let's go this way." Shep pointed to a passage on the left.

"Okay."

They went down the passage, which was dimly lit and had loops of wires hanging from the ceiling. Pipes ran along the walls. The passage ended in a room full of crates.

"Ooh, jackpot!" Shep said.

"They're crates."

"Yeah, let's open some."

They went over to the nearest crate and pulled the lid open.

"What are those? Do those look like bandages?" Bailey asked.

"Kinda. Like bandages with goop on them."

Bailey picked up a bundle. There was writing on the back.

"Emergency sutures," she said.

"We don't really need those. But good to know they're there," Shep said.

"Let's open some more crates."

They went to the next crate, opened it, and found more emergency sutures. They moved across to the other side of the room and opened another crate. It was full of something called a "sonic spanner."

"I have no idea what that is," Shep said.

"Me either. Probably some sort of medical tool," Bailey said.

"Let's check another crate."

They moved deeper into the room and started opening more crates. After going through eight additional crates they found: gauze and tape, calamine lotion, surgical clamps, scissors, iodine, surgical steel screws and rods, some type of crazy-strong glue, something called Unna's Boot, Foley catheters, and sigmoidoscopes.

"Wow, this is crazy. It's like some kind of hospital," Bailey said.

"Maybe they're delivering it somewhere," Shep said. He paused for a moment. "You know, the emergency sutures look useful. And the scissors too." He grabbed a pair of scissors and a pack of emergency sutures and shoved them in his pocket.

"Oh, you know, iodine is supposed to be good in case you cut yourself," Bailey said.

"Okay, grab a bottle."

Bailey took one of the smaller bottles.

"Okay, let's go to another room, I don't think there's any food in here. I'll bet every single crate is full of medical stuff," Bailey said.

"Okay, let's go."

They went back to the main corridor and started going down other passages and into other rooms. The passages all led off from the main corridor, so they didn't really have to worry about getting lost.

They came to another room with more crates. Each crate was stamped with the label *Athos Vineyards*. Shep and Bailey opened up a crate. Inside were dozens of bottles.

"Is this wine?" Bailey asked.

"I think so," Shep said. He picked up a bottle. "Made from the finest Merlot grapes in the vineyards of Mount Sinai II. Hand picked and crushed by the monks of the local monasteries, and fermented using the best old-world methods as passed down by the original colonists."

"Wow, sounds like a lot of work to make it."

"Yeah, and gross. Monk feet stomping on it. Eww."

Shep put back the bottle.

"Let's go, this stuff is no good," Bailey said.

"Alright. Next room."

They went further down the main corridor, then turned down another side passage. Here, a smaller room was lined with shelves. Boxes and baskets sat on the shelves. One shelf had a crow-bar and some other large tools on it. Another shelf had multiple tool boxes. Shep opened one of the tool boxes. Inside there were hammers, screwdrivers and wrenches, as well as different tools that looked unfamiliar.

"This is kind of weird stuff. I've never seen half of it before," Shep said.

"Let me see," Bailey said. She pushed past Shep and peered into the toolbox. "Yeah, you're right, I'm not sure. Is that a laser?"

She picked up a small cylinder. She pointed it at the wall and pressed a button. A red dot of light appeared.

"Cool. I'm keeping it," she said.

"Okay. I wonder what else is in here."

The two of them started going from shelf to shelf, looking into the different boxes and baskets, hoping for something interesting or useful.

"Hey look at this!" Bailey said. She pulled a dusty brown brick from a box. There was a latch on the brick. She pressed it and the brick split in half. One half of the brick had a smooth reflective surface and the other half had a keyboard. "Shep! This is a computer!"

"Wow, think it works?"

"I don't know. It's really old, but you know what? I could use it. My mom gave me one just like it when I was little. I've been using it forever."

"Think it can help us?"

"I don't know. But we could play games on it at least."

"Oh cool."

Shep started walking out of the room.

"Where are you going?"

"To check the next room. We still have lots of rooms to check."

"Okay, I'm coming," Bailey said. She shoved the laser into her pocket and carried the computer under her arm.

They checked dozens more rooms, which they were able to do very quickly because each room was empty.

"I'm getting tired," Bailey said.

"Me too.... Just a few more rooms."

They kept moving further along the main corridor, combing through more of the side passageways and the rooms attached. They were most of the way back to the stairs that they'd originally come down when they found a room full of small crates labeled 'rations'.

"Yes!" Shep yelled.

He ran to the first small crate and opened it. Inside there were small containers with eggs. "What's a century egg?" he asked.

"I don't know. I'll eat it. Eggs are good," Bailey said.

"Okay, let's see what else there is."

They went to a few more small crates.

"Biscuits," Bailey said.

"Meat paste," Shep said.

"There's water in this crate over here."

"Let's get a bit of everything and put it into one crate. We could carry one of these little crates all the way back."

"Okay," Bailey said. They gathered some packages of biscuits, some tubes of meat paste, and some bottles of water, and put them in the crate with the eggs.

"This is going to be yummy. Ready?" Shep asked.

"Okay. Go."

They each took one side of the crate and picked it up together. They walked carefully out of the room, down the side passageway and then along the main corridor back toward the room where Balraj was resting. The walk back along the corridor seemed to take forever - it was a much longer trip with the extra weight of the crate.

"Oh wow, this is getting heavy," Bailey said. With one arm carrying the crate and another arm cradling the computer, she was prone to running into things. At least five or six dangling wires smacked her in the face, but she couldn't use her hands to push them out of the way. "Ouch! This sucks," she said when the last one hit her on the nose.

"We're almost there. Listen, you can hear the intercom now," Shep said.

"Yeah, I hear it. Okay, we'll make it."

Less than a minute later they were in the room with Balraj, who was lying down near the windows. Balraj sat up when he heard them come in.

"Oh, you found stuff?" Balraj asked.

"We found some neat stuff," Shep said.

"And we got food," Bailey said.

"Oh that's really good news. Can we eat?" Balraj asked,

"Sure. There's biscuits, meat paste, eggs, and water. Here, take some," Bailey said. She took out a package of each and gave them to Balraj. Shep reached in and took some for himself, and Bailey took some for herself.

The three kids sat down together and ripped open the packages. Balraj squeezed the meat paste onto the biscuits and ate them like a sandwich. Shep tried squeezing the meat paste straight into his mouth.

"This meat stuff is gross," Shep said.

"It's not so bad on the cracker," Balraj said.

"Yeah, maybe I'll do that."

Bailey put one of the eggs in her mouth.

"Oh guys, this egg tastes good. It's salty. It smells a little weird but it's good."

"That's the way they smell. I've had them before. My mom likes them as a treat or something. Oh, I miss my mommy," Balraj said.

"Me too," Shep said. He put a whole egg into his mouth and smiled at Bailey with his mouth open.

"You're so gross," Bailey said.

"Well, at least we have food," Shep said.

They ate some more of the eggs, biscuits, and meat paste, and then drank some water.

"I feel so much better," Bailey said.

"Me too," Balraj said.

Shep smiled and put one last egg in his mouth. Bailey shook her head.

"So now what should we do?" Balraj asked.

"I don't know. I found this computer. We could try seeing if it works," Bailey replied.

"Oh, cool. Can I take a look?" Balraj asked.

"Sure, you just need to –"

The floor lurched beneath them and the room was flooded with light from outside.

On the speaker someone announced, "*Captain, we've arrived at Labia Minor.*"

All three of them ran to the window. The sun was large and bright in the sky, and a planet sat below them, covered in blue oceans and lush green continents.. Dozens of ships of various shapes and sizes seemed to almost fill the space around them. Some of them were coming and going near a large circular object that dwarfed any of the ships. Some of them were heading to the surface of the planet or returning from it, and some of them were flashing away as new ships popped into space to replace them. Some of the ships seemed to be getting repaired. They could see little sparks and flashes of light, like lasers or welding torches.

"Is this some sort of army?" Balraj asked.

"Well we did have a whole war with the Labians, so if this is Labia Minor, well then I guess this is their army," Shep said.

"You mean fleet," Bailey said.

"What?"

"Fleet. You know? It's a fleet of ships. Not an army."

"Oh, okay. Sure, it's a fleet then," Shep said.

"Yeah... I just... I just think 'army' is not the right word for it."

"Okay."

"Okay."

Balraj stared out at the large circular object.

"That's a space station, right?"

"It looks huge," Bailey said.

"Gigantic," Shep said.

"I've never heard of a space station like that before," Bailey said.

"Me neither," Shep said.

"We've never even seen a space station before," Balraj said.

"Yeah that's true. Is that big for a space station?" Bailey asked.

"I don't know. It looks big to me," Shep said.

There was a vibration in the floor and a few seconds later a shuttle passed overhead. It turned toward the planet and headed into the atmosphere.

"I wonder what they're doing," Balraj said.

The trio got tired of staring at the fleet of ships. They sat down and started looking at the things they'd collected.

"I've got iodine," Bailey said.

"I've got scissors and emergency sutures," Shep said.

"I have this little laser," Bailey said. She pulled it from her pocket and handed it to Balraj. "And the computer."

"That computer looks old," Balraj said.

"Yeah, it is, but I know how to use it. At least I think I do. It looks kind of like the one mom gave me."

"What's it good for?" Balraj asked.

"Probably nothing. But I thought, why not bring it."

"Hey Balraj, there's wine back there somewhere."

"Ewww, that's gross."

"I know."

They had been talking for about an hour, when Bailey pointed at the window.

"Look guys, the shuttle is coming back," she said.

The shuttle passed overhead, very close to the windows. They ran for cover, afraid they might be seen.

"Wow, he came really close. Think they know we're here?" Bailey asked.

"Wouldn't they just come down if they did?"

The shuttle was gone. There was another slight vibration in the floor.

"I guess that's the shuttle landing, or the doors of the ship are closing," Shep said.

A few minutes later they heard something very interesting on the loudspeakers.

The voice sounded like it belonged to an old man.

"*My meeting with the Imperatrix went well. They are carrying out their side of the deal. Her ships and people are in place. We are ready to proceed as planned.*"

There was silence on the loudspeaker for a moment.

Then, the old man said, "*Set coordinates for Uranus.... Flash.*"

The planet and the fleet of ships vanished, and the outside of the window became entirely black.

"Oh, we're heading back to Uranus," Balraj said.

"That's good news, right? Better than being here, right?" Shep said.

"Yeah, but now what? I guess sit around and wait," Bailey said.

"Sure. In the meantime, I guess we could have some more meat paste."

28

HAMLET, OBERON

"Wayland, we've touched down at the Hamlet Spaceport," Commander Tajiki said.

"Good luck, Commander Tajiki. *The Doctor and I will keep the lights on for you,*" Wayland Hauer replied from Horatio Station, which was in orbit five-hundred kilometers above.

"Thanks Mister Hauer, we'll talk again soon."

Lauressa turned off the transmitter and sighed. *Here we go.* She pressed a button on her console and the hatch on her shuttle opened. Steven Wang was outside with ten men from his private garrison.

"Your escort, Commander Tajiki," Steven Wang said. He raised his hand toward her.

"Oh, thanks Wang. Anything suspicious on the way over here?"

"Nothing at all. I have men deployed throughout the area and along the route back to my office. They'll let us know if they see anything to be concerned about."

"Good," Lauressa said. She turned and pressed her hand against a panel on the side of the shuttle. The shuttle hatch closed. "Okay, let's go."

"Chang, you stay here and keep an eye on the Commander's shuttle," Steven said. One of his men stepped forward and nodded. "Alright, let's get back to the office."

Steven turned and started walking toward the exit of the spaceport. Two of his men ran ahead and checked around the corner. The other men surrounded him and Lauressa. So far, they were more organized than Lauressa had been expecting.

"I'm impressed so far," Lauressa said.

"That's what I live for," Steven said.

"Are these guys former Stellar Corp?"

"Some of them."

Two men up ahead sent hand signals to the main group, and then moved farther ahead to an intersection.

"They seem well trained."

"In this line of work they have to be. You never know what's in the next cargo ship you inspect."

The lead pair crossed the intersection and met up with another group of men. There were more hand signals. The group fanned out ahead.

"Any mercenaries?"

"If someone has been a soldier for hire I won't hold it against them. Those kinds of skills can be useful."

"So, ex-mercenaries."

"I should hope so. Our employment contract explicitly forbids secondary employment. You seem quite interested in my squad," Steven said.

"I'm curious. But it's good to know I'm in strong hands."

"You mean good hands?"

"That's what I said."

"Oh I thought you said..."

"*Suspicious activity on 12th Avenue*," a voice said over a hand-held communicator.

A man just to the right of Steven Wang replied, "Do we need to change our route?"

"*Stand by, we're investigating.*"

Steven pointed at the man and said, "That's James Royson, the garrison's commander."

James Royson looked at Lauressa and said, "Hi there, Commander."

Lauressa nodded. She stood a little straighter and tightened her stomach. *That man is sculpted from hard ebony. Stop it. You've got work to do.* She shook her head.

"Something wrong?" Steven asked.

"No, no, Wang. I was just thinking about something."

Steven shrugged slightly.

"*It's just some teenagers messing around, we're good.*"

"Roger that. But keep an eye on them," James said.

"Will do, over."

"That's good news. We're almost there. The office is just another block that way."

"Okay. So what do we do once we get to your office?" Lauressa asked.

"I'll give you a tour while the garrison gets ready, and then we'll go looking for your engineer."

"That sounds great."

The rest of the walk to his office was uneventful. The men who had guarded them went off to their garrison. Steven led Lauressa to the elevator to his suite. The doors opened to reveal Carol sitting at her desk.

"Oh, Steven!" Carol said. She hurriedly put away the sandwich she had been eating. "Oh, and uh, Commander Tajiki, hello." There was a spot of mayonnaise on the edge of her mouth.

"Hello, Carol. So this is the office. Nice view," Lauressa said.

A window behind her desk looked out over most of downtown Hamlet. The neon-colored signs of different businesses glowed in the distance and the colony dome glittered in its daylight cycle.

Carol turned and looked out the window.

"Oh, yes, it is a nice view," she said. She turned back to Lauressa, but they had already moved on to Steven's private office.

"So this is where the magic happens," Steven said.

"Magic."

"Sure, from here I oversee all of the operations of Hamlet Customs Brokers. I also have a fine selection of drinks."

He walked over to a panel on the wall and slid it open. Dozens of bottles, all in different sizes and colors, filled the shelves.

"Can I offer you anything? I have a lot of things that are hard to come by."

Lauressa looked at the drinks. *You really shouldn't. You have a job to do. But he's offering. Well just one won't hurt.* "Alright, just a small one. What do you recommend?"

"I have a bottle of Laphroaig twenty-five year old. But it was bottled in 2800, so you can think of it as - let me do the math - three-hundred-and-thirty years old."

"I'm sold," Lauressa said.

Wang poured a small amount into a glass and handed it to Lauressa. It was a deep gold color and smelled like medicine. She took a sip. It evaporated up her nose and left behind an aftertaste that made it feel like she was eating caramel while smoking a cigar.

"Wow," she said.

"Incredible, isn't it?" Wang asked. He watched Lauressa take another drink.

"Thanks," Lauressa said. *That hit the spot.*

"So, how long before the garrison is ready?" she asked.

"They should be ready now, but I wanted to have a minute to talk with you in private, just the two of us."

"Okay, go ahead."

"Lauressa, are you sure it's the Labians?"

"As sure as we can be."

"How far does this thing go? Your engineer, and who else?"

"I don't know. That's why I want to talk to him."

"Okay, we'll find him. Lauressa, who do we know we can trust? I mean, when it really counts?"

"I trust you," Lauressa said. Steven smiled. "I also trust Doctor Poisson."

"You never call him by his first name."

"I just always think of him as Doctor," Lauressa said.

"So just him and me," Wang said.

"That's it. I suppose I can trust the captain of the Applegate. He's off now trying to see if he can get help. And the Captain of the Johnson. He's in orbit right now. I think he's trust-worthy, or at least I don't think he'd cross me."

"It wouldn't be smart to cross you, would it. Okay, so it's a small group of people we can trust. I'll tell you who I trust: James Royson and Garret Chang. That's why I left Chang with your shuttle."

"What about the rest of your men?"

"I don't know them well enough to trust them. I've known Royson and Chang for a long time. I know their families. I know their history. They've proven their loyalty. And that's what I'm worried about. If the Labians are out trying to start some kind of war, and if they've got plants in Stellar Corp, then we can't trust anyone we're not absolutely sure of."

"I get it," Lauressa said.

"Alright, let's get down to the garrison. We're both going to get ourselves some proper gear."

They headed out of his office and down the elevator. They were met at the garrison by James Royson.

"Hi there, Commander," Royson said.

"Hi," Lauressa said. She paused for a minute. *Say something. Say Something!* "Uh, how are you, Commander Royson?"

"I'm fine. You know I don't have an official rank."

"Are you sure? You look like you're made of the right stuff," she said. *Oh god, I'm losing it, this is pathetic. But look at him, dammit! Stop it. Just stop it right now.*

Royson smiled. "Thank you, Commander. Well, let's get you and Mister Wang properly outfitted. Follow me to the armory," he said.

He led them into the back of the barracks. There was a door that had a keypad and a biometric hand scanner. Royson entered a code and then placed his hand on the scanner. The door unlocked and they went inside.

"Mister Wang told me a little bit about who you're trying to find. We need to be prepared for anything. Here, put this on first."

Royson handed Lauressa a combat jumpsuit. It was a thin one-piece outfit consisting of pants and a long-sleeve top that was reinforced against both laser and bullet impact.

The suit shimmered in multiple colors.

"Wow, this is shiny," Lauressa said.

"Those are prisms. They reflect the photons from a laser. So if someone tries to hit you with a laser, it will spread the beam around the suit and then disperse it harmlessly in all directions."

"Stellar Corp doesn't have this kind of suit, at least not that I know of."

"Stellar Corp isn't willing to pay the cost during peacetime," Wang said. He put on an identical suit. "Tell her about the bulletproof part," he said.

"The inner lining has multiple layers of carbon nanotubes. There are also layers filled with a liquid that reacts to incoming physical impact, hardening or softening as required."

Steven Wang turned to Lauressa, and said, "hit me." He pointed to his Stomach.

"Hard?"

"Not too hard, I don't want you to hurt your fist. But give it a good hit."

"Okay," she said. She punched him in the stomach. "It feels like a metal plate," she said. She rubbed her fist.

"Pretty cool stuff, right?" Steven said. He grinned widely.

"Alright, these aren't toys, you two. We need to finish getting you outfitted. These are your helmets," Royson said.

Lauressa and Steven both put on combat helmets. They had the same shimmery look as the suits. The visors in the helmets had an internal display that could overlay thermal and other imaging on top of their normal sight.

"Okay, weapons," Royson said.

He handed them several different side arms. The first was a black pole a half-meter in length with a dial on one end and a button on the side.

"This is a stun stick, police use them in the colonies. It's also a favorite of smugglers. It's small and useful in close quarters. You can set it to discharge up to a hundred thousand volts to incapacitate an attacker. You can use it at lower voltages just to get your point across. You can also use it as a blunt object to hit with."

They secured the stick on the belt of their suits.

Royson gave them both a small handgun. "This is a subsonic nine millimeter handgun. It's accurate, lethal, and nearly silent. There's twelve rounds in the clip."

"I've never had to carry a gun before," Lauressa said.

"Never?" Royson asked.

"Only during training."

"You're lucky, then. Maybe this is something you'll feel more comfortable with."

He produced a pair of long hand guns.

"This is a long-range stealth rifle. If you can get a clean shot at some unarmored skin, you can deliver an anesthetic dart from two-hundred meters. Perfect for getting in somewhere without having to shoot your way in. Or taking someone prisoner without a fight."

"I feel so deadly. Wait, why aren't you dressed?" Lauressa asked.

"I'll get my suit and gear together now, while the team assembles outside. See you in a minute," Royson said. He left the armory and headed back to his mess.

"Let's go outside," Steven said.

Just outside the entrance of the barracks, a team of ten men were gathered in full combat gear. Some had the same weapons that Lauressa had, but there were some who seemed to be carrying lasers or assault rifles.

Royson came out of the barracks behind them.

"Alright men, we're ready. We're following Commander Tajiki's lead here," Royson said. He turned to Lauressa. "You lead the way, and I'll keep you out of trouble and watch your back."

"Thanks Commander Royson," Lauressa said.

"I'm not a comman... never mind," Royson said. He smiled and turned and walked over to his men.

"Where to?" Steven asked.

"I'm not sure," Lauressa said.

"Uhh, okay."

"I suppose we could start at the space port. I assume he landed his shuttle there."

"How about I just check the spaceport logs?"

"Oh, that's a good idea."

"Hold on," Steven said. He retrieved the spaceport logs and displayed them on his helmet visor. "Oh, there's nothing here. No shuttles."

"Are you sure?"

"In the last twelve hours there are records of only cargo ships, some larger transports, and your own shuttle."

"But he flew inside the colony dome."

"He must have landed somewhere else."

"Great."

Steven raised his visor.

"Royson," Steven said.

Royson walked over from his group of men.

"Mister Wang. Ready?"

"So, Royson, the shuttle that we're looking for doesn't show up on the spaceport logs."

"He landed somewhere else," Royson said.

"That's what I'm thinking. Do you think your friend at Hamlet Security would be able to check the colony's internal radar?"

"Let's give him a call," Royson said. A few seconds later he said, "Hey Snaggletooth, it's Jackal. Can I get your help with something?"

Steven smiled and leaned in close to Lauressa's ear. "They've got these nicknames, from some kind of team they were on together. I think it's funny."

"Are you sure?" Royson asked. "Hey, would I doubt you? I just want to make sure you're sure. No. Snaggletooth. No. I've got a squad ready to go right now so I just want to be sure. Yeah, okay, I owe you a beer. And another for the last time. Yeah, it's been too long. Well, you know, we've been busy. Okay, okay, next weekend. Fine, three beers. Thanks, gotta go. You too."

"So?" Steven asked.

"My contact says that the colony radar tracked a small shuttle that came in a few hours ago. It landed out in the industrial district past the smelters. It hasn't left."

"Great. That's pretty far from here, let's get the transport ready."

"Okay."

"Oh, did you get coordinates?"

"Right here," Royson said. He pointed at the visor on his helmet. He turned and hollered at one of his men to go get the transport. A minute later an eight-wheeled armored truck rolled up in front of them.

The transport had four forward-facing seats at the front, and two long side-facing benches in the rear. Royson, Steven, and Lauressa sat up front. The squad of ten men sat on the long benches.

"You guys ready, Sym?" Royson asked.

One of the men, presumably Sym, replied that they were ready. Royson hit the accelerator and the transport moved forward.

"This is going to be a long ride. The smelters are nearly a hundred kilometers from here," Royson said.

The transport wound through the streets of Hamlet. They drove past the spaceport, then on through the main business district. They passed the commercial center of the colony, where there were so many neon-colored signs that the streets were as bright during the day as they were at night. They went on through the residential neighborhoods, which alternated between gleaming high-rise towers and quiet tree-lined streets buttressed with two, three, and four-story walk-ups. Beyond the residential neighborhoods were a series of parks, marshes, and lakes. Beyond that stood the smelters. These were dozens of large, dark, hulking buildings that created different kinds of metals and ceramics and let out a portion of their exhaust into the colony to help maintain its atmosphere. The air in the transport began to smell like burning copper mixed with sulfur. Lauressa put her hand up to her nose, but the smell soon dissipated as they left the smelters behind.

Past the smelters there was the industrial district. The area was a rabble of low-rise factories and warehouses. The streets were extra wide to make room for the trucks that shipped items to and from the spaceport. Royson took the transport around a corner and stopped.

"Alright folks, the shuttle landed just a few blocks away. Let's proceed on foot," Royson said. "Sym, I've transferred the landing coordinates to everyone's visor displays. Move out."

"You heard the man, let's move," Sym said. He hit a button and the back hatch of the transport opened downwards and became a ramp. Sym headed out along with the rest of the squad. They took up positions around the transport. A few went across the street and crouched along a wall.

"Okay, here we go," Royson said. He climbed out of the transport. Lauressa and Steven came out after him.

Royson nodded at Sym, and Sym pointed forward. The squad began to advance along the street, in the direction of the shuttle.

"Remember, if we get into a fight, you get down," Royson said.

"I can take care of myself," Lauressa said.

"I'm sure you can, but the two of you are my responsibility. So if things get hot, I'm keeping you safe."

"Well I can't argue with that logic," Wang said.

"Then why bother with the combat suits and the weapons?" Lauressa asked.

"We'd be foolish to go into an unknown situation unprepared. But like I said, I'm not interested in putting you in the line of fire," Royson replied.

Lauressa shrugged and continued on silently.

"Point sees the shuttle," Sym said over their helmet intercoms.

"What's his position?" Royson asked.

"At the next block. He's peeking around the corner into a side-street."

"Alright, let's do this," Royson said.

The squad took up positions at the corner. Some ran across the street so that the side-street was covered from both sides.

"Ready?" Royson asked.

Lauressa nodded. Sym gave a thumbs up.

"Okay," Wang said.

"Move in," Royson said.

Sym made a hand gesture and the squad advanced down the side-street toward the shuttle. The shuttle was in the middle of the street and seemed to be unattended. The squad moved up to the shuttle and surrounded it. Two of the men went further down the street, well past where the shuttle was, and crouched in some doorways.

"The shuttle is secured," Sym said.

"Let's go," Royson said. He led Lauressa and Steven to the shuttle.

"Commander Tajiki, can you get in?"

"I should be able to," Lauressa said. She took off a glove and pressed her hand against a scanner. The hatch unlocked. Lauressa was about to push it open when Royson pulled back on her shoulder.

"Hold on," he said. He stepped in front of Lauressa and opened the shuttle hatch. He stepped inside and looked around. "It's clear, come in."

Lauressa entered the shuttle.

"Anything in here look helpful?" Royson asked. Lauressa looked around but didn't see anything useful.

"No. Let's check the communications logs," Lauressa said.

She went to the pilot's console and entered a code. The last communication was recorded in the computer's memory. She played it back.

"*I'll be there in a few minutes... pffft ... do you read me ... pffft ... interference ... pffft ...*"

"That sounds like Petty Officer Davis," Lauressa said.

"*Come in ... pfft ... I'm almost there ...*"

There were a few seconds of silence, and then a different voice was heard.

"*We'll meet you as planned ... pfft ... don't say another word ... pfft ... not secured ... pfft ...*"

"That's the end of the recording," Lauressa said.

"I know that voice," Royson said.

"You do?" Steven asked.

"I think so. He's a soldier for hire. I've worked with him a few times in the past."

"Do you know where we can find him?" Lauressa asked.

"I know where his office is."

"He has an office?"

"It's a small one-room office with a back-room for supplies. He uses it to meet with clients. It's a ten minute drive from here."

"Okay, well I'm ready when you are," Lauressa said.

"What about the shuttle?"

"I'll lock it down and we'll worry about it later," Lauressa said. She entered a code into the pilot's console and the power shut down. "It's not going anywhere without my code."

"Sym, let's get back to the transport."

"Moving," Sym said.

Royson walked out of the shuttle. Lauressa and Wang followed behind. The squad began to retrace their steps and headed back the way they'd come.

"*Movement back here,*" said one of the men who had been crouched down in the doorways.

"Hold up," Sym said.

"*Five men.*"

"Defensive positions," Sym said.

"Get back in the shuttle," Royson said.

Lauressa and Steven Wang turned to run back to the shuttle. Lauressa's suit suddenly glowed blue all over.

"Laser!" Royson said.

"*No weapons visible on the five men. They're running. It's not them.*"

"Are you okay?" Wang asked.

"Where did it come from?" Sym asked.

"I'm okay. There's smoke," Lauressa said. Parts of the skin of the suit looked melted. They ran inside the shuttle.

"*Target on the roof!*"

"I see him," Royson said. He brought up his weapon and fired. The person on the roof stepped back to safety.

There was a popping sound.

"Gunfire! I'm hit!" said one of the men.

"Jarvis, get yourself to cover!" said Sym.

A squad mate's suit glowed blue and he fell over.

"*I'm burning!*"

"Get Khaala to the shuttle!" Royson said. Sym ran to the fallen soldier and dragged him into the shuttle. He came back out of the shuttle and just as he did a large object hit him in the chest. Sym landed on his back.

"Aggggghhh!" he yelled. "Heavy projectile. On the other roof," Sym said. He pointed in the direction of the roof. He looked down and an entire section of the suit was leaking liquid.

"On it." One of the squad crouched and pointed a heavy laser up at the roof. He fired at a spot below the roof and the wall crumbled, bringing the roof and a person down with it.

At the same time, one of the other squad-mates was propelled backward. The force was so violent that his helmet flew off. He held his head and curled up into a ball. Two others gathered around him and fired up at the roof. There was a scream from the roof and then silence.

In the distance, they heard someone shout, "pull out! Pull out!"

"They're falling back. Squad, report," Royson said.

"I took a big hit, but I'm okay. My suit is fried," Sym said. "Jarvis was hit in the arm, but he'll be okay. Khaala has burns. His suit didn't dissipate enough of the laser. What happened to Silver?"

"Silver? Silver!" Royson said. He ran over to him. He was still holding his head.

"I've been hit," Silver said. His voice seemed distant.

Royson knelt down.

"Let me see your head."

Silver lowered his arms. The right side of his face was pulverized. His right ear was missing and his cheek was crumpled inwards.

"Everybody in the shuttle now," Royson said.

The squad carried Silver into the shuttle. It was a tight fit with all thirteen people in the shuttle.

"Get us out of here Commander Tajiki."

Lauressa sat in the pilot's chair and entered a code. The engines powered on and the doors closed.

"Where to?" she asked.

"The hospital. I'll send the coordinates to your visor now."

29

ABOARD S.C. APPLEGATE

The Applegate appeared in normal space almost a million kilometers from Earth. The Sun warmed the hull of the ship and light poured in through every window.

"We're home, boys," Smitty said.

"Get Stellar Corp on the line," Captain Bach said.

"On it."

Smitty sent the standard Stellar Corp message packet. He waited.

"No response yet."

"That's odd. Try it again."

Smitty re-sent the message packet. And he waited.

"Still no response."

Jeremy looked at Smitty, who was frowning and turning red.

"Smitty, maybe there's a communications problem."

"Doubt it."

"Mister Mulligan, take us closer to the moon," Jeremy said.

Smitty walked over to the pilot. "Nice and easy, no sudden moves. Just drift on in."

"What are you worried about?" Jeremy asked.

"I'm worried that something's happened, and I don't want to get noticed. I recommend we run silent."

"Good thinking. Go ahead," Jeremy said.

Smitty went over to his console and entered in a few commands.

"We're running silent now. Active sensors are shut off and all external lights have been turned off."

The pilot nudged the ship toward the moon with a few quick bursts of the maneuvering thrusters.

"I'm scanning for ships with the telescopic cameras. I don't see anything." Smitty said.

They were drifting toward the moon on a course that would take them past the dark side.

"Try to get Stellar Corp again," Jeremy said.

"Alright Captain," Smitty said. He sent the message packet again. No response.

"It's been more than a minute. Their communication system should have sent us an automatic response within a few seconds."

"Maybe we should try again," Captain Bach said.

"Let's wait. If anybody out there wanted to find us they could triangulate our position. The risk goes up as we send more transmissions."

"Good call Smitty. We'll wait."

The pilot kept an eye on the ship's course. There was no real need to do so, since its course wouldn't change without his input. Smitty used the telescopic cameras to scan for ships. He concentrated on the inner orbital zones around Earth – the space between the earth and the moon where most ships tended to gather. If the angle was right, another ship would either glow as a tiny point of reflected sunlight or appear as a black spec crossing over the blue and white planet in the background. If the angle was wrong the other ships could be virtually invisible.

Jeremy sat and stared at Earth. He got up and began to pace.

"How long has it been? Smitty? Anything?"

"No ships visible yet. And it's been five minutes."

"Shouldn't we have seen something by now? Earth should have ten or even a hundred times the traffic that Oberon has," the Captain said.

"Seeing as we're nearly a million kilometers from Earth, that means we're looking for ships that are most likely eight or nine hundred thousand kilometers away from us," Smitty said.

"You're right. They'd be nearly invisible at this distance."

"We're beginning to transit across the moon's dark side," the pilot said.

"Distance?" Smitty asked.

"We're about five hundred thousand kilometers away."

"Let me take a look with the telescopic camera. One second."

Smitty scanned across the surface of the moon. He could see the dark-side colony, but only a few lights were visible.

"The dark side colony doesn't seem to be very active," Smitty said.

"I see a flashing light," the pilot said. He pointed at the screen.

"I see it too. That's odd. Wait, that's a laser transmission."

"Laser?" Jeremy asked.

"That's right. Give me a second, I can decode it."

Smitty took the video feed from the camera and passed it to the communication system.

A voice came through on the loudspeakers.

"Stellar Corp ship, can you read us? Stellar Corp ship, are you there? Please respond."

"How do we respond?" Captain Bach asked.

"Let's try a tightly focused radio transmission. Say something."

"This is Captain Jeremy Bach, on the S.C. Applegate. Can you hear me?"

A few seconds passed.

"Captain, we hear you. Is your radio transmitter secure?"

Jeremy looked at Smitty.

"There's nothing between us and them to intercept it, as far as I can see."

"We think it's secure. Who is this?"

"We're scientists on the dark side colony. We've had no contact with Stellar Corp for several hours."

"What happened?" Jeremy asked.

"We overheard emergency transmissions from different Stellar Corp facilities in orbit and on earth. Then our communications satellite at the L2 Lagrange point was destroyed. A hit and run."

"Do you know who did this?"

"Our telescope captured video of the attack. I'm transmitting it now."

"What kind of emergency transmissions did you hear?"

"Multiple Stellar Corp facilities sabotaged. Space Station disabled. Different ships were either sabotaged or under attack. Close-quarters combat at headquarters."

"This isn't good. Hold on, we have the video now."

Smitty played the video on the main screen: a static image of some satellites illuminated by the sun. Then a black ship with shimmering skin appeared on screen. A missile sped toward the satellites, which were engulfed in a fireball that quickly faded to darkness. The ship sped away.

"Fucking Labians. They've infiltrated Stellar Corp," Smitty said.

"Captain, are you an advance scout for the response fleet?"

"What fleet?"

"One of the last transmissions we heard – rushed talk about a response fleet being assembled. But we don't know where it is."

"We don't have a fleet."

"Then you're on your own? Get out of here, Captain."

"We're here to try to find out what's going on. Are you sure you don't know where the fleet is?"

"Nobody here knows. Get out of here before they see you. Maybe you can find the fleet."

"Do you need help?" Jeremy asked.

"No, they've left us alone. Everything here is okay for now. Don't worry about us."

"Captain, we should go," Smitty said.

"Go where?"

"Back to Oberon. Back to Horatio Station and the S.C. Johnson."

"Hold on. What kind of work is done at your colony?"

"We're a research facility for advanced military applications."

"Do you have weapons?"

"We do."

"Can we borrow them? We could use any advantage you can give us."

"Yes, if you're sure you can get here undetected."

"Stand by. Smitty?"

Smitty shook his head, then threw his arms up.

"Look, we can try. But at the first sign of trouble we're flashing away," Smitty said.

"We'll be there shortly."

"Use landing bay five. It's inside a crater, so it offers more camouflage."

"Roger that, see you soon," Jeremy said.

Smitty leaned forward toward the pilot's station. "Ease her in, Mister Mulligan. Keep the lights off." The pilot nodded and guided the ship slowly toward the moon. After twenty minutes of only the smallest course adjustments possible, they brought the ship into the gravity well of the moon.

"Go ahead, take us into landing bay five."

The pilot descended toward the crater that housed the landing bay. He rotated the ship as he went down, so that the docking ports of the ship would align with the port in the landing bay. Thrusters fired as they got close and the ship slowed until it touched the ground softly.

Captain Bach smiled at Smitty. "You want to come too?"

"Of course I do, but I'm bringing a marine with me."

"Alright."

They went to the docking port five levels down. A panel near the hatch indicated that there was a good seal with the docking extender. Smitty pressed a button and the hatch unsealed. It slid open with a slight hiss. There was a small breeze as the pressure equalized between the two newly connected bodies of air. The three men walked along the docking extender toward the wall of the lunar base. Once at the other end, they pressed another button, and the moon base hatch opened.

They were greeted by a short bespectacled man.

"I'm Doctor Eaglefeather. Welcome to our research facility."

"Miigwech. I'm Captain Jeremy Bach. Pleased to meet you. This is Smitty."

"Oh, we spoke earlier then. Good to meet both of you in person. Let me show you some of the technology that may be of use to you," the Doctor said. He turned and began to walk down the hall. Captain Bach and Smitty followed him. The marine trailed behind.

"Are these walls carved into the bedrock?" Captain Bach asked.

"Yes, they are. We used tunnel boring machines. They built the tunnels and coated the walls with a five centimeter layer of bio-sealant. It's cost effective and quite safe."

"Self repairing?"

"Yes, self-replicating bacteria and enzymes in the coating create more bio-sealant under the presence of oxygen. So any crack large enough to admit an oxygen molecule gets rapidly sealed off. I'm glad you're interested in our construction techniques, but it isn't exactly leading-edge."

"This isn't something we see very often. We spend all our time in space-stations and ships, so seeing a station like yours is a bit of a treat."

"Thank you, Captain. Here we are. This is our main testing area," the Doctor said. He led them into a large room with dozens of workstations. A few scientists were scattered among the tables, focused on their work.

"What's this?" Smitty asked.

"Just a laser pistol. Standard Stellar Corp issue, the same as the one on your holster. The experimental technology is back here."

He led them to a black jumpsuit. It shimmered and reflected the light in different colors, as if it was covered in millions of tiny mirrors.

"We're in the process of fabricating these for Stellar Corp."

"It's a combat jumpsuit. Laser dissipation," Smitty said.

"That's right. Stellar Corp doesn't presently employ these. There are some corporate manufacturers who sell them to private security forces, or to mercenaries. But their effectiveness is limited."

"Are yours any better?"

"Judge for yourself."

The doctor pressed a button on the nearest table and a laser fired at the jumpsuit. The laser appeared as a dull blue glow spread out across the entire front of the fabric.

"How powerful is this laser?"

"It's the equivalent to a small ship-mounted cannon."

"That can't be possible. One shot from a laser *that* powerful and the suit should be fried, along with the person wearing it."

"It is possible. We've rebuilt the refractive mesh from the ground up. It's extremely efficient at dissipating the laser energy. It takes a lot of punishment before the material can heat up enough to start to break down. In fact, it can take this level of energy for about five minutes before it fails," Doctor Eaglefeather said. He turned the laser off.

"We'll take them."

"I have four of them ready. You can have them all."

"We can't let these fall into the hands of the Labians."

"I agree. We'll blow the station's air into space to protect our secrets, if we have to."

"Thank you, Doctor Eaglefeather."

"There's one other project we've been working on that's ready for use."

The Doctor moved across the room to another table. A black box sat at the center of the table. He opened the box and withdrew a pistol. He pointed the pistol at a target on the wall and pulled the trigger. In a fraction of a second the target vanished along with a few centimeters of the wall it had been attached to.

"Is that a death ray?" Captain Bach asked.

"Not at all. We were working on a way to apply quantum teleportation to large-scale matter. But it doesn't work."

"What do you mean? It sure looks like it vanished."

"It did. The teleportation project was a failure. We had two problems that we couldn't overcome. First, as you can see, it's not easy to teleport a specific object while leaving the matter around it, like the wall, intact. The universe just doesn't distinguish between the matter at the tip of my finger and whatever it is I'm touching with my finger. And second, we don't know where the teleported object goes."

"You don't know where it goes..." Smitty said.

"Right. There's a variable that we haven't accounted for yet. Our formulas tell us that the object should re-appear instantaneously three feet to the left. Instead, it vanishes."

"Have you tried teleporting a transponder?"

"Of course. It vanished as well. So wherever it's reappearing, it's showing up so far away that the transponder can't be detected, if it's reappearing at all."

"So, it's basically a death ray," Captain Bach said.

"No it's a quantum teleporter, but... Yes, it's basically a death ray."

"I'll take it."

"Good luck, and be careful with it. I'll walk you back to your ship. I hope we were able to help in some way. Things don't sound very good for us right now."

"We'll come through, we just need to – "

Doctor Eaglefeather suddenly crumpled to the floor.

"Doctor!" Smitty yelled. He went to reach for the doctor.

"Leave him!" yelled one of the scientists. He walked forward with a pistol in his hand. "Step back from him. Don't worry, he'll be fine. It was just a small electrostatic charge."

"Who are you?" Captain Bach asked.

"Does it matter? I'm just a scientist. The kind that wants to live. I have no intention of letting Eaglefeather here kill us all to protect our secrets."

Smitty took a step forward, to try to insert himself between the Captain and the scientist.

"Don't you move. I'll hit you with a bigger charge. Stay there."

"So, what's your plan?" Smitty asked.

"I'm going to notify the Labians. If we help them then we'll be safe."

"You don't know that. They might leave you alone. They might kill you for sport. They might take you back to one of the home planets and force you to mate with them for the rest of your life. That's a fate worse than death."

"I'll take my chances. Now don't move, I'm just going to program a message to go out. Hopefully they receive it and then – Aaahhhhhh!"

The scientist dropped his pistol. His hand had been suddenly burnt. The marine stepped forward with his laser pistol drawn.

"Damn you and your marine! Look at what you did to my hand. Do you know how much a new hand will cost? I don't have that kind of money! I'm just a researcher!"

"You should have thought about replacement hand costs before you held up Stellar Corp officers at gunpoint. Secure him," Smitty said. The marine took hold of the scientist.

Doctor Eaglefeather was sitting up now.

"I'm so sorry. I had no idea this would happen," the Doctor said.

"It's not your fault, it's his. We'll be taking him with us, to make sure he stays out of trouble," Smitty said.

Smitty helped the Doctor to his feet. They took the four combat jumpsuits and the teleportation pistol, and headed back to the ship with the marine and their prisoner. Doctor Eaglefeather wished them luck, and left them to return to his work. They walked through the landing port and back onto the S.C. Applegate.

"Take him to the infirmary. See about treating that hand. Then throw him in the brig," Smitty said. The marine led the scientist away.

The pilot's voice came on over the intercom.

"There's a ship headed our way. Are we ready to disembark? Please advise."

Smitty ran to the nearest intercom panel.

"We're all aboard. Get us out of here now. We're on our way to the bridge."

"Yes sir."

The ship's thrusters fired and it began to lift out of the crater that it had landed in. Once it was safely clear of the crater, the pilot accelerated as fast as possible. The Applegate sped away from the moon.

Captain Bach and Smitty stepped onto the bridge. On the screen behind them was a rapidly shrinking moon. A Labian ship was now visible, part way between them and the moon. But instead of turning to pursue them, it turned and headed toward the moon.

A cluster of missiles launched from the surface of the moon.

"Oh those fools!" Captain Bach said.

"He was serious about protecting their research," Smitty said.

The missiles reached the Labian ship. Most of them missed their target, but a few hit. The ship was struck and two separate explosions were visible. The ship seemed to be drifting.

"Finally a win. Those scientists punch above their weight," Smitty said.

A second Labian ship came into view from the other side of the moon.

"They called for backup," Smitty said.

The second Labian ship immediately fired lasers at the moon. There were multiple bright explosions across different parts of the facility.

"Those poor souls," Captain Bach said.

Smitty looked away from the screen, and whispered, "They did their duty."

The bridge was silent for a moment, then the pilot said, "Captain, the Labian ship is turning toward us. Wait, it looks like it's firing missiles at us."

"Deploy chaff, then flash, Mister Mulligan."

"Yes, sir."

The pilot launched chaff, and thousands of metallic objects scattered in a cloud behind the ship.

"Flashing in three, two, one."

He engaged the engines and the ship's skin began to glow. The first missiles hit the chaff and exploded safely away from the Applegate. The ship's skin glowed brighter and finally flashed an intense white light.

A cluster of missiles passed through the chaff. A few exploded, but a few more carried on. The missiles headed into the white glow in front of them. Then they passed the location where the ship had been only an instant before, but where now there was only empty space.

30

HAMLET, OBERON

"Silver is going to be okay," Royson said.

"He better be," Sym said.

"The doctors said all the damage is fixable. It's going to take some time to grow a new ear though. Commander Tajiki, these guys were organized. They were ready for us," Royson said.

"I agree," she said.

"This isn't good," Royson said.

"This is beyond not good. We've got a guy in there getting his face reconstructed. We got off real lucky," Sym said.

"Sym, stay here with Silver. Keep an eye on Khaala too. Let me know when his burns have healed," Royson said.

"Alright. I suppose you're going back to the barracks?"

"Yes. We need to regroup and plan our next move. Uh, if it's okay with Commander Tajiki."

"Yes, it's okay with me."

Royson started down the hospital hallway, toward the exit.

"Hey Royson!" Sym hollered.

Royson stopped and looked back.

"Yeah Sym?"

"Pay them back for me, okay? Pay them back big time."

"Agreed, one hundred percent. Coming, Commander?"

Commander Tajiki had been standing, watching the exchange between Royson and Sym.

"Coming," she said. She hurried off after Royson.

Steven Wang was sitting on a bench outside the hospital. His head was in his hands. He looked up when he heard Royson and Commander Tajiki approach.

"How are they?" Steven asked.

"Silver is in pretty rough shape, but he'll make it," Royson said.

"Oh, that's good. That's good."

"What are you doing sitting out here?" Royson asked.

"I don't know what else to do. It was so bad. What if I had lost..." Wang paused and looked at Lauressa. He put his head back in his hands.

"Get up," Royson said.

"What?"

"Get up. Come on, stand up."

Wang stood up.

"You need to support your men. You're no good to anyone hiding out here."

Royson smoothed out Steven's outfit.

"There you go," Royson said. "Now go visit Silver and Khaala."

"Okay. You're right, I'll do that. What are you doing now?"

"We're going back to the barracks to do some planning. We can't let them have the tactical advantage again."

"Okay, I'll come join you when I'm done here," Steven said. He went into the hospital.

Royson and Commander Tajiki walked over to the shuttle.

"That was interesting," Commander Tajiki said.

"What, the pep talk?"

"Yes."

"Wang pays me to keep his men organized and to maintain his authority."

"Okay, that makes sense. I get it. I just wasn't expecting it. I don't know how I'd react if one of my subordinates talked to me like that."

"It's part of my job. And we're not Stellar Corp," Royson said.

Commander Tajiki entered her code on the side of the shuttle and the hatch opened. The barracks were nearby, so the flight took only a few minutes.

The barracks were about half-full. Some of the men who had recently been with them were lying on their bunks or cleaning their gear.

"My office is back there," Royson said.

He led Commander Tajiki through the barracks to a room in the back.

Royson's office was a small room with just enough space for a desk and a bed. A stand-up shower was off in the corner.

"Private shower," Lauressa said.

"The wonderful perks of being in charge."

"I think I need a shower."

"Feel free to use it," Royson said.

Commander Tajiki unzipped her combat suit. She pulled the suit down to her feet and stepped out of it. She walked over to Royson and put her hands on his arms.

"I think you need a shower too."

"Commander Tajiki, I'm not sure..."

"It's Lauressa," she said. She pulled down the zipper on his combat suit and it fell to the ground.

"Commander, uh, Lauressa, I'm..."

"You're like black marble," she said. She ran her hands down his stomach and into his underwear.

"I'm married," he said.

Lauressa placed his hands on her shoulders. Then she got down on her knees and pulled off his underwear.

"No, I can't," Royson said. He pushed her away. "I'm married. Go have a shower." He bent down and gathered up his clothes.

"Who cares if you're married! What does it matter? What's the point of it? We live! We just live and live. It just goes on and on and it doesn't stop until we get lasered or shot or whatever. But until then it's just more of the same. So how can you just go on being married and act like it matters?"

"What's wrong with you? Of course it matters. Every day that I risk my life, it matters. Just because it seems like you can live forever doesn't mean that you should live like you will."

Lauressa ran at Royson. She jumped up and wrapped her legs around him. They fell onto the floor. She tried to maneuver him inside of her but he was soft, so she thrusted hopelessly.

"This is all there is! This is what matters!"

Royson laid there for a few seconds. Then he pushed her off with all of his strength. She fell backwards onto her butt.

"You have no right!" Royson yelled.

Lauressa sat on the floor.

"What's wrong with me.... We're all going to die," Lauressa said. She began to cry. "I'm sorry. I'm sorry."

"Go have a shower. Clean yourself up. This is no way for an officer of Stellar Corp to behave."

Lauressa got up from the floor and took a quick shower.

She came out a few minutes later. Her eyes were bloodshot.

"I'm sorry. I'm a fool. To think I can just go around having sex with anybody," Lauressa said.

"You're not a fool. But you need to be careful. It isn't safe."

"There's no disease..."

"But you don't know who you can trust. How do you know I wasn't working for the enemy? You're putting yourself in a situation where you're vulnerable."

"I trust you."

"And I trust you too, as long as you have your clothes on. The people we're up against, they're organized. Who knows what they'll do. Be careful."

"You're right. I just have these urges. And when I think about a war breaking out, I can't control myself. I just need to do something with my body. How will I live with this...."

"Live with what."

"What?"

"I'm not telling anybody. This is a little embarrassing for me too."

"I hadn't thought of that."

"I'm going to shower now. Then we'll plan our next move. I wonder what's keeping Wang."

Royson walked off to the shower. Lauressa sat on the bed and stared at the floor. *Damn, I'm a fool. A tired fool.* She laid back and fell asleep almost instantly.

Royson came out of the shower a few minutes later.

"Commander," he said.

Lauressa began to snore.

"Commander. Really? Okay, I'll give you a few more seconds."

Royson finished getting dressed.

"Commander."
Lauressa didn't move.
"Commander!"
Royson grabbed Lauressa and shook her.
Lauressa sat up suddenly and she butted her face into his.
"Ahh!" she yelled. "Dammit!"
"My nose! What the hell."
"What were you doing?"
"Trying to wake you up."
"Sorry. Ouch, that hurt."
"Who said you could sleep in my bed," Royson said.
"I'm sorry, I –"
"I'm just messing with you."
"Oh."
Lauressa walked over to the mirror and looked at her face.
"That'll bruise," she said.
"That's what you get."
"Thanks."
"Commander, I think I'll call my old friend at Hamlet Security."
"Snaggletooth?"
"Right."
"Let's do it."
Royson walked over to his desk. He picked up a handset and connected to Hamlet Security.
"*Hamlet Security. Lieutenant Sher –*"
"Snaggletooth, it's Jackal."
"*What's the code.*"
"I need your help."
"*Close enough. How'd it go?*"
"We were ambushed. We've got men in the hospital."
"*How can I help?*"
"Can you tell me if there was any movement where we were?"
"*Let's see, one moment. I've got a small shuttle that flew straight to the hospital.*"
"That was us. Anything else?"
"*Hold on. I'm looking. I see. Hmm, this is interesting.*"

"What is it?"
"There's a hole in the sensor network."
"They took out the sensors?"
"Maybe. There's a blind spot."
Lauressa hit her fist against the table. "Shit!" she yelled.
"Jackal, who the hell is that?"
"She's the one we're helping. Bit of a temper problem."
"Okay. I'm looking at the sensor data. Whoever tampered with the sensors did an amateur job."
"What are you saying?"
"The blind spot in the sensors moves over time. I can't see what's inside that blind spot, but I can see where it ended up. I'm sending you the location."
Royson's handset beeped.
"Thanks. Jackal owes you."
"Jackal owes me a vacation on earth at this point."
"We'll do that one day. Thanks. Gotta go."
Royson disconnected the handset from Hamlet Security.
"Look at these coordinates," he said. He passed the handset over to her.
"That's on the other end of the colony. On the edge of the park district," Lauressa said.
"We'll need to be careful. We don't want to get into another firefight in a residential area."
"What do you suggest?"
"A small group. Strike fast. In and out before they can put up a fight."
"You and me?"
"And two of my men. We'll go in fast and quiet."
"When?"
"Now."

Royson, Commander Tajiki, and two of the garrison men got into a small shuttle. It was a tight fit. There were two seats up front but only a small space behind the seats. The two men – Jefferson and Capshaw – were crouched down and almost sitting on eachother.

"Sorry about the accommodations guys," Royson said.

"Don't worry about it," Jefferson said.

"This is an interesting shuttle. I'm not familiar with this design," Commander Tajiki said.

"It's a custom build. Small, fast, silent, and armed."

"What use would you have for something like this on Hamlet?"

"Sometimes you need to get somewhere as quickly and quietly as possible. Sometimes you need to be able to defend yourself."

"Or run guns?"

"Don't be silly. Ready? Hold on."

Royson hit the altitude controls and the shuttle shot up into the air. The only sound was the movement of air around it. He pressed forward on the accelerator and the shuttle moved forward. Capshaw grunted.

"Sorry about that," Royson said.

"We're fine, let's just get there."

Royson turned on the map overlay. A map of the colony projected onto the front window, overlaying itself on the view outside. Icons indicated different buildings, security barracks, power stations, and other points of interest. A glowing blue dot on the map indicated their destination.

Royson hit the altitude controls again and took the shuttle up to nearly the top of the colony dome. He accelerated forward again and the shuttle flew across the colony. After a few minutes they were almost directly over their destination. The houses and streets were tiny beneath them.

"Let's take a look," Royson said.

An image of the ground projected onto the front window. He zoomed until he had a closeup view of the neighborhood. Tree-lined streets and large houses ran in a grid. A large series of parks were nearby.

"There's nothing obviously wrong here," Royson said.

"They're holed up in the house. How about we drop in on them?" Capshaw said.

"The park is only two streets over and it would offer very good cover," Commander Tajiki said.

"We can get closer," Royson said.

"What do you mean?"

"We're going to land right on their roof."

"Isn't that risky?"

"Risky but very fast. We'll keep the shuttle hovering so they won't hear the weight of the shuttle on the roof. They won't suspect a thing until we're breaking through their windows. When we do this you're going to stay behind us. Are you ready?"

"Ready."

Royson began to descend. He kept an image of the ground below them projected on the window.

"If they look up we'll see them on the screen."

After a few minutes they were hovering only a meter above the roof.

"Jefferson, Capshaw, you go first. Step lightly. Don't spook them with your footsteps."

"Not our first pony ride," Jefferson said.

"What's a pony?" Commander Tajiki asked.

"Never mind. Let's move."

Jefferson reached over and hit the hatch release. The side hatch of the shuttle slid sideways. He stepped out and lowered himself as gently as possible. There was almost no sound at all when his feet hit the roof. Capshaw followed.

Capshaw and Jefferson moved across the roof toward the back of the house. A ladder led down to a balcony below. There was nobody around. Capshaw made a hand signal to Royson.

"Let's go," Royson said. He slipped down onto the roof, followed by Commander Tajiki.

Capshaw and Jefferson went down to the balcony first. A sliding glass door led to a large bedroom. The door was unlocked. They went into the bedroom. Royson and Tajiki followed. There was nobody to be found. From the bedroom they went into the hallway. Then they moved slowly down the stairs to the ground floor. The house was well built and the stairs didn't creak or otherwise give away their presence.

The main floor seemed quiet.

Jefferson heard a faint murmuring coming from another room. He held his hand up and pointed to his ear. Capshaw listened for a second, then nodded. Capshaw and Jefferson crept forward through the house. Two men were standing talking to each other. Capshaw made a hand-sign for "S" or stun. They pulled their stun sticks and dashed forward, pressing the sticks into the men, who dropped to the floor.

Capshaw and Jefferson returned to Royson and Tajiki.

"We're good," Capshaw whispered.

The rest of the ground floor was empty.

The door to the basement was closed. Royson stood behind the door and slowly opened it, while Capshaw and Jefferson peaked in. It was dark but there was a faint light coming from the bottom of the stairs. Two people, a man and a woman, sat together under the light in the basement. A small table held food and drinks. One of them heard movement on the stairs and turned.

"Davis?" he asked.

Capshaw stepped into the light.

"Don't move," Capshaw said.

The woman gasped.

"Oh no! Don't hurt us!" she said.

"Stay quiet."

She nodded and began to cry. The man put his arm around her.

Commander Tajiki walked up to them. "You know Davis? Where is he?"

"We don't know. He went out," the man said.

"Who are you? You're not from my station," Tajiki said.

"We're –"

A man came down the stairs quickly.

"Hey guys, I got the chips and Titania Cola you asked for," he said as he walked down the stairs.

He was nearly to the bottom of the stairs when he saw Commander Tajiki.

"Fuck!" he yelled. He threw the chips and cola and ran.

"That's Davis! Get him!" Tajiki yelled.

Capshaw took off up the stairs after him.

Davis ran out the front door and into the street. Capshaw ran after him. He got a few steps out of the house when he noticed a van. Davis was running toward it. Several people jumped out of the van. Capshaw turned and ran back into the house. He closed the door and locked it. He ran to the top of the basement stairs.

"We've got company! Pull out now!" he yelled.

Jefferson ran upstairs.

"Move," Royson said. He pointed at the man and woman.

"Please don't hurt us," the woman said.

The man stepped in front of her.

Royson raised his stun stick.

Commander Tajiki stepped in between them.

"We won't hurt you, we promise. But you need to come with us now, okay?"

They could hear pounding at the front door upstairs.

"Let's go!" Jefferson yelled from the top of the stairs.

"Okay?" Commander Tajiki asked.

The man nodded and took the woman's hand.

"Let's go," she said. She led them upstairs. Royson followed behind them.

They came out of the basement and started to walk back toward the stairs to the upper floor.

The front door blew open with a loud bang.

"Covering fire!" Capshaw yelled. He and Jefferson unloaded a torrent of projectile weapons fire at the front door.

"Go!" Royson said. He pushed forward on the back of the man and the woman. They ran up the stairs behind Commander Tajiki.

Capshaw and Jefferson fell back and ran up the stairs.

Outside, men were making their way into the house. A few of them began to run up the stairs.

Capshaw fired down the stairs and they backed off.

"Get them to the shuttle, we'll be behind you," Jefferson said.

Capshaw and Jefferson fired down the stairs again. Tajiki, Royson, and the man and woman ran through the bedroom, onto the balcony, and up the ladder to the roof.

Capshaw dropped a stun grenade down the stairs, and he and Jefferson ran toward the balcony. On the floor below there was the sound of men scrambling for safety. Then silence. Then the grenade exploded.

Capshaw climbed the ladder to the roof, followed by Jefferson.

"In the back," Royson said. He pushed the two captives into the space behind the seats. Tajiki got in, and then Royson hopped in and powered up the shuttle systems.

"Let's go!" Royson said.

"One second!" Jefferson said.

Capshaw ran back to the shuttle. Jefferson looked over the roof. Someone peaked out of the bedroom window and looked up.

"Hi there," Jefferson said. He dropped a stun grenade onto the balcony and ran toward the shuttle.

The stun grenade rolled off the balcony onto the ground below, and a man with a weapon popped up on the ladder. He shot at Jefferson.

"Fuck!" Jefferson yelled. He fell to his knees.

Capshaw returned fire and the attacker ducked out of view. He grabbed Jefferson's arm and pulled him up. They hobbled back to the shuttle and Jefferson crawled in. Capshaw fired in the direction of the ladder again and climbed into the shuttle and hit the hatch button. The shuttle hatch slid shut.

"We're taking fire," Royson said. The shuttle was getting hit by projectiles. It sounded like pebbles against a metal roof. He hit the controls and the shuttle lurched up and forward and accelerated at a high rate.

"This is really quite comfortable," Jefferson said. He was lying on top of the man and the woman. Capshaw was pressed up against the shuttle hatch.

"How's your leg?" Royson asked.

"Bleeding."

"We'll be home in a few minutes."

Royson flew the shuttle at a high speed, but not in a straight line. He at times brought it down to within a meter of the ground, then drove it through the streets – as if it were a car – for a minute or two, and then took off again after a few blocks. He did this a half-dozen times. Once he was close to the barracks, Royson landed the shuttle a few blocks away and drove it through the barracks gates.

"If they have access to the space traffic network they'll have trouble figuring out where we've gone, hopefully," Royson said. He reached back and hit the hatch release. The hatch slid open and Capshaw stumbled out of the shuttle.

Capshaw took hold of Jefferson and helped him out.

"Let's get inside," Capshaw said.

Jefferson hobbled along with Capshaw into the Barracks.

He laid down on the nearest cot.

"Let's take a look," Capshaw said. He used a knife to cut off Jefferson's pant leg.

"It went clean through," Capshaw said.

"That's good news," Jefferson said.

"I'm going to cauterize it now," Capshaw said.

"Fuck. Okay, do it."

Capshaw pulled out his stun stick and pressed it against the wound. He adjusted the voltage down and the amperage up. He pressed the trigger and it launched a beam of burning electricity into the wound. It lasted less than a second.

Jefferson cried in pain.

"Looks good. I'm going to pack it with carbonic bandage powder and wrap it up."

"Sounds great."

Capshaw poured powder into the wound, until it seemed completely filled. He used his finger to pack it in deeper.

"Fuck!"

"Sorry, need to get it packed in there."

He poured more powder in and pushed it down again.

"Looks good," Capshaw said. He wrapped Jefferson's leg in a bandage.

"That should feel a lot better in the morning."

"I think I'll just take a nap. Let me know if you need me," Jefferson said.

"Sounds good."

Capshaw walked out of the barracks. Royson and Commander Tajiki were standing by the shuttle. The man and the woman were sitting on the shuttle floor, with their legs hanging over the side.

"Everything okay?" Royson asked.

"Just a scratch, he'll be fine," Capshaw said. "Do you need me at the moment?"

"We're fine. We've got some talking to do with these two. Actually, could you grab us a pizza? They look hungry."

"Pizza?" Capshaw asked. Royson nodded. "Sure... Okay, I'll be back in a bit," Capshaw said. He walked off.

"So, how do you know Davis?" Commander Tajiki asked.

"You know Davis?" the woman asked.

"Yes. What's your name?"

"Maris," she said.

"Maris, Davis works for me. But he stole a shuttle and ran away."

"Oh," Maris said.

"It's very important for me to find him."

"Okay. Well, we work for him."

"Work for him?"

"Yes. We do what he needs us to do. We helped him with breaking into the sensor network to cover his tracks."

Commander Tajiki looked at the man. "So you both work for him? What's your name?"

"I'm Jordan."

"Jordan, why do you work with Davis?"

"Because we were hired to," Jordan said.

"Hired? By who?"

"We don't know. Someone came to us one day at our home and said there was a job for us and we'd be rewarded if we did it. They didn't say who they worked for though."

"What kind of reward?" Commander Tajiki asked.

"Our freedom."

"Your freedom? Where are you from?"

"Luyten's World," Maris said.

"Luyten's World?" Commander Tajiki asked. She looked at them again. Of course, there was no visible sign of it.

"Yes," Maris said.

"You're not human."

"We're Transgenic Utilities," Jordan said.

"Those laws aren't changing any time soon," Royson said. "Who would promise you freedom and hope to be able to give it to you? How could you believe them?"

"We didn't believe them. But we were paid good money up front, so we decided why not, it would be an adventure and probably better than whatever else would be in store for us," Jordan said.

"But now we believe them. They can do it. Free us," Maris said.

"Why is that? Why do you believe them now?"

"Because since we've been here we heard them talking a little bit. We think we know who we're working for," Maris said.

"Who is it?" Commander Tajiki asked.

"Promise you won't hurt us?"

"I promise."

Maris put her head down and began to sob.

"I'm sorry. She just wanted to be free," Jordan said. He embraced Maris.

"It's okay, you're safe with us."

"We heard them talking about a war; about taking power. We think we're working for the Martians," Jordan said.

"Oh. No," Commander Tajiki said.

"We just wanted to be free. We didn't want to be in a war."

"Are you sure about this?"

"No."

"We need to be sure."

"We're not sure. Because of the money they paid us. It came from an Amish bank on Mount Sinai II."

"Amish?" Commander Tajiki asked.

"Yes."

"This makes no sense," Royson said.

"Why would the Amish pay you to help start some sort of war with Mars?" Commander Tajiki asked.

"We don't know. This is all so confusing. We really didn't want any of this," Jordan said.

Royson was about to speak when Capshaw returned.

"Pizza!" Capshaw said.

"I'm starving, can I have some?" Maris asked.

"We'll all have some. Then we'll talk some more," Commander Tajiki said.

Maris wiped the tears from her cheeks. She grabbed the largest slice and bit into it with wide excited eyes.

31

Aboard S.C. Applegate, in orbit over Oberon

"Horatio Station, this is S.C. Applegate," Smitty said.

"This is Horatio Station, Wayland Hauer here. Good to see you're back."

"Thank you. We need to speak with Commander Tajiki."

"Commander Tajiki is on Hamlet. I have a secure communications channel to her handset if you need it."

"Thanks Mister Hauer. Put us through."

A few seconds of silence was followed by a short beep.

"The system indicates we have a secure connection to Commander Tajiki," Smitty said.

"Commander Tajiki? This is Captain Bach, can you hear us?" Jeremy asked.

"Jeremy? You're back? Oh good. You don't know what I've been dealing with. Did you bring help?"

"Not exactly. Commander, we've got a problem."

"What is it?"

"I don't know how to say this. I guess I'll just say it. Stellar Corp may be unable to help us. They've been attacked, or sabotaged, or both. The space station in earth orbit wouldn't respond to us."

"You couldn't reach anybody?"

"We managed to make contact with a research colony on the dark side of the moon. That's as far as we got before the Labians moved in. They bombarded it."

"No."

"Yes. And Valhalla base on Callisto – the long range communications base – has been disabled too. Stellar Corp, or whatever bits are left of it, are isolated from each other. We're deaf and blind."

"Do you have any good news?"

"There could be a fleet assembling somewhere to respond to the threat. But we don't know where."

"That's not encouraging."

"It's not. We did pick up a few prototype weapons from the dark-side base. It's not much, but it's something I guess."

"Jeremy. Captain Bach. I have some news for you. We tracked down my missing engineer. We were able to capture two of his conspirators."

"That's great news."

"No. This is not good. The two people we captured, they're Transgenic Utilities."

"What?"

"They're not human. Not officially. But they're working for people who promised to give them their freedom."

"The Labians? I'm sure the Labians would look at them as inferior."

"No, not the Labians. They think they're working for some sort of Mars resistance."

"Mars? Really? Are you sure?"

"We're not sure. They got paid via an Amish bank on Mount Sinai II."

"What's the connection to Mars?"

"We don't know. We're still talking to them. But it makes sense that a Martian uprising would consider Transgenic Utilities to be free humans. It fits their ethos of religious and personal liberty. But we don't have any actual evidence yet.

"Thanks Lauressa, uh, Commander."

"Bye, Captain."

There was a beep.

"Commander Tajiki disconnected," Smitty said.

"Thanks," Captain Bach said.

"Mars," Smitty said.

"Let's not jump to conclusions."

"The force-field unit we photographed underneath Adriana Colony. It was registered to a Martian company. And there was the crate with a Martian flag."

"Maybe it's true. But what about the Labians?"

"They're working together somehow," Smitty said.

"But why? That makes no sense. They should see the Martians as breeding stock at best."

"Isn't it obvious? They have a common goal: power. The question is, what can we do about it?"

Jeremy put his hands on his face and rubbed his temples.

"I don't know, Smitty."

Captain Bach began to pace across the bridge.

"Smitty, do you think they need our help with the interrogation?"

"I doubt it."

"We could head to Mount Sinai II."

"We could. It's far. The superlight drive is old but it should be able to handle it."

"Okay, let's do it. We don't have much to go on, but we can't just sit here doing nothing."

"Right Captain. Pilot, prepare to flash."

"Yes sir," said the pilot.

An incoming message icon flashed on the main screen.

"Hold on pilot," Smitty said.

Smitty hit a button on his console and retrieved the message.

"This is Volaris Gollari on Adriana Colony. Captain Bach, we need to discuss something privately. Please come right away."

"Well that was unexpected," Captain Bach said.

"Your call," Smitty said.

"Let's go visit Volaris Gollari."

"Pilot, take us to Titania, whenever you're ready," Smitty said.

"Yes, sir," the pilot said. He turned the ship away from Oberon and started navigating toward Titania. "We'll be there in thirty minutes."

"You're not going to flash?" Smitty asked.

"Smitty, I could use that time to get a bite to eat," Captain Bach said.

"Okay," Smitty said.

"I'll be back in thirty minutes. Enjoy the perks of command while I'm gone."

Smitty nodded.

Jeremy went down to the pantry. He got some bread and milk. He was alone in the room. He sat down, dipped the bread into the milk and ate quietly.

"This isn't going to end well," he said.

32

Aboard S.C. Applegate, in orbit over Titania

"We've arrived at Titania, sir," the pilot said.

"Good. Put us in orbit over Adriana colony," Smitty said.

"Yes, sir."

Captain Bach walked onto the bridge holding a sandwich.

"Oh good, we're here," he said.

"Ham?" Smitty asked.

"Salami."

"Very good."

"Smitty, let's see if we can reach Volaris Gollari."

"One second," Smitty said. He hit a few buttons on his console and Volaris Gollari appeared on the screen.

"Oh great, you're here," Gollari said.

"We're here. What did you want to talk about?" Captain Bach asked.

"*Can you come down here to meet me? Or I can come up there. I don't want to speak about this over the air.*"

Jeremy looked at Smitty. Smitty nodded.

"Alright, we'll be down there shortly. Send me the location you'd like to meet at."

"*I'll meet you at your shuttle.*"

"Okay. See you there. Applegate out."

Smitty broke the connection.

"Smitty, let's go. Let's bring John Dvorak and David the mechanic as well."

"You think they'll be needed?"

"I don't know. I just thought since they'd been to Adriana twice it would be useful to have them along. Who knows what Gollari has to say."

"Fair enough. We should bring a few marines as well."

* * *

Smitty navigated the shuttle toward the colony. The crater was still clearly visible in the center of the city, but the smoke had largely subsided. Smitty brought Adriana's traffic controller on the line.

"This is Adriana port traffic control, go ahead."

"This is Applegate shuttle. We'd like permission to land at the next available landing bay."

"Welcome back Applegate. Permission granted. Proceed to landing bay fourteen."

"Thank you traffic control. Applegate shuttle out."

Smitty brought the shuttle through a port in the colony dome and flew it down to landing bay fourteen. He opened the shuttle hatch. The two marines on board walked out of the shuttle and took up positions on either side of the ship. Smitty walked out next, followed by Captain Bach, John Dvorak, and David.

"Nobody here," Smitty said.

"I don't get why we're down here. Shit's hitting the fan and we're standing in an empty landing bay," John Dvorak said.

"Relax. We'll wait for a few minutes," Captain Bach said.

"Sorry."

"Don't worry about it. Just relax. And look. There he is."

Volaris Gollari jogged into the landing bay.

"Volaris, good to see you –," Captain Bach began to say.

Volaris Gollari jogged past him straight into the shuttle.

"Hey, hold up!" Captain Bach said. He walked back into the ship.

"Sorry," he said. He was breathing hard, and he looked nervous. "I've been watching my back all day. It's safer in here."

"Watching your back? What's going on?"

"Things are bad. Really bad. I'm not sure who to trust."

"You can trust me. Just tell me what's happening."

Volaris Gollari sat on one of the cockpit seats.

"I hope you don't mind. Just need to sit for a minute."

"Okay."

"I'm being watched. It's been happening since the explosion a few days ago. I first noticed when I was working on the initial response. I saw the same faces repeatedly. At first I thought it was my imagination, but it's not. And I know why. It's because of what I've discovered."

"What did you find?"

"Not so much found, but overheard."

"Oh?"

"I was on my way to Governor Shull's office – you know, the mobile one that he had set up at the beginning of the crisis. So I was about to walk into his office when I heard voices coming from inside. I couldn't make out everything, but I heard two words that made me very afraid: Mars, and revolution. I turned around and started to walk away. And just then someone popped his head out and saw me as I was leaving. From that moment I think I've been watched almost continuously."

"Are you sure about this?" Smitty asked.

"Yes, absolutely."

"Okay, let's take this one step at a time," Captain Bach said.

"Okay."

"Mars."

"Yes."

"Revolution."

"Yes."

"Anything else?"

"That's it. Other than being followed."

"What about your security team?"

"A lot of them have been with the governor long before I took this job. I can't trust them."

"Okay, we'll look into it."

"Thank you, Captain Bach. I'd better go. I think I lost them, but I'd better get back before it's obvious that I'm talking with you."

"Alright. We'll let you know what we find."

"Thanks, thanks."

Volaris Gollari stepped out of the shuttle. Suddenly he cried in agony and crumpled to the ground. Blood spilled from his right shoulder.

"Gollari!" Captain Bach said.

"Covering fire!" Smitty yelled.

The two marines outside the shuttle ran toward either side of the hatch while firing their weapons at the landing bay entrance.

Smitty picked up Volaris Gollari and pulled him into the shuttle. John Dvorak and David stepped inside, and the two marines followed last.

"Hatch!" Smitty said. Captain Bach closed the shuttle hatch.

"We're getting out of here," Captain Bach said. He sat in the pilot's seat and powered up the shuttle. "Hold on," he said. The shuttle lifted off the ground and accelerated straight up.

"Applegate shuttle, this is Adriana port traffic control. You haven't received clearance to take off."

"We've just been shot at. We need to get back to the Applegate now. We've got injured on board."

"What? Hold on."

There was talking in the background between traffic controllers.

"Applegate shuttle, you're requested to land outside Central Hospital. Medical personnel are standing by."

Captain Bach muted the connection.

"What do you think?" he asked Smitty.

"No way."

"Sorry, this is Stellar Corp business. We're returning to the ship," Captain Bach said.

The shuttle reached the top of the colony dome.

"Adriana port traffic control, please open the hatch."

"Negative, I don't have authorization to do that."

"Traffic controller, we need to get out of here."

"I don't have the auth – what? – he what? – you can't do that – the governor doesn't –"

"Traffic control?"

"*Something's going on here. They're coming up. I'll keep the hatch open as long as I can. Go now.*"

The hatch on the colony dome opened. Captain Bach pushed the shuttle forward. But as soon as it had opened the hatch began to close again.

"Push through!" Smitty said.

Captain Bach throttled the shuttle up and slipped through the dome.

"*This is Adriana port traffic control. Return to Adriana immediately,*" a different voice said. Jeremy disconnected the line.

"How's he doing?" Captain Bach asked.

"I've stopped the bleeding, but he's lost a lot of blood," John Dvorak said. He was kneeled over Volaris Gollari, with a hand pressed down over the wound.

"S.C. Applegate, this is Applegate shuttle. Tell Doctor Smith we have someone with a gunshot wound to take care of," Captain Bach said.

"*Acknowledged Applegate shuttle.*"

Captain Bach flew the shuttle into the hangar. Doctor Smith was waiting for them. The shuttle hatch opened and the Doctor stepped into the shuttle.

"Let me see," the Doctor said. He pushed John Dvorak back and cut open Volaris Gollari's shirt with some scissors. The wound was slowly oozing. The Doctor felt his skin. It was cold and clammy.

"He's in shock. Help me get him onto the stretcher so we can move him to the infirmary."

Doctor Smith and John Dvorak lifted up the wounded man and carried him out of the shuttle and placed him on the stretcher. The doctor pulled a thermal blanket from a pack underneath the stretcher and laid it over his shivering patient.

"Okay, let's go," he said. They headed off toward the infirmary.

The doctor looked again at the oozing wound as they wheeled Volaris Gollari down the hall.

"What did you use to stop the bleeding?"

"Cauterizing agent from the first-aid kit and pressure from my hand," John said.

"That will do for now. You know how to use an MRI?"

"I do," John Dvorak said.

"Good, you'll be my assistant."

* * *

Captain Bach, Smitty, and David the Mechanic stood on the bridge looking at maps of Adriana colony.

"We should go to the infirmary," Captain Bach said.

"We'll only be in the way. Give doctor Smith some time to do his job," Smitty said.

Captain Bach nodded, and said, "Okay, you're right. So let's figure out how to get down there and have a talk with the Governor."

"Let's just try to give him a call first," Smitty said. He went over to his console and opened a line to Adriana. "This is S.C. Applegate for Governor Shull."

"*This is the governor's office. The governor is unavailable at the moment.*"

"This is urgent. We need to speak to him," Smitty said.

"*I'm sorry, the governor is not available.*"

"I repeat, this is urgent. Interrupt whatever he is doing, this is a Stellar Corp matter."

"*One second.... I'm sorry the governor is not available.*"

"Oh? When will he be available?"

"*I don't know.*"

The line disconnected.

"That's not a good sign," Smitty said.

"I'm done playing around," Jeremy said.

"What?"

"They shot Volaris Gollari, tried to keep us from flying out of the colony – who knows what happened to the traffic controller who helped us – and the governor won't talk to us."

"Right."

"That's enough evidence for me. Governor Shull is acting against Stellar Corp. We're going down there and arresting him and bringing him back up here. He'll tell us what he knows and if he still resists, he'll rot in the brig."

"Good enough for me. David, your thoughts on the best approach?" Smitty asked.

David looked at the map of Adriana colony. He spun the map around, zoomed in and out, and put different overlays on top of the map.

"The governor's offices are here, in the main government compound. He's got barracks of local security forces on two sides of the offices. Any land approach from the space port will be difficult. There are barricades at the entrances to the compound, so we'd have to go in on foot from that point," David said.

He changed the overlays on the map, and three triangles glowed in different parts of the compound.

"Approach by air is defended by these anti-aircraft emplacements. Our shuttles can take a hit, but I don't know if I'd trust our shuttles offensive capabilities to be strong enough to neutralize them."

"So a combined ground and shuttle attack," Smitty said.

"No," Captain Bach said.

"No? Okay, what's your proposal?"

"Let's not take any chances. Let's go down there with the one thing we know they won't be able to stop."

Smitty nodded.

"Let's go pay the governor a visit."

* * *

"I've got a grip on the bullet fragment," Doctor Smith said.

John Dvorak held the MRI against Volaris Gollari's shoulder. A holographic image floated above them. The doctor rotated the image with one hand, while he held the forceps in his other hand.

"There, got it. Hold the MRI there."

Doctor Smith slowly pulled the bullet fragment out. A dark area spread across the image.

"He's bleeding internally," John said.

"I see it. Hold on."

The doctor retrieved the fragment and dropped it onto a tray. He picked up a small cauterizing wand and a vacuum.

"I'm going to suction the blood and cauterize the wound directly. I think I see the main source of the blood. Move the MRI a little to the right. There. Hold there. See it?"

"I don't see it."

Doctor Smith rotated and zoomed in on the holographic image. An artery became visible and the blood was clearly spurting from it.

"See it now? Hold there. Here comes the wand... and... done."

The edge of the artery turned black and the bleeding stopped. The doctor removed the wand and the suction.

"Hand me that packet of carbonic bandage powder," the doctor said.

The doctor took the packet and poured the contents into a cup. He added a bit of water to turn it into a paste. Then the doctor placed a syringe into the cup and withdrew the paste into the syringe. He inserted the syringe into the wound on Volaris' shoulder. The syringe was visible on the MRI.

"I've got the syringe embedded well into the wound now, so I'll inject the paste until I've filled up the wound."

The doctor injected the contents of the syringe into the wound. He then held the edges of the wound together and began to stitch it up.

"Stitches?"

"Old but effective. This will make sure that the carbonic bandage paste stays put while it does its work. The stitches themselves will just break down over a few days. Mister Gollari, how are you feeling?"

Volaris turned and looked at the doctor. His eyelids drooped.

"I'm okay, I think. I feel so relaxed."

"Are you cold?"

"No. I feel warm. Did you put stitches in me?"

"Yes."

"Old fashioned doctor," Volaris said. He smiled and closed his eyes.

"Go ahead and rest for now. I'll check back on you in an hour." Doctor Smith pulled the blanket up to his patient's neck. He walked out of the room. John Dvorak followed.

"Thank you Mister Dvorak. Having someone hold the MRI makes the job easier."

"How is he really?"

"He'll need to rest for a few days while his body replenishes the lost blood and the wound heals. But he'll be okay."

"What now?"

"We wait. Actually, I'll wait. There's no need for you to be idle here."

"Okay. Let me know if you need me."

John Dvorak headed out of the infirmary. He was walking down the hall when he was paged on the ship's intercom.

"John Dvorak, report to engineering and call the bridge."

He reached engineering and went to the nearest console.

"Bridge, this is Dvorak. I'm in engineering."

"Good. We're going to raid Adriana colony. Are all systems go?" Smitty asked.

"Stand by. Verifying now.... Verified. All systems are go."

* * *

"Pilot, take us down," Smitty said.

The pilot throttled forward and the ship headed toward Adriana colony.

"Adriana port traffic control, this is S.C. Applegate. We're headed to the colony. Please open an entry port for us."

"S.C. Applegate, you don't have permission to enter the colony."

"Pilot, head for the nearest port. And tell me which port it is once you can read the number printed on it."

The ship headed closer to the colony dome. Multiple ports of different sizes became clearly visible. The nearest one was labeled "7" and was just large enough for the Applegate to fit through.

"Adriana port control, we're outside port 7. We require you to open the port, on authority of Stellar Corp."

"*Sorry S.C. Applegate, you don't have permission to enter the colony.*"

"David, prepare to fire at port 7."

David sat at a console to Smitty's left. He moved his fingers across the console.

"Lasers are ready to fire, Sir."

"Open port 7 now, or we'll blow it open," Smitty said.

"*No, this is a violation of Adriana's sovereignty.*"

"Sorry if that's how you feel. David, fire."

"WAIT!"

The doors on port 7 began to part.

"*Stellar Corp thanks you.*"

Smitty disconnected the link to Adriana port traffic control.

"Pilot, take us through quickly."

The Applegate sped through the entry port and turned toward the government compound. The ship arrived at the compound in under a minute.

"Here they come," Smitty said.

Anti-aircraft fire hit the ship from all sides.

"What a nuisance. David, whenever you have a firing solution."

"I have one now," David said. The ship's lasers lashed out at the anti-aircraft batteries, crippling all three simultaneously.

"Take us down. Put us right on that open field outside the governor's office."

The pilot landed the ship on the field. Some monuments on the field were crushed beneath the hull. The landing pylons sank into the dirt as it compacted under the weight of the ship. The main disembarkation stairway descended from the underside of the ship. The distance to the governor's office was less than one hundred meters.

"Insertion team go," Smitty said.

Ten men ran down the stairs and across the open space to the governor's office.

"There's a security team heading over from one of the barracks," David said.

"Fire a warning shot."

David fired the laser at a spot of ground about thirty meters in front of the approaching security force. The laser etched a three meter wide valley into the dirt. The security force ran away.

"Good work. Keep an eye out for anyone else. Hopefully warning shots are all that we need," Smitty said.

The insertion team opened the doors to the Governor's office and went inside.

"Five minutes," Smitty said.

* * *

Inside the governor's office the ten men spread out in the main foyer.

"Upstairs. Let's go," Captain Bach said.

Captain Bach took four men with him up the nearest stairs. The other five men went up a different set of stairs at the back of the foyer. A pair of government security officers stood waiting for them.

"Halt on the order of the governor!" one of them said.

"Really? Look behind you," Captain Bach said.

The security officer turned around and saw the other five men. His face turned white.

"This doesn't have to get messy. Stand down and lead us to the Governor. That's an order from Stellar Corp."

The security officers looked at each other.

"Yes, sir. He's in his office, just two doors down the hall."

"Lead the way."

The security officers walked down the hall, to the second door on the right.

"Knock."

The security officer knocked.

"Yes?" Governor Shull said from inside the office.

"Go in," Captain Bach said.

One of the security officers opened the door and walked in.

"Shouldn't you be guarding the perimeter?"

Captain Bach stepped into the room.

"What!?"

"Let's go," he said.

"How dare you! I'm the lawful governor of this colony. You don't have the authority."

"I have all the authority I need. You're under arrest for violating the Stellar Corp code against treason."

"That code only applies to Stellar Corp personnel."

"Really? Well we'd better go back to the ship and sort it out together. Let's go."

"I'm not going anywhere with you, Stellar Corp."

Captain Bach fired his laser at the desk that Governor Shull was standing behind. Papers and various objects on the desk burst into flame.

"The next one is hitting you in the stomach. Let's go."

Governor Shull silently moved toward the door.

"After you," Captain Bach said.

* * *

The insertion team exited the building with Governor Shull. Smitty and David watched from the bridge.

"As soon as they get aboard, retract the embarkation ramp and lift off."

"Yes, Sir," the pilot said.

The team was crossing the hundred meters toward the ship. Three trucks sped toward them.

"David, slow them down please."

"Yes, Sir," he said. The lasers fired immediately in front of all three trucks. The drivers were unable to react quickly enough and the trucks drove into the gullies created by the lasers.

"Good work. Alright, they're coming up the stairs."

"They're all in, I'm retracting the embarkation ramp now," the pilot said.

"Let's get out of here."

The ship lifted off and headed back toward colony dome port 7.

"Adriana port traffic control, we're leaving now. Please open port 7."

"*We obviously can't stop you, so go ahead,*" the traffic controller said.

The doors on port 7 opened and the pilot took the ship through the dome and out into open space.

"David, please stay here on the bridge with the pilot. I'm going to meet the governor in the brig."

Smitty headed for the doors.

33

Hamlet Customs Brokers, Hamlet, Oberon

Sym walked to the shuttle and grabbed a slice of pizza.

"How are they?" Royson asked.

"Khaala's burns are healing well. He's sitting with Silver, watching over him. Silver is awake. He's pumped full of drugs. He told me to come back here and take care of the gremlins that shot him. Hey, who are these two?"

"Sym, this is Jordan, and Maris. They're transgenic utilities. We rescued them from the people they're working with."

"Did you get Commander Tajiki's missing man?"

"He got away, but we got these two. Sym, there was a firefight. Jefferson is resting on his bunk."

"I'll go check on him. So, Tajiki, do you want to make another attempt on this engineer of yours?"

"I do. But they'll be more prepared this time. We need to go in force," Commander Tajiki said.

"Royson, what do you think?" Sym asked.

"We're already in it, so let's finish it," Royson said.

"I'll get the men together," Sym said. He walked off toward the barracks where Jefferson was resting.

"Maris, are you enjoying your pizza?" Tajiki asked.

"I am, thank you."

"Good. We're going to go out for a bit. So the two of you will need to stay here. Can you do that?"

Maris nodded.

"You two can stay in the barracks with Jefferson. He'll take care of you. And the mess has all sorts of food and entertainment," Royson said.

"Oh that sounds fun," Jordan said.

"Okay, let's go. Don't forget the rest of the pizza."

Royson and Tajiki walked toward the barracks. Jordan and Maris followed. Maris turned around, ran back to the shuttle, and picked up the pizza box. She hurried back to Jordan's side.

Inside the barracks, Jefferson, favoring his wound, was talking with Capshaw.

"Hey there Royson," Jefferson said.

"Hey. Good to see you're doing okay."

"I'm fine, fine. Just needed to rest for a few. I'm ready to go murder this engineer of yours."

"Woah!" Tajiki said.

"I appreciate your enthusiasm, but this is a recovery mission, not a hit. Besides you're staying where you are. You'll be watching Jordan and Maris while we're gone," Royson said.

"We're told your mess has food and entertainment," Jordan said.

"It does. So, I'm watching you two?" Jefferson asked.

Jordan nodded.

"They look like they can take care of themselves. Besides, I'm ready for action," Jefferson said. He stood up. Then he cringed and sat down. "Damn. Looks like I'll be staying here with you."

"Great!" Maris said.

Sym walked out from one of the offices at the back of the room.

"The garrison will be ready in ten minutes," he said.

"Good, how many will be ready?" Royson asked.

"Forty-seven, including you, me, and Capshaw."

"So everyone except Jefferson, Khaala, and Silver."

"That's right."

"Did you hear from Wang?"

"He says he's gone back to the hospital. He sounded winded. Maybe he's been crying."

"Fine, we'll go on without him. I'll call Snaggletooth. We'll see if he has any info." Royson said. Royson walked away from the group. He was talking quietly, but gesturing passionately. A few seconds later he returned. "Snaggletooth has been tracking all air and ground traffic to and from the location where we got these two. He thinks he knows where Davis is, but he also thinks that someone else might be looking for him. He says the information has been accessed from the outside, but he doesn't know who it is."

"Is that it? You seemed pretty emotional," Tajiki asked.

"That's it. Oh. I convinced him to give us some backup. Hamlet Security Officers are on their way to secure the roads to and from Davis' hideout. We'll be able to go in without worrying about reinforcements catching us off-guard."

"That's great news!"

"It helps."

"Okay, let's go," Sym said. He walked out of the barracks.

"Jefferson, are you good?" Royson asked.

"I'm great. Going to the mess with Jordan and Maris to get some lunch right now. Let's go guys," Jefferson said. He used his rifle as a crutch and the three of them headed slowly to the mess.

Outside, Sym was doing roll-call with the garrison. Three armored vehicles sat beside the shuttle.

"Where did these come from?" Tajiki asked.

"The parking lot, behind the barracks. Royson, the garrison is ready," Sym said.

"Capshaw, take the shuttle. You'll provide aerial surveillance. Sym, take sixteen in a transport. Tajiki, you take fifteen. I'll take fifteen in the third transport. Here's the coordinates of Davis's hideout."

Royson transmitted the coordinates to Tajiki and Sym. Sym reviewed it on his handset.

"We've got our jobs to do," Sym said loudly to the garrison. "There's a reason we're all here. We're the best. That's all there is to it. Now let's go mop the floor and bring back our prize. Move out!"

The shuttle took off into the air, and the three transports lumbered out of the garrison compound. The transports moved through the streets, winding their way to a part of the colony almost one-hundred kilometers distant. The shuttle kept pace above.

"All clear from up here. I can see the hideout; so far nothing out of the ordinary," Capshaw said.

"Thanks Capshaw. Let us know if you notice anything in the next hour," Royson said.

"Next hour? Can't these things go any faster?" Tajiki asked from her transport.

"Sure, if you want to risk hitting other vehicles on the road," Royson said.

"Of course, right. It's just a little anticlimactic," Tajiki said.

"It's pre-climactic, if you think about it. Because the climax is coming. When we find Davis. A long, slow pre-climax," Sym said.

"That was insightful. How about we just observe tactical silence until we get there?" Capshaw said. A clicking sound indicated that he'd disconnected.

"Tactical silence," Royson said.

The team proceeded in silence down the streets of Hamlet for around an hour, until it was only a few blocks from where Davis was suspected of hiding out. Hamlet Security Officers had set up checkpoints at an intersection and waved them through.

"Here we go. They're on the next block. Sym, take your team down that alley so that you can come in the back way," Royson said.

"*On our way.*"

Sym's transport rumbled off down the small lane behind the row of houses.

"Capshaw, how does it look?"

"*Looks all clear.*"

"Okay, deploy," Royson said.

The transports sped down the street and stopped in front of a small bungalow. The men jumped from the transports and took up positions around the house. More men from Sym's transport swarmed into the back of the property. Royson made a hand signal, and they stormed in through every door and window in the house. But instead of a firefight, it was quiet in the house. One of the men came out and made an all-clear sign. Sym went into the house, followed by Royson and Tajiki.

"What the hell!" Royson said.

Sitting at the kitchen table were two men. Petty Officer Davis, pale-faced and flush, was sitting upright and staring at the barrel of a laser pistol. The man holding the gun was leaning against the table. He had one hand pressed against his side.

"Hi Lauressa."

"Wang! What the hell!" Tajiki said.

"I got him for you," Steven Wang said. The area where he held his hand against his body was red and wet.

"God, what have you done Steven!"

Lauressa crouched and put her hand over his hand.

"I couldn't put anyone else in danger again. I almost lost Silver, and Khaala, and you."

Steven Wang cringed and started to lower his gun. Petty Officer Davis began to move.

"Don't even think about it," Royson said. He placed a hand on Davis's shoulder.

"Wang, what were you thinking," Lauressa said. Her hand was red with blood now.

"Let's talk about this back at the barracks. Sym, get Wang to the shuttle. Go back with him and get him patched up. We'll bring Davis back the long way," Royson said.

"Sounds good. Wang, can you walk?" Sym asked.

"Sure, just give me a hand."

Sym reached out and Wang took his arm. He pulled himself up. His knees started to buckle. Sym put an arm around Wang and held him up.

"One foot after another. It's only a few steps to the shuttle," Sym said. He led Wang out the front door. Capshaw brought the shuttle down and landed it in the street. They hobbled into the shuttle and seconds later took off at a very high speed.

"Davis, you can come with us on your feet, or we can beat you and drag you to the transport," Royson said.

"Woah, hold on," Commander Tajiki said.

"I'll come willingly. I won't fight," Davis said.

"Good move," Royson said. He led Davis to the nearest transport. The rest of the team followed them out. They got into the three transports and drove off.

"Why did you sabotage the station?" Tajiki asked. They sat with fifteen of Wang's men in the rear of the transport.

"For freedom," Davis said.

"What are you talking about."

"Stellar Corp has controlled the fate of dozens of planets and colonies for too long. It's time we took a stand against their totalitarian rule."

"Who are you working for?" Tajiki asked.

"I don't know."

"How can you not know?"

"I was recruited anonymously. I stumbled on a source of information. It was a storehouse of all of the transgressions of Stellar Corp. I read through the whole thing. I reached out to other people with questions. And then one day I was contacted. I was given even more condemning evidence. I was convinced. The people you work for, the organization that you represent, it's rotten to the core. So when they sent me instructions, I did as they asked."

"Just like that. Without knowing who they were?"

"I know who they are, in general, but not specifically who they are."

"So who are they?"

"They are the resistance. People from the colonies and from Mars, who are tired of this solar system being dominated by the strong arm of Earth. The sun is rising on freedom. Freedom to have our own beliefs and our own thoughts, without fear of being condemned for our views."

"Is that all?"

"I'm a pawn I guess. But I'm a willing pawn. Unlike you. You're a pawn for Stellar Corp and you don't even know it."

"I'm no pawn. Besides, at least I know who I work for."

"Are you sure about that?"

The transport continued to rumble through the streets in silence. It reached the barracks of Hamlet Customs Brokers some time later.

"Move," Royson said. He pushed Davis out of the transport and guided him toward the barracks. Inside, Jefferson was playing checkers with Jordan, while Maris was watching a video comedy about Martian soy farmers called The Settlers. Capshaw and Wang were eating. Maris heard them come in. She turned to see who it was.

"Oh no, we're in trouble!" she said. She stood up and froze.

"Don't worry Maris, it's fine. You're safe. You're safe. Okay?" Jefferson asked.

Maris nodded and sat down.

Royson led Davis to the office at the back of the barracks.

"Those two have no idea what they're doing, they were hired just like me, but they know nothing," Davis said.

"Why does it matter to you?" Royson asked.

"I like them. They must have led sheltered lives or something, because they have a child-like innocence about them."

"So?"

"So, go easy on them."

"You don't have much say in what we do. Sit down."

Davis sat in a chair beside a small side-table. Tajiki sat down in a chair opposite the side-table.

"You're in a lot of trouble. A lot of trouble," Commander Tajiki said.

"I don't care about that."

"Why not?"

"Because there are higher principles at stake than my own safety. I'm fighting for the freedom of everyone who is under the thumb of Earth's central control."

"You're so wrong."

"No I'm not. You represent oppression and control."

"We fight against oppression. We safeguard freedom. You know that, or at least you did at one point."

"You represent the opposite of freedom, whatever that is called. Tyranny? Your day is coming to an end. A new day is dawning."

"Davis, you've been deceived. These people you've been helping have coordinated attacks on multiple colonies. They've detonated a nuclear weapon on Adriana Colony. They've killed hundreds on ships and space stations, maybe thousands. Is that the freedom you're hoping for?"

Davis looked away, then looked at Lauressa.

"Maybe there will be some initial injuries, some casualties. But it's for the greater good. The sun will rise on freedom and there will be peace."

"Do you know who has been attacking our ships? Our space stations? Do you know who they are?"

"The resistance, the freedom fighters," Davis said.

"No. That's not who they are. They're the opposite of that. The space stations, the ships, the colonies that have been attacked, at least the ones that we know about, were attacked by a fleet of Labian war ships."

"No. No. You're lying. You're lying!" Davis said. He stood up. Royson pushed him back down. "It's not possible, the resistance...."

"You've been used. You're a pawn. You helped them to start a war when you blinded our long-range communications. I need you to tell me everything that you know."

Davis slouched in his chair. He put his hands to his face.

"I don't know anything. I just received instructions and was told to rendezvous with the resistance cell on Hamlet. I was to use my engineering expertise to help them. That's all I know."

"So you don't know anything else."

"No."

Lauressa stood up and walked to the door.

"I'm going to take a walk," she said.

"I'll take care of Davis. Him and I are going to have a chat," Royson said.

"Commander, don't leave me with–" Davis said.

Lauressa walked out and closed the door before he could finish. She walked over to Wang, who was eating a type of meat pie manufactured locally on Hamlet.

"Feeling better?" Lauressa asked.

"A lot better. Sym patched me up on the flight back. It wasn't that bad really. Just a scratch."

"Let me see."

Lauressa knelt down and lifted his shirt. A large clear bandage covered the injury. Underneath, a dark red and brown clot pressed against the bandage.

"He just shoved some carbonic into the wound and put this plastic sheet over it. I'll be mostly healed by the morning."

"You can't do this. It's too dangerous," Lauressa said.

"I had to."

"I don't understand."

"You got shot with a laser because of me. You were okay thankfully. But Khaala wasn't so lucky, and Silver.... You know, I sat there at the hospital and I kept thinking, what if it was you in the hospital. What if it was you all burned up? All smashed up. And I couldn't imagine letting that happen... and so I had to go out and do something. So I found him for you."

"You risked your life. It's not your job to do that. That's my job."

"You know, I'm three-hundred-and-one next month. I've had a lot of life and when I see you I feel like I.... Like I have a purpose. I...."

"But I've been cruel to you for years," Lauressa said.

"It doesn't matter."

Lauressa, still kneeling, trembled slightly. She crumpled the hem of his shirt in her hand. She leaned forward and pressed her lips against the back of his hand.

"I'm... I'm sorry," she said.

Steven put his hand on her head. They were silent and still for a moment. Royson walked up behind them.

"He knows nothing," he said.

"You sure?" Tajiki asked.

"Either he knows nothing or he's an excellent liar."

"Okay, I'll take him back to Horatio Station. He'll sit in the brig until this war is over."

Commander Tajiki stood up. Wang grabbed her arm.

"It's too dangerous up there," he said.

"More dangerous than on this colony?"

"Maybe. At least here we can watch your back."

"I can't stay here."

"I know. Lauressa, this might not make a difference one way or another, but take half my garrison with you."

"What?"

"Twenty men, and Royson."

"Are you sure? What about your security down here?"

"We'll be fine. We're not a target of any sort."

"Well I suppose so. I mean.... Thank you, Steven."

"You're welcome. Now go on and get back to the station."

Royson picked up his hand-held.

"Chang, you there?" he asked.

"*Chang here.*"

"We're on our way back to the shuttle. How are things over there?"

"*Absolutely uneventful. Boring actually.*"

"You're fortunate. We're bringing prisoners and a team with us. When we get to the shuttle, head back to barracks. You'll be taking over for me."

"What's that?" Garret Chang asked.

"You'll be taking on my role while I'm gone. I'll be spending some time on Horatio Station."

34

Aboard S.C. Applegate

"Governor Shull, you're in pretty serious trouble," Captain Bach said. Smitty leaned against the wall behind him.

"That depends," Shull said.

"Depends on what?"

"On who is doing the writing of the history books after this war is over."

"Who will that be?"

"I don't know, but I've picked my side."

"And you're ready to live with the consequences?"

"I'm ready to die with them, if need be."

"Governor Shull, in my power as an officer of Stellar Corp, I'm charging you with the bombing of Adriana Colony."

"Nonsense. I have done no such thing."

"You're a Mars sympathizer and a traitor!" Smitty said.

"I am a Mars sympathizer. But I'm no traitor. A man can't be a traitor to a government that is against the people it is supposed to represent. Stellar Corp – and the Earth government that it is an extension of – is corrupt. Where is the freedom that we have guaranteed by our constitution?"

"We're plenty free, you piece of –"

"Relax Smitty. Governor, how could you let your own colony be bombed?" Captain Bach asked.

"I did not let it happen, I did not aid it, in any way. I wouldn't want to hurt anyone here. The colonists are under the thumb of Earth as much as any other colony; as much as Mars is under Earth's thumb."

"So who did it, then?"

"You did."

"What!? I'm going to throw this guy out an airlock!" Smitty said.

"Earth's central government must have found out that Mars is planning a new revolution. They carried out this terrible act of terrorism to pin it on Mars, to make us look bad and to ensure the public supports Earth."

"That's nonsensical," Captain Bach said.

"Captain, I don't know who bombed my colony. Earth is as good a suspect as anyone. Remember when we first talked, on the day of the bombing? I pointed out that it happened on a Sunday, when the observatory was closed and most people in the area were out at the market. Do you remember?"

"I do."

"Remember, I said the timing seemed too convenient. As if it was done to purposely minimize casualties. Think of it, if Earth wanted to do this to frame Mars, wouldn't it make sense to do it at a time when as few people as possible would be hurt? After all, if it was meant as a marketing tool, then actually killing people wouldn't be necessary. Just the shock of the event would be enough."

"I don't buy it."

"You don't have to. But I wasn't involved in the bombing, and I don't think Mars was either. But when I received news that the resistance was starting a new revolution, I sent word to the others in the colony to take over in places like space port control, security, and so on. Adriana is free of Earth oversight now. We're joining the Martian cause, and I think most of the population will go along willingly to support our freedom."

"You're still a traitor. You took an oath to Earth when you became governor," Smitty said.

"Like I said, I'm not a traitor. I'm a liberator. And when this is all over I will be free, unless Earth is able to crush us again. In which case I'm sure I'll be convicted for treason and spend the rest of my life in a cell or working on an asteroid mining rare metals somewhere."

"There's just one thing. If you care so much about freedom, then why are you working with people who believe in building an empire?" Smitty asked.

"Excuse me?" Shull asked.

"The Labians. They've attacked Stellar Corp facilities throughout the solar system."

"What? No, that doesn't make sense. Why would Mars work with the Labians?"

"I don't know. But it fits. You get word that a revolution is starting, and at the same time dozens of Labian ships make attacks on multiple locations simultaneously."

"You lie."

"We're not lying. And the ships look the same as the one that bombed Adriana Colony. The Martian revolutionaries are working with the Labians somehow. They're responsible for the bombing of your colony."

"No, I don't see how –"

"You're not a liberator. You're delivering your people into the hands of the worst kind of oppression possible – servitude at the feet of the Labian Empire."

"No, it's not possible."

"It is possible, and it's happening. Captain, let him rot in the brig."

"We need him out of our hair. We've got places to go. Shull, you're going to be transferred over to Horatio Station, where you'll stay until the war is over. You'll either go to trial or you'll be a slave to some lucky Labian. Smitty, let's go drop this prisoner off."

"Sounds good to me."

Smitty grabbed Shull's arm and led him away.

* * *

"Horatio Station, this is S.C. Applegate," Smitty said.

"S.C. *Applegate*, *Horatio Station* here," Wayland Hauer said from the bridge of the station.

"Horatio Station, we're on approach now. Permission to dispatch a shuttle, we have a prisoner to transfer."

"*Did you say a prisoner to transfer? Please confirm.*"

"That's right."

"Go ahead S.C. Applegate. A security team will be waiting in the hangar for you."

"Thank you."

Smitty dropped the connection to Horatio Station.

"Did you hear that, Captain?"

"I did, thank you Smitty. I'm opening the hangar doors now," Captain Bach said from the pilot's seat. David the Mechanic sat to his right. Behind him was Governor Shull, flanked by two marines. The hangar doors opened and the shuttle eased out of the ship. The station loomed ahead, only a dozen kilometers away.

A few minutes later the shuttle touched down in one of the station's hangars. Jeremy got up from the pilot's chair and walked to the hatch. He hit the release and the hatch opened. Commander Tajiki stood not far from the shuttle, flanked by a half-dozen marines.

"Captain, welcome back to Horatio Station," she said.

"Thank you, I wish it was under better circumstances. I have the prisoner for you," Captain Bach said. He leaned back into the shuttle and waved. The marines led the prisoner out.

"But that's..." she said.

"Governor Shull. He's working with the Labians."

"I'm no Labian sympathizer. I support the Mars resistance," Governor Shull said.

"Either way, you'll be staying in a cell for the foreseeable future. Take him away."

The security team took Governor Shull's arms and led him out of the hangar.

"He seems to have not known he was working for the Labians," Captain Bach said.

"We found the same thing – we retrieved my engineer, and he said he was working for the Mars resistance too."

"It could be some kind of alliance between the Labians and Mars. It doesn't make much sense that they'd work together, but they do share a common goal."

"Overthrowing Earth and Stellar Corp," Commander Tajiki said.

"What's your next move?"

"We're going to keep interviewing our prisoners. We'll work on any leads we can that are local to this system."

"Okay good. Now that you've got Governor Shull in your hands, I'm going to get back to our original plan – to take a trip to Mount Sinai II and track down the people behind the Amish bank payments. But do you need us to stay here to help protect the station?"

"No, we'll be fine. We've got the S.C. Johnson to protect us, and with your superlight drive you've got an advantage. You're actually safer out there traveling between the stars, rather than sitting here waiting for the inevitable to come."

"You're right."

"Of course I am. Good luck Captain," Commander Tajiki said. She leaned in and kissed Captain Bach on the cheek. "That's for in case –"

"I know. Good luck to you too, Commander."

Captain Bach returned to the shuttle and piloted it back to S.C. Applegate. A few minutes later the ship glowed white and was gone.

35

Aboard Horatio Station

"There's a ship heading our way at a high speed," Wayland Hauer said.

"Talk to them," Commander Tajiki said.

"This is Horatio Station, slow your approach immediately."

The ship didn't slow down and did not respond.

"Weapons ready," Tajiki said.

Wayland entered a few commands at his console. A crew member in engineering appeared on the corner of the screen.

"Fire control ready," the engineer said.

Suddenly the approaching ship turned and headed toward Oberon.

"S.C. Johnson, do you have them?"

"Intercepting," the Commander of the S.C. Johnson said.

The Stellar Corp ship accelerated toward the interloper.

"Commander I've got a good image of the ship, it matches the description of the ship that bombed Adriana," Wayland said.

"Labians! S.C Johnson, that's an enemy ship. You're free to engage as needed."

"Thank you Commander."

The Labian ship launched a missile toward Hamlet. It careened off course and landed harmlessly on the surface of Oberon. The ship turned and fled.

"Pursuing," S.C. Johnson's Commander said.

The ship disappeared over the curvature of Oberon. S.C. Johnson followed and also vanished.

"Another ship approaching. Another Labian ship," Wayland said.

"Weapons ready!"

The ship sped toward the station.

"They're firing!" Wayland Hauer said. Beams of light flew at Horatio Station. The beams hit their stationary target and began to vaporize the outer layers of armor.

"Counterfire!" Tajiki said.

The engineers in fire control activated their weapons.

Multiple lasers fired at the Labian ship. It maneuvered away and its lasers moved off target, sparing Horatio Station.

"We've got armor damage," Wayland said. "Shit, they're turning toward us again."

"Keep the pressure on!" Tajiki said. Horatio Station's lasers reached out and burned the hull of the Labian ship. It veered off again.

"They're moving closer," Wayland said.

"Fire again."

Lasers hit the Labian ship again, and it once more veered off. But it managed to get closer to the station. Suddenly a barrage of missiles launched from the Labian ship.

"Missiles incoming, five seconds," Wayland said.

"Take them out!" Tajiki said.

The lasers managed to shoot down most of the missiles. But four made it through and hit the station in different spots. Three only caused some minor damage to the armor. The fourth hit hard. The station groaned and the overhead lights went out and the main screen went dark.

"One of the missiles just overloaded our power grid. Some kind of EMP maybe," an engineer said. "Backups are online now. Main power is being rebooted and should be restored in thirty seconds."

"We're blind," Wayland said.

"No outside cameras at all? Fire control, do you have anything?"

"We're blind down here too," the engineer said.

Tajiki stood in silence. *What does a good leader do, when there's nothing you can do?* She began to pace in the dark, with only the emergency light strips embedded in the floor to provide some light.

A few seconds later an alarm sounded.

"It's the brig," Wayland said.

"What? Get a team down there."

"Commander Tajiki, this is Royson. I'm in the brig. It's bad," James Royson said over the intercom.

Just then the main power came back online, and the view of space became visible again on the screen. The Labian ship was not visible.

"Where's the ship?" Tajiki asked.

"It's not on any of our cameras or sensors," Wayland said.

"Check the hull-facing cameras."

Wayland put the hull-facing cameras on screen and rapidly flipped between them.

"There," he said. The Labian ship was stuck to the side of the station. It detached and a jet of air and debris blew out of a small hole in the station's skin.

"Emergency bulkheads are closing," Wayland said. The jet of air and debris stopped.

"Fire on that ship! All weapons!" Tajiki said.

The station's lasers lashed out. At this close range they could actually see the outer layers of the ship begin to melt. The Labian ship changed direction. The lasers struggled to keep up. Then, the Labian ship began to glow.

"No! Hit them! Stop them!"

The lasers hit the Labian ship again. The ship changed direction again. The glow grew brighter. Then it flashed and was gone.

"Royson, what happened down there?"

"They stormed the brig in force. Broke out Shull and Davis, and fled," Royson said.

"The crew?"

"They're all alive, but there are injured. We're taking them to the infirmary now."

"Thanks Royson."

"Mister Hauer, does it seem to you that they knew exactly where to hit us?"

"It does. They seemed to know how to take down our defenses, and also the best place to break into the hull to get in and out of the brig with minimal resistance."

"Davis must have given them schematics.... Any word on S.C. Johnson?"

"They must still be behind the moon. Wait, hold on – there they are."

"Connect me to them, Mister Hauer. S.C. Johnson, did you have any luck?"

"No, *they skirmished and ran. It's like they were playing with us*," the Commander said.

"They were. While you were out of range we were attacked and the prisoners were broken out of the brig."

"Are you okay?"

"For the most part."

"*Good. So it was a feint. We were lured away so that they could minimize their risk.*"

"I agree. We can't let this happen again. We have to stick together. We're too vulnerable alone."

"*Yes Commander. We'll be back in a few minutes.*"

"Good. Please come aboard when you get here. Meet me in the infirmary. Mister Hauer has the bridge."

Commander Tajiki walked off the bridge and threw herself against the elevator wall. Once the door closed she let out a wailing cry. *Fuck, fuck, fuuuck!!! They outmaneuvered you Lauressa, and you let them win. You're going to end up dead if you keep this up. Fuck!* She punched the wall a few times. The elevator door opened and Commander Tajiki walked out, composed and looking like a leader.

The infirmary was a hub of activity. Royson was holding down an injured crew member while Doctor Poisson injected the injured man with a sedative. Ashley Chung was applying dressing to a wound.

"Hi Commander," Ashley said. She waved at Lauressa.

"Oh, hi Ashley, did you get hurt?"

"No, I was just here with the doctor when all these people came in. So I'm helping and–"

"Ashley, over here please," Doctor Poisson said. Ashley went over to the Doctor and took Royson's place holding onto the injured person. Royson walked over to Commander Tajiki.

"Three people are hurt. The brig security guard and two people the Labians crossed paths with on the way. They came in, made a surgical strike, and left," Royson said.

"We need to prevent this from happening again."

"This is a big station, and your crew – even augmented by my garrison – isn't big enough to defend it."

"We'll have to pick our battles, defend the critical places."

Royson nodded. Doctor Poisson stepped away from the injured person. Ashley held the patient's hand.

"Commander Tajiki. The brig security guard had his femur broken. He's hopped up on pain-killers and the break had been set. It will take some time to heal though. The other two have injuries from some sort of energy weapon. There are actual burns on the skin," Doctor Poisson said.

"Will they be okay?"

"Yes, the burns will heal nicely. There doesn't seem to be any internal injuries. The guard took the worst of it."

"Can he talk?"

"No, he's out of it, but he gave me a rundown of what happened."

"Okay, what happened."

"He says at least seven women rushed into the brig. He said he shot one with his sidearm, but they swarmed him so fast that they overran his position. They hit him in the leg with some kind of baton or pipe. Then they broke out Davis and Shull and retreated."

"The one that he shot, where is she?"

"Gone. She got out."

"Thanks Doctor. Take care of them. And prepare your infirmary as best you can for more of this."

"I will, but I'm not looking forward to it. I should get back to work."

"Okay. Oh, Doctor, please tell Ashley Chung that I'm drafting her into service. She is now officially your assistant."

"I think she's already made that decision," Doctor Poisson said. He smiled and walked back to his patients.

Commander Tajiki headed for the door. Royson followed. A man walked through the doorway just as she was about to head through it.

"Oh! Excuse me, Commander Tajiki," Captain Thomas said.

"Captain Thomas, I was just about to look for you. This is James Royson, my garrison commander."

"Mister Royson," Captain Thomas said. He extended his hand. Royson gave it a brief shake.

Commander Tajiki headed out the door.

"Let's get back to the bridge," she said.

The two men followed behind her.

"So, you have your own garrison now?" Captain Thomas asked.

"On loan to us," Tajiki said.

"On loan? From who?"

"Hamlet Customs Brokers."

"What? Wang's company?"

"You know him?" Royson asked.

"I think Commander Tajiki mentioned him previously. And, I have heard of his private security before. Your group has a reputation for getting the job done, whatever that job is."

"It's a reputation we've earned."

"Stellar Corp has investigated your boss once or twice for suspected black market dealings. But nothing stuck. In any case, I'm glad we have you in our corner."

"Thank you."

They got on the elevator to the bridge.

"We need to be prepared for the next attack," Commander Tajiki said.

"I agree. The Johnson will stay close to Horatio Station. We won't be baited again," Captain Thomas said.

"Royson, let's distribute a few of your men to the most important areas – engineering, weapons, the infirmary."

"What about the bridge?" Royson asked.

"Not that important. Myself and Mister Hauer are the only people you'll find there on most days, and honestly, we're not very tactically important. Other parts of the station are more important than the bridge if we're boarded. We can also lock down the bridge rather easily if required."

"Okay, I'll set up a few sentries. We should keep a unit together as well, so that they can rapidly travel anywhere in the station and respond in force."

"Okay," Commander Tajiki said. The elevator doors opened and they walked onto the bridge. Wayland Hauer turned around.

"Everything okay down there?" he asked.

"The doctor is doing his best. A broken leg, some burns," Commander Tajiki said.

"Engineering says their repairs are complete. There's some damage to the armor, which will take some time to patch up, but otherwise we're fully operational and ready for action."

"Okay, that's good news. Could you work with engineering on something for me?"

"Of course. What is it?"

"We need to change every single password, and regenerate every encryption key. We also need to reprogram the main computer to wartime specifications. That means no remote access, and the commands need to be changed so that their names and purposes are hidden. Someone like Davis is a weapon in the hands of the Labians."

"Uhh, I'll get started on it. Passwords and encryption won't take very long. I don't know why we didn't think of changing them before. But reprogramming the computers, well I don't know if this is something we can do in any reasonable amount of time."

"Please do your best."

"I will."

"Also, we should see about bringing on-line the old anti-ship batteries and EMP evasion systems."

"I don't know if they're working. They were installed, but I don't think they were ever connected to the main computer or main power."

"Lucky for us, one of the people who was present when Horatio Station was being built is still here."

"You're right. I won't bother him about it yet. But as soon as he's free I'll ask for his help."

"Good. We've got to have this station ready for war. The next time the Labians show up they won't know what they're up against. I have something to take care of. I'll be back shortly," Commander Tajiki said. She left the bridge.

Lauressa looked at her reflection in the mirror in her office. *That's it Lauressa. Leadership. You were foolish to have not thought about bringing the station up to its full wartime specs days ago. But now you're doing it; now you'll be ready. All these decades of experience are leading up to this moment.* Lauressa stared at her face in the mirror; at the face that had witnessed those one-hundred-and-sixty years of experience. A young reflection, seemingly thirty-seven at most, stared back.

36

Labia Minor, on Gliese 832c

"What news do you bring?" Imperatrix Shauna Lone asked.

"The Advance Fleet has encountered resistance on the Uranus colonies," Mei Lun said. Her face filled the screen that Shauna Lone was currently looking at. Mei Lun was Supreme Commander of the Core Fleet, and the Advance Fleet was under her control.

"Tell me."

"A Stellar Corp battleship attacked the Adriana Colony and extracted the governor. A small strike-force also attacked operatives on Hamlet and managed to steal away three of our assets."

"And this concerns me, how?"

"The Uranus system, as you know, is central to our plans."

"Of course I know this!"

"I apologize, Imperatrix, I did not intend to suggest anything," Mei Lun said.

"Please, continue."

"Thank you, Imperatrix. We launched a rescue operation. We raided the space station where they were being kept. We rescued the governor and one of our Stellar Corp assets."

"Good."

"We were unable to locate the other two – they are a pair of Transgenic Utilities that work for us under the guise of Martian sympathy for their lack of human status."

"You don't know where they are?"

"We do not. We have our network looking for them, but wherever they are, they are well hidden."

"Do those two Utilities know much?"

"No. But even the smallest bit of information could lead Stellar Corp to guess our plans."

"Keep looking. The two that you rescued, what have you learned?"

"Our assets – Shull and Petty Officer Davis – really believed that they were solely working toward the rise of a Martian hegemony. They had no idea we were involved."

"So our recruitment network has been successful in its deception."

"Yes, Imperatrix. At least with these two."

"And what have you learned from them?"

"Nothing of use – too low of a level in our network. However, the governor did say he was kidnapped by a ship called the S.C. Applegate."

"Is it a threat?" the Imperatrix asked.

"At this time, no. By his account it is a local patrol ship, of antiquated design and with a small, inexperienced crew."

"Good."

"Now, this space station, why didn't you destroy it?"

"A tactical decision, Imperatrix. Our main goal was rescue only – to move in quickly and retreat with minimal commitment of our fleet. We didn't want to launch a full-scale attack on the Uranus system Stellar Corp assets, due to its strategic importance. If we destroyed their space station, would that bring the attention of any Stellar Corp reconnaissance that may be in place? We still don't know where the main Stellar Corp fleet is – assuming it is still functional – and we did not think it wise to risk a fight that could place their fleet so close to our primary goal."

"Thank you, Mei Lun. I knew you were the right choice for Supreme Commander. What are your plans now?"

"We continue to search for the Transgenic Utilities. As for the ones that we rescued, they have no further useful information to offer us. We're transferring them to more comfortable residences, where they will be made to service the needs and indulge the attentions of our warriors. For the moment they are terrified, but they will come to appreciate the benefits of Labian servitude."

"Very good. Return to your work. Update me if you have any other useful information."

"Thank you, Imperatrix. I pledge my blood to the empire," Mei Lun said. She saluted.

"May the Labian Empire never fall," Imperatrix Shauna Lone said. She cut the transmission and the screen went dark.

High above Labia Minor, the Supreme Commander's ship flashed away into interstellar space.

Shauna Lone turned and walked toward her advisors. A flurry of helpers descended upon her – makeup, wardrobe and more. The moment of her coronation was near.

37

Mount Sinai II

ARCHIVIST'S NOTE: *The planet Mount Sinai II is a self-governing territory, with articles of incorporation specifying that Stellar Corp will appoint a 'Lord High Appropriationer', to ensure that the interactions between the various religions on the planet do not result in risks to the purity of said religions. The Lord High Appropriationer is concerned with two primary spiritual risks: the 'twin cardinal sins' of syncretization and appropriation. All visitors to the planet are also screened by the Appropriationer's Office; this gives Stellar Corp de-facto control over all external affairs of the government.*
-- Ashley Chung, Archivist

S.C. Applegate flashed into space outside the orbit of Mount Sinai II. The planet was a small blue and brown ball off in the distance.

"Smitty, anything?" Jeremy asked.

"Nothing unusual, Captain. Hold on. The planet is calling us."

"Okay, let's see what they have to say."

"This is Mount Sinai II territory control. You appear to be a Stellar Corp vessel. Please state the nature of your visit."

"This is Captain Jeremy Bach. We're investigating an attack on Adriana Colony. We're following a lead here."

"Have you received clearance from the Lord High Appropriationer for your visit?"

"Stellar Corp official business doesn't require clearance. I believe the articles of incorporation for Mount Sinai II state that."

"Hold please."

They waited for a minute or two. Captain Bach began to absentmindedly play with the sleeve of his uniform.

"Sorry, I just had to confirm that with my superior. You're correct. I'm sending you an orbital slot and landing permission now."

I've been asked to remind you that Mount Sinai II is a self-governing territory, and as such Stellar Corp has no authority to act without approval of the Lord High Appropriationer."

"Thank you, we understand. We're traveling to Amish territory. Is there someone who can meet us there?"

"I'll have one of our sheriffs meet you at the landing site."

* * *

"I'm Sheriff Raber, welcome to the Amish territory."

"Thank you, Sheriff. I'm Captain Jeremy Bach. This is Smitty."

"Pleased to meet you. How can the Amish assist you?"

"We're investigating a bombing on Adriana Colony, among other things. Our investigation has led us to believe that some of the people involved have been paid via an Amish bank."

"Surely that can't be."

"That's what we're here to look into."

"We should speak with the Finance Minister."

"Okay."

"It's a short drive. We can take my car."

Sheriff Raber pointed to a four-wheeled vehicle. It looked like an archaeological curiosity.

"We don't adopt new technology so readily. This kind of car has served us for almost a thousand years now. Please, get in."

The Sheriff drove away from the landing site toward the center of town. Smitty looked back toward the shuttle. A dust cloud, kicked up by the tires, obscured the road behind them and the shuttle disappeared into the expanding brown cloud.

"Rain much here?" Smitty asked.

"There's a short rainy season. But most of the year it's nearly a desert. You haven't been here before?"

"No."

"Oh, well I could see this entire planet being a little bit alien to you. Most of the planet has a similar climate. Earth's government wasn't very interested in a dust bowl. But it seems to be the best weather for spiritual contemplation. So it worked out well."

"How big is the Amish territory?"

"About ten percent of this continent. Much more than we'll ever need. There's a lot of buffer space between us and the Jews, who live to the south of us... or the Muslims to the north."

"Do you ever cross paths with them?"

"At special events, holidays, government meetings. But on a day-to-day basis we mostly stick to our own folk. There are always a few travelers – those who syncretize the different faiths. We're almost there. The Finance Ministry is just ahead."

Sheriff Raber pulled the car up beside a two-story brick house.

* * *

"Finance Minister Imhoff, this is Captain Bach from Stellar Corp," Sheriff Raber said.

"Gentlemen, pleased to meet you. Stellar Corp usually doesn't take much interest in Mount Sinai II," the Finance Minister said.

"These are not typical circumstances. Finance Minister Imhoff, Stellar Corp is under attack. We're hoping you can help us figure out who is behind it," Captain Bach said.

"Under attack?"

"Yes, on multiple colonies in multiple locations. We have one lead. A pair of Transgenic Utilities we captured said they were given a cheque written against an Amish bank."

"Transgenic Utilities? Are you sure?" the Finance Minister asked.

"Yes."

"Some Amish support Transgenic Utilities financially. They have sympathy for their plight. But that's at an individual level. And I haven't known any Amish to seek out violence. Our people work for change via strictly peaceful means."

"This time it may not be true. These Utilities believed they were working for a Martian resistance movement. However, our fear is that the actual money behind it comes from the riches of the Labian Empire."

"The Labians? Oh that's not good. Not good at all. I can't see how any Amish would want to associate with them. They enslave. We support peace and freedom. Unless...."

"Unless what?"

"The Amish banking sector is the most mature and diversified of the ones that are not regulated by Earth. And Mount Sinai II is situated between the Labians and Earth. If these Martians, or Labians, or whoever they are, wanted an easy way to move financial transactions across all the colonies, then this would be one of the few banking sectors capable of doing it."

"Can you help us track them down?"

"We'll do our best. If the payments themselves are not strictly illegal then I may not have authority to do anything about it. But we'll look. Please give me any documentation you have and we'll check."

Jeremy handed a pad of data to the Finance Minister.

"We'll wait outside while you search," Jeremy said.

"Oh, I'm sorry, that won't work. We keep most of our records either on paper or on local databases on a per-bank basis. We have no central way to search."

"That sounds inconvenient."

"It has worked for us for centuries, so why change it? The only problem is this search could take up to a week to complete. Can you come back then?"

"I don't see any other option. We'll be back in a week. Thank you for your help, Finance Minister."

"Captain Bach, I hope things work out. I'll see you in a week."

* * *

They left the Finance Minister and headed back to Sheriff Raber's car.

"I suppose I should take you back to your ship, unless you want to do some sightseeing."

"That would be nice, but I think we should –" Jeremy began to say.

"Actually," Smitty said, "if you don't mind, I have a cousin who lives not far from the Amish Territory. I haven't seen him in years."

"Smitty, I didn't know you had family here. If it's alright with the Sheriff, I guess we could take a quick detour."

Sheriff Raber nodded. "I'm happy to. I'm assuming you mean the Canadian outpost that we host on our land."

"How did you guess?" Smitty asked.

"You aren't Amish, and they're the only non-Amish around here."

"Fair enough."

Sheriff Raber smiled and began the drive out of town. It wasn't long before they were driving through scrub land, and not a building was visible for miles around. Eventually they came over a hill, and upon getting to the top, a few dozen buildings came into view.

"Here we are. Who are we going to see?" the Sheriff asked.

"Do you know where Charles Sacré-Coeur lives?"

"I know Charles," the driver said. He turned the car down a street lined with modest homes and stopped at the fifth house in.

Smitty got out and jogged to the door. His cousin must have heard them stop outside, because he opened the door and shouted, "Smitty? Smitty!"

Smitty and Charles embraced tightly.

"I haven't seen you in years, this is incredible! How are you here?"

"We're on a mission, and we were just at the settlement next door."

"Okay, okay. Who's your friend?"

"This is Jeremy Bach, captain of my ship."

Smitty turned to Jeremy, and Jeremy noticed that Smitty was smiling, really smiling. This was something he wasn't sure he'd really seen before.

Charles extended his hand, and said, "Pleased to meet you, Jeremy, welcome to Canada."

Jeremy shook his hand.

"Canada?"

"I say that for fun. This outpost is made up of mostly Anishinaabe from Canada. Come inside, have a drink."

Charles led them into the living room. He poured a few drinks from a pitcher of water that had strawberries added to it for flavour.

"I didn't know that there were any Canadians here."

"We don't publicize it, I suppose. It's not a very dramatic story anyways. A group of Anishnaabe thought it would be a good idea to take the opportunity to leave, as an insurance policy against things going horribly wrong on Earth. Which they nearly did, as you know."

Charles took a photo from the wall and handed it to Jeremy. "Take a look at this photo. That's my uncle George in his crew uniform. See the flags on his uniform? That's the Canadian flag, that's the Métis Nation flag, and that is the Anishnaabe flag."

"I can see the family resemblance."

"Miigwech. Uncle George is a striking guy, so I'll take that as a compliment. Now, tell me, why are you here? I'm happy to see Smitty, but it's odd, don't you think, that he brought his captain with him?"

"Oh, I can't really say."

Smitty put his arm on Charles' shoulder. "Cousin, things are happening. I know I teased you when you decided to move to this outpost, but I think you made the right decision."

"I see," Charles said. He held eyes with Smitty, and with a lowered voice, he continued, "Sounds vague and serious. You are welcome here any time. If things get bad, come here. Your captain can come too."

Charles turned to Jeremy. "Smitty here has you in good hands. He won't admit it, but he has *minose* coming out of his ass."

"Minose?"

"Oh, it means that he has good luck. He has so much of it that it's probably just coming out of all the holes."

Smitty shook his head, and said, "What the hell's wrong with you, Charles."

"What, it's not true? I'm being a little vulgar, but really, you've survived way too many near misses."

"Maybe. Let's hope it stays that way. Oh, I brought a little something for you. It's some tobacco grown on an organic farm on Adriana Colony. It smells quite lovely."

Smitty held a small pouch in his left hand. Charles picked it up and smelled it.

"It has a delicate smell. A little bit floral. Thank you, Smitty, you didn't need to. But I appreciate it. Miigwech."

Charles embraced Smitty in a big bear hug. Smitty clenched his lower jaw tightly as he said goodbye. Outside, Sherif Raber waited patiently.

"That wasn't long. All done?"

"Yes, thank you Sherif. It's time to go."

Dust peeled up from the tires, obscuring the receding view of the outpost and of Charles watching them drive away, one arm raised above his head in a motionless wave.

38

Labia Minor, on Gliese 832c

Shauna Lone stood under the proscenium arch of the Great Hall. Thousands of the highest ranking warriors and politicians faced her impatiently. Shauna muted her microphone and cleared her throat.

"My companions in life and battle. My fellow warriors. We are here today to witness the birth of a new empire, and a new way of life. Today we throw off the shackles of our past defeat, and rise to a new dawn for the Labian people. Because of your support we are on the verge of victory over Earth and Stellar Corp. Our allies, the Martians, have lent themselves to our common cause: a galaxy free from the domination of Earth politicians. Together we will crawl out from under the oppressive boot of Earth. The Martians will have their freedom, and the Labians will have living space to expand our empire – an expansion which will provide us with the resources and genetic variety that we so greatly require."

Shauna paused, and the assembled guests applauded.

"We are reclaiming our empire, one planet at a time. We are reclaiming our self-respect, one victory at a time. We will be the rulers that our ancestors intended us to be. Because of your support – the support of those of you gathered here with me, as well as those of you on our planets who are watching this right now – I am your Imperatrix. So I now take the official oath."

Below her one of the senators moved toward the stage. In her hands she held the Imperial crown. Shauna Lone placed her hand on the crown.

"I am Imperatrix. I pledge my life to the Empire. I pledge my soul to the Empire. I pledge my blood to the Empire. The Glory of the Empire comes first. I lay my life down for the Empire, just as my subjects lay their lives down for their Imperatrix. May the Labian Empire never fall."

The senator placed the crown on Shauna Lone's head, stepped back, and bowed. Imperatrix Shauna Lone raised her hand and saluted the crowd.

"As your Imperatrix, I ask you: return to your ships, to your factories, and to your training grounds. Work toward fulfilling the purpose of the empire. Thank you for being here to witness this event. May the Labian Empire never fall."

Shauna Lone walked away from the crowd, went behind the proscenium arch and descended the stairs into the back-stage area of the Great Hall.

"Imperatrix, we must speak," Supreme Commander Mei Lun said.

"Mei Lun, what are you doing here?"

"I wanted to bring news to you in person. I'm concerned."

"What is it?"

"One of our spies on Mount Sinai II told us that a Stellar Corp vessel was in orbit. They had gone to speak with the Amish."

"The bankers?"

"Yes."

"How did they know that we use them?"

"I don't know. And I'm not sure that Stellar Corp is even sure of it themselves. From the spy's description it sounds that they were following a lead without being sure of the value of the lead."

"And now?"

"They left. We don't know where."

"Thank you for telling me about this. It is troubling. If our ability to move money out of the empire were to be curtailed, it could be a serious problem."

"That's why I wanted to let you know."

"Keep an eye out for any more activity on Mount Sinai II."

"We have a ship in the system now, to respond to any future Stellar Corp activity."

"Good."

"Imperatrix, there's one other aspect to this situation that is troubling. The Stellar Corp vessel was reported to be called S.C. Applegate."

"The antique patrol ship from Uranus?"
"It appears to be the same one."
"They have interstellar superlight capability?"
"It doesn't make sense. But if it is the same ship, then it appears that they do."
"They could cause trouble for us. If they learn too much, and if they are able to communicate with the main Stellar Corp fleet, then they could be much more than the minor nuisance that they appeared to be. Mei Lun, return to the fleet. If you find this ship, destroy it if you must. I don't want to focus attention on Uranus needlessly, but act if you are forced to do so."
"Yes Imperatrix. I pledge my blood–"
"To the empire."
"To the empire."

39

ABOARD HORATIO STATION

Lauressa was looking at a stray gray hair in the mirror. *Well it could be worse. This isn't the time to be thinking about this. Damn you're vain.* The door chimed. She left the mirror and walked over to the door.

"All done," Doctor Poisson said as the door opened.

"Already?" Lauressa asked.

"Yep, it wasn't that difficult really."

"So what did you have to do?"

"I went down into the computer core and flipped on some switches that activated the war-time logic. Then I went down to the sub-levels of engineering and flipped the circuit breakers that are dedicated to operating the war weapons."

"That's it?"

"That's it. As far as I know they were turned off by Stellar Corp to save energy."

"The fusion reactors can handle it right?"

"They'll be fine. They'll probably burn through their fuel faster, but what does it matter, really? At this point survival in the short-term is more important. We can worry about fuel later."

"You've got a point."

"So what weapons and defensive systems do I have access to now?"

"The first thing you'll notice is that with the war-time logic enabled, remote access to the network has been disabled. The logic also has hardened a lot of the low-level commands, which means anybody wanting to do something like sabotage the hangar doors will have a much harder time of it."

"Okay, so the system is more secure. That's great. But tell me about my guns."

"The anti-EMP system is automated. It automatically shuts off power to any system that is beginning to overload, and sensors turn power back on as soon as the EM pulse has passed. So instead of the entire station being down for minutes, you're down for a few seconds at a time, and only in sections that have been targeted by the pulse."

"Good. But what do I get to shoot back with?"

"The station is outfitted with sixteen plasma launchers."

"Holy shit! What!?" Lauressa jumped up and down and pumped her fist in the air. "We'll be ready the next time the Labians come calling! How does it work?"

"The plasma launchers propel spheres of super-heated plasma, accelerated via electromagnets to a fraction of the speed of light. It's a ball of lightning basically: twenty-eight thousand degrees and extremely high amperage and voltage. It's a crude weapon but powerful."

"Strange that the station wasn't outfitted with lasers, but I'll take this."

"I think the goal was to be able to engage multiple targets rapidly. Imagine if sixteen ships are heading toward you. Firing sixteen lasers at once would drain too much power, and the delay in charging the laser could be an issue. With the plasma launcher a continuous series of plasma spheres can be created rapidly and fired very quickly – the electromagnets will guide the sphere to the appropriate launcher. I've never seen it in action, but the idea is that the switching and firing is so rapid that it's an almost simultaneous delivery of large quantities of energy to every target; basically an avalanche of fire on any ships that come too close."

"What's the drawback?"

"Other than the high energy cost? I imagine the main drawback is a higher chance of hitting your allies by accident – once the plasma is fired it continues in that direction until it hits something or eventually dissipates. I would imagine that a friendly ship could stray into the path. With laser-based systems the laser can be shut off automatically if the system detects a friendly ship getting too close. After all, a laser travels at the speed of light, so turning it off stops the beam at the speed of light. With plasma it takes a lot longer to reach its target, and it can't be turned off once fired."

"Okay, so we'll be careful, and we'll keep an eye on the reactor fuel levels."

"Absolutely. Well, I'd better get back to the infirmary. I've been gone long enough," Doctor Poisson said. He started for the door.

"But everyone there is okay, right?"

"They're all stable, and Ashley is with them. She'd call me if there was an emergency."

"Good... Can you stay? Just for a minute?"

"Sure," Doctor Poisson said. He walked over to a chair and sat down. Lauressa sat on the bed.

"Why don't you come over here?" Lauressa asked.

"I'm fine here."

"But I thought...."

"I like where things are with Ashley right now. I don't want to do anything to complicate that."

"I see. I understand. But we're going to die."

"I'm planning on staying alive, Lauressa, for a long time to come."

"I hope you're right. Why do I always rush into sex like this?"

"Haven't we had this discussion before?"

"Maybe we have."

"I suppose it's a reaction, a safety mechanism of sorts."

"Flight or fight."

"It could be."

"What would I do without you?" she asked.

"I'm not going anywhere."

Lauressa smiled and her eyes welled up. She got up and walked over to the doctor. She put out her hand.

"You're a true friend. Thank you. Thank you."

Doctor Poisson stood and took her hand. He kissed her cheek and said, "Of course. Always."

Lauressa nodded.

The intercom beeped.

"*Commander, Captain Bach from the S.C. Applegate is here.*"

"Thanks Mister Hauer," Lauressa said. "Doctor, I'll go meet with the Captain. I'll let you know what I find. You go take care of your other patients."

* * *

"I'm at a loss. I've got no idea what our next move should be," Lauressa said.

Jeremy sat beside her at one of the cafeteria tables. He held a hot chocolate with both hands.

"I don't know. Wait, I guess. Then go back to the Amish bank in a week. But I can't imagine being idle for that long, not while the rest of Stellar Corp is in disarray."

"I don't like the idea of just waiting around either. While you're here, you're welcome to all the comforts that my station has to offer, for what it's worth."

"Well, your hot chocolate is better than what I've got on my ship."

"I wasn't referring to the hot chocolate," Lauressa said. She leaned toward Jeremy and put her hand on his arm.

The intercom beeped.

"*Commander Tajiki, this is Doctor Poisson. Please come down to the infirmary right away.*"

"Let's go," Lauressa said. She got up from the table and headed for the door.

"You want me with you?"

"Yes. Coming?"

Jeremy grabbed his hot chocolate and hurried after her.

They made their way down to the infirmary, which was not very far from the cafeteria. They entered the infirmary and saw Ashley Chung tending to the injured.

"He's in his office," Ashley said.

"Thanks."

Commander Tajiki and Captain Bach walked through the infirmary to the office. Doctor Poisson was kneeling beside his office couch. Wayland Hauer was lying down with a cold cloth on his forehead.

"He came into the infirmary to see me and passed out before he could say anything."

Wayland lifted his head slightly.

"Oh Commander...." he said.

"Lie back, Wayland," Doctor Poisson said.

"What happened?" Lauressa asked.

"Wayland, can I tell them?" the Doctor asked. Wayland nodded.

"When Wayland passed out I put him on the couch. I checked his vitals and did the usual blood tests. The tests showed that he had just ingested a large quantity of pills. I administered a neutralizing agent, which has eliminated most of the drugs from his system. The blood analysis also showed me something else – it tested positive for Transgenic Utility DNA."

"What?" Lauressa asked. She kneeled down beside Doctor Poisson. "Wayland, you're not a Utility, are you? And why did you try to kill yourself with pills?"

"I'm not a Utility. My father was. My mother registered me at birth as having no father, so that I wouldn't have to live with the stigma. My father left, for my protection. I never saw him. But...." Wayland said. His voice trailed off.

"You need to rest. You've been through a lot," Doctor Poisson said.

"No, I have to tell you first. People found out. They came to me. Said they were fighting for Utility rights. But I wouldn't go along with them. They brainwashed me. They programmed me. Turned me into a kind of sleeper agent. Wherever I went, I'd observe and send back information. They sent me a message today. They wanted me to destroy the station. But I wouldn't. I fought their programming. I took the pills. I thought that was... for the best."

"I'd rather have you with me, Wayland. I'm glad you're alive. Okay?" Lauressa said.

"Okay."

"But why attack the station now?"
"They have plans. And the plans are happening right now."
"Do you know what their plans are?"
"I have some information. Not enough to put the whole thing together. I've picked up bits and pieces and I can tell you what I know."
"Thank you, Wayland."
Lauressa took Wayland's hand. "Go on," she said.
"The weather station on Adriana Colony was destroyed because it was the observatory dedicated to Uranus weather. They wanted to stop anyone from having a close-up view of Uranus, so that they could operate without being seen."
"Something's happening on Uranus?" Lauressa asked.
"I think so. It's happening today. Soon. Or maybe it's already started. It's something huge. Something critical to their entire strategy. Critical to this war they've started."
"Do you know what it is?"
"I don't know. But I know roughly where it is. It's inside the orbit of Miranda at least. Maybe even inside the orbit of Cordelia. And from what I can tell, whatever they're doing has an orbit roughly in sync with Miranda."
"That's a large area to search," Captain Bach said.
"I'm sorry Captain, I wish I knew more," Wayland said. He closed his eyes.
"He needs to rest," Doctor Poisson said.
"You get better, Wayland. Captain Bach and I have work to do. We'll check on you later, okay?" Lauressa said.
Lauressa and Jeremy left the infirmary and headed for the elevator.
"You really seem to like him," Jeremy said.
"He's been with me for years. He's been very loyal."
"Until now."
"I wouldn't say that. I'd say especially now. He tried to kill himself rather than hurt us."
"You have a point.... I'd better get back to my ship. We'll get started on the search right away."

"The S.C. Johnson can join you."

"I wouldn't want to leave you exposed."

"We've got our weapons online now. We'll be okay."

The elevator stopped.

"This is your floor. The hangar is down the hall to the left. Good luck Captain," Lauressa said.

"Thank you," Jeremy said. He paused for a second, then hugged Lauressa quickly, and made off down the hall.

40

Aboard S.C. Applegate

Jeremy Bach stepped onto the bridge of his ship.

"Welcome back, Captain," Smitty said.

"Thank you. Smitty, the intercom please."

Smitty hit a few buttons.

"Go ahead," he said.

"This is Captain Bach. We've just learned the location of a Labian operation. We're headed there now, and we can probably expect a fight. General Quarters."

"General Quarters," Smitty said. He entered a command and a tone sounded.

"Pilot, set our destination to Miranda and prepare to flash."

The pilot, Jerry Mulligan, entered the coordinates for Miranda and brought the superlight drive to full power.

"Flash in 3... 2... –"

The intercom at Smitty's console beeped.

"S.C. Johnson is calling," Smitty said.

"Pilot, hold. Put them on, Smitty."

"This is Captain Thomas. We've got an engine calibration problem that we're working on. It's going to be about thirty minutes before we can set off. Since we can't leave right away, Commander Tajiki has decided to send over James Royson and his men to my ship. I'm not sure I like that. But either way, we'll be ready in a half-hour."

"Thanks for letting me know Captain. But we can't wait. We'll go on ahead and start the search. Join us as soon as you're able."

"If you're sure about that. I'll see you there."

"See you there."

Smitty disconnected the call.

"Pilot, flash when you're ready," Smitty said.

The pilot entered in the command and the ship's skin glowed, then flashed, and the ship winked away into the void. A second later it appeared outside the orbit of Miranda.

"Pilot, keep the engines ready to flash at all times," Smitty said.

"Let's begin the hunt," Captain Bach said.

They did one orbit around Miranda, focusing their cameras on its surface. The face of the moon was barren of any artificial structures, except for the small abandoned modular base they had previously discovered.

"Let's turn the cameras toward Uranus."

Uranus loomed large on the screen. The space in front of them to be searched was enormous: a roughly shaped box 130,000 kilometers on each side. The space in front of them was dominated by Uranus. The sun was behind them, and so anything that traveled in front of Uranus either showed up as a bright object or as a dark spot over the blue background of the planet. Thousands of objects were visible and they all appeared to be traveling in normal orbits. None of them looked suspicious.

"This could take awhile," Smitty said.

"We could use active scanners – the radar, the laser rangefinders," Captain Bach said.

"We could, but that would light us up. Anything out there would see us right away."

"You're right, of course. Let's keep looking."

Smitty entered in some commands at his console and the camera zoomed and began to pan.

"Maybe we'll notice something with a bit of magnification," Smitty said.

They stared at the screen but didn't see anything that resembled a ship of any kind.

Then the pilot yelled, "Incoming!"

The thrusters fired and jerked the ship sideways. A missile flew by the ship.

"The ship flashed in and fired," the pilot, Jerry Mulligan, said.

Smitty zoomed the cameras out. A ship was closing in from the left.

"Show them our nose!" Smitty said.

"Yes sir."

The ship spun toward their attacker.

"Fire!" Smitty yelled. He pounded his console and lasers lashed out at their attacker.

"We're hitting them," the pilot said.

The enemy ship rolled sideways and moved closer.

"They've slipped off target," the pilot said.

"Let's get them again," Smitty said.

Jerry Mulligan adjusted the ship's position and the lasers sped out through space again.

"Another hit. Hold on," he said.

"What is it?" Smitty asked.

"Their reflective armor is holding according to the sensors. 90% of the laser energy bounced off them."

"Show me the data," Smitty said.

The pilot threw up a spectrograph on a corner of the main screen.

"Shit, you're right," Smitty said.

"They're moving closer," the pilot said.

"They're taking hits so they can move in," Captain Bach said.

"Show them our side," Smitty said.

The pilot hit the thrusters and rotated the ship so that the length of the Applegate was visible to the attacking ship.

"Fire!"

The broad-side canons fired and four high-velocity projectiles sped toward their attacker.

"They've fired rockets," the pilot said. "Incoming!"

The Applegate spun and accelerated away from the rockets. They passed harmlessly by.

The attacking ship had already maneuvered out of the path of the projectiles as well.

"They're still moving closer," the pilot said.

"Show them our sides again. Fire as soon as you can," Smitty said.

The Applegate spun and launched its projectiles immediately. The attacking ship began to glow and flashed away.

"They're gone! I'm pretty sure one of the projectiles hit though," the pilot said.

"Stay ready," Smitty said.

"Incoming!" Jerry Mulligan yelled. He spun the ship violently around. The attacking ship had flashed in immediately behind them, only a few thousand kilometers away. At this distance they could see debris floating out of a gash in the side of the ship - one of the projectiles had in fact hit their target. A rocket sped past the Applegate. As the ship spun out of the way of the rocket its lasers came into line-of-sight.

"Firing lasers," Smitty said.

At this close range the reflective armor wasn't nearly as effective and the skin of the enemy ship began to burn off. The ship - now clearly visible as a Labian ship - thrusted away and out of the range of the lasers. They fired back with their own weapons.

Multiple rockets launched out from the Labian ship, along with simultaneous laser fire.

"Back us out!" Smitty yelled.

The pilot started to put distance between the two ships and moved to avoid the lasers and rockets. The laser hit briefly and the ship shook. One of the rockets hit the rear of the ship. Alarms sounded.

"We're losing main engine power," the pilot said.

"Keep pulling back. I'm returning fire," Smitty said.

The lasers fired again and hit the Labian ship; a flash of light indicated something had exploded.

"The Labians are still moving closer. I can't accelerate fast enough," the pilot said.

"Keep them busy," Smitty said.

He fired the lasers again, and the Labians fired theirs. Both ships moved to evade. A beam briefly touched the Applegate and tore off a chunk of armor. The Labian ship was even closer now. They somehow managed to cross into the Applegate's beam. One side of the Labian ship ruptured and armor plates flew off along with puffs of escaping air. The Labian ship turned away from the lasers.

"Show them our side, now!"

The pilot spun the ship, and the projectiles launched.

The Labian ship fired its rockets.

One of the projectiles hit the Labian ship, but it avoided the rest.

The Applegate moved to evade, but with reduced engine power it was sluggish.

"They're going to hit!" the pilot yelled.

Two of the rockets hit the Applegate and the ship went dark. The bridge was dark, except for an emergency light. The ship kept moving in the direction it had been going in, but was now powerless to make any change.

"We're dead," the pilot said.

"Get those engines back online! Engineering, get to work repairing whatever you can," Smitty said.

The Labian ship closed in.

"We need to abandon ship," Captain Bach said.

"We're not done yet. The Johnson should be here in a minute or two," Smitty said.

"They'll rip this ship apart before then," Captain Bach said.

"We'll make it," Smitty said.

He hit commands on his console and all the remaining lights on the ship went dark. A laser blazed out and hit the Labian ship dead on the nose. The nose buckled and sparks flew out. But the Labian ship kept moving closer. The ship stopped only a few kilometers from the Applegate.

The Labian ship fired their lasers.

"I think they've hit our laser," the pilot said.

"We need to abandon ship. Now!" Captain Bach said.

Smitty nodded. He turned on the intercom.

"This is the bridge. All crew –"

He stopped talking when the image on their screen changed. The Labian ship went dark.

"Hold on," Smitty said.

He brought up an energy readout. The Labian ship showed all systems offline.

"All crew. The Labian ship just lost power. We need to get the engines back on now," Smitty said. He disconnected the intercom.

"You'd better be right," Captain Bach said.

41

INSIDE A SPACESHIP

Shep was chewing on some biscuits when the light from Uranus painted the inside of the room in a blue glow.

"*Captain, look at that, there's a ship orbiting Miranda,*" a man said over the intercom.

The ship turned and started to head toward Miranda.

"What do you think is going to happen?" Balraj asked.

Shep walked over to the window and looked out.

The ship began to glow.

"We're going to –" Shep said. Then the ship flashed.

The ship came back to space in only a second, and Miranda was just off to their right. A ship was in front of them. It was very small, but just visible. They heard a scraping sound from the floors above, and a bright light passed by the window above them.

"They fired a rocket," Shep said.

Balraj and Bailey came over to the window and watched. In a few seconds the rocket seemed to pass by the other ship.

"They missed?" Bailey asked.

The skin of the ship suddenly shimmered in different shades of blue.

"*Lasers. Evade,*" the man on the intercom said. The ship turned and sped out of the path of the lasers.

"*Move in,*" the voice said.

The ship turned and moved closer. The ship shimmered blue gain.

"*Evade. Move in.*"

Again, the ship moved out of the path of the laser and moved closer. The ship shimmered again.

"*Evade. Fire rockets.*"

The ship turned out of the path of the laser once again and fired its rockets.

Suddenly the ship jerked to the left.

"What's happening?" Bailey asked.

"Good work. Damn it, our rockets missed. Wait. Incoming! Flash!"

The ship glowed and flashed, but just as it did there was a loud popping sound followed by the sound of metal twisting and crushing.

"Oh, no! This is bad!" Balraj yelled.

A second later the ship returned to space, and now the other ship was closer and easier to see. The scraping sound happened again.

"Rocket," Shep said.

A trio of rockets sped toward the enemy. They appeared to miss.

The ship was bathed in blue light again.

"Evade! The armor is taking damage."

The ship turned away.

"Fire lasers and rockets."

There was a flash of light in the distance where the laser hit its target. Then there was a small orange glow from a rocket that had impacted something solid.

"Good work. Move in."

The ship moved closer. A laser hit them again. The ship shook and Balraj sat on the floor and hugged his knees.

"Fuck! The armor is losing its effectiveness. Avoid those lasers. Return fire."

Sparks flared from the other ship where the lasers had hit. But almost as quickly, their ship shook again. There was the sound of an explosion. Shep could see bits of armor and debris float by the window.

"Hit them with the rockets!"

The rockets launched out at the other ship, but at almost the same time something tore through one of the floors above.

"The rocket launchers are offline. Wait. Our rockets hit them. They're losing power."

"Move in closer. We'll finish this with our lasers up close."

The ship began to move in closer. The other ship appeared a lot larger out the window now.

"Bailey, I can sort of make out that ship now," Shep said.

Bailey squinted and pushed her face to the window.

"Is that a Stellar Corp ship?" Bailey asked.

"I think so," Shep said.

"We have to help them."

"But we're on this ship."

"We're the good guys. They're the good guys. I think."

"I don't want to get blown up."

"We have to help them!" Bailey repeated urgently.

"But what can we do?"

"Let's rip up all the wires down here."

"Okay."

Bailey and Shep ran out of the room. They ran down the hallway. There were axes in one of the storage rooms. They were heavy but they could still swing them.

"Just hit the wires," Bailey said.

"Which ones?"

"All of them."

They ran from room to room, swinging at any exposed wires they could find.

Shep hit a bundle of wires with his axe and the lights flickered. Machine sounds that could be heard from the floors above went quiet.

"We hit something!" Shep said.

They ran back to the room at the front of the ship.

"*We just lost power. I don't know what happened.*"

"Fix it!"

"*As soon as we figure out what's going on. Oh great, the bridge doors won't open.*"

"We're stuck in here?"

"Yes, Captain."

"Balraj, we did it!" Shep said.

"The Stellar Corp ship might fire again," Balraj said. He was rocking, with his arms still wrapped around his knees.

"He's right," Shep said.

"I could send them a message," Bailey said.

"How?"

"With that old computer and the laser. I can hook up the computer to it and then we just point the laser at the ship."

"Okay, let's try it."

Bailey picked up the computer and took it to the window. She sat down, placed it on her lap and powered it on.

"Okay, plug in the laser to this port here, and keep it pointed at that ship."

"Okay, I'll try," Shep said.

Bailey typed a message on the computer and hit 'send'. The laser pulsed.

"Now what?" Shep asked.

"Let's send it again. We don't know if they received it."

Bailey re-sent the message.

"I just saw a light flicker on their ship," Shep said.

"Did it flicker twice? And then a second later flicker twice again?"

"Yeah."

"That's what I asked them to do if they got the message."

"What did you tell them?"

"I told them we're three kids, that we're stowed away in the lowest level of the ship. That we cut some wires and sabotaged the ship. And oh yeah, please don't shoot at us and come rescue us if you can."

"Wow! So we're saved?" Shep asked

"Yeah I think so," Bailey said.

"Oh I hope so," Balraj said.

42

URANUS

"Flash," Captain Thomas said. The S.C. Johnson flashed away from Horatio Station and a second later appeared in orbit around Miranda.

"Captain, look! It's the Applegate and another ship," said the pilot.

"Take us in. S.C. Applegate, this is Captain Thomas, can you hear me?"

"*We hear you. This is Captain Bach. The Labian ship is without power, but so are we. Captain, there are some children on that ship who sabotaged it. They're hiding in the lowest storage level. We would have been finished without their help. Their names are Shelp, Balraj, and Bailey.*"

"Thanks Captain Bach. We'll take care of them. Do you need any help?"

"*We need help with repairs, to get the engines jerry-rigged. We could also use some medical supplies. Our infirmary is overrun.*"

"We'll send over a shuttle now."

"*Thank you Captain.*"

* * *

James Royson hit the hatch release on the shuttle. The hatch ramp lowered and they were in a dark hanger.

"Go," he said.

His team, twenty men strong, left the shuttle and took up positions around the shuttle and the hangar doors.

"I'm going to find those kids. You two are with me," he said. Royson headed toward a maintenance door with two of his soldiers. "The rest of you, secure the ship."

The team left the hangar and headed toward the bridge. There was no resistance until they reached the bridge. They stormed the bridge, only to find there were no Labians to be found. Instead, they found a half-dozen men.

"How did you get aboard?" an old man asked. He was sitting in the Captain's chair.

"Identify yourself," one of Royson's men said.

"I'm Jensen Mandala, and you're trespassing on a sovereign Free Martian ship."

"There's no Labians here?"

"No."

"Get over there against that wall. All of you. You're all under arrest."

"What authority gives you the right to arrest me?"

"Stellar Corp."

"I don't recognize the authority of Stellar Corp," Mandala said.

"It doesn't matter what you recognize. We either arrest you or shoot you."

Mandala's face turned bright red. He slowly stood up. His knees appeared to strain under the effort.

"Very well, you win. You win. Arrest us," he said. He moved slowly toward the wall. He waved at his companions. "Don't resist, there's no point now."

The rest of the Martians moved to stand beside Mandala.

* * *

"Kids, are you down here?" James Royson asked.

There was silence, except for the sounds of distant mechanical systems echoing down from the floors above. Wires hung in bundles from the hallway ceiling, intermingled with flickering lights. Royson moved down the hallway carefully.

"Kids? It's James Royson. I'm here with Stellar Corp."

There was more silence, but he thought he caught the slight sound of feet shuffling at the far end of the hall. He stopped and looked at his two soldiers.

"Check the rooms one by one. I'll keep moving along the hall."

The soldiers disappeared into the storage rooms. The glow of their flashlights dimly illuminated the hallway as they moved in and out of each room. Royson walked forward. He could see the end of the hall more clearly now – at this distance it seemed to be washed in a blue glow. He moved closer and could see that the blue glow was light from Uranus drifting in through a window. He stopped near the end of the hall and waited for his two companions. In a moment they caught up to him. They both shook their heads – there was nobody to be found in any of the rooms behind them. Royson walked forward out of the hall and into a large room. The window ran from the floor to the ceiling and Uranus filled up the entire view. He looked around. He heard a sound, like air moving in and out – breathing.

"Kids, it's okay, you can come out. We're here from Stellar Corp. We're here to take you home," he said.

One of the children peaked out from behind a crate: a little girl. Her hair was tousled and matted and her face was grimy.

"You're not the space pirates?" she asked.

"No. We're here to help you. It seems that you kids saved a whole bunch of people today. There's a whole ship full of people who are worried about you and want to meet you. What's your name?"

"Bailey. It wasn't me," she said.

"Oh? Who was it?"

"My friends. I just sent the message to tell them we're here."

"Oh? Where are your friends? Hiding around here somewhere?"

"They're here. Hey guys, come out."

Two boys came out of their hiding places. One was behind another crate. The other popped open the lid and stood up from inside the crate.

"Hey, there you are. I'm James Royson, from Hamlet. How did you three end up on this ship?"

"It was an accident," one of the boys said.

"Are you Shep?" Royson asked.

"Yes, um... James... um... sir... um... Royson," he said.

"Just James, okay? So that makes your friend here Balraj," Royson said.

Balraj nodded. He began to cry.

"It's okay, you're safe now," Royson said. He walked over to Balraj and put out his hand. Balraj jumped up and grabbed on to Royson, with both arms around him.

"My mom is going to be so mad," Balraj said between sobs.

"It's okay. You're okay."

Bailey and Shep walked over and put their arms around Balraj and cried too.

"Let's get you off this ship," Royson said.

* * *

Volaris Gollari was trying to hop out of his bed in the Applegate infirmary. The infirmary was swamped with people injured during the fight. Half the crew was down there, while the other half was busy working on repairs.

"Don't even think of it," Doctor Smith said. He was cauterizing a wound on one of the crew.

"I'm fine," Volaris said.

"That's because of the drugs you're on. You lost a lot of blood, and it hasn't been very long since the operation. Now stay in bed and rest."

"No, I can help, just give me a second."

Volaris got up on both feet and stood up straight.

"See, I'm fine. Now give me something to do. I can't just sit while other people in worse shape than me need help."

"I'm too busy to fight with you, so just take it easy. Go to the supply closet and get some sterile water packets. Hand them out to the injured."

"On it," Volaris said. He moved slowly toward the supply closet. He held his hand against his injury, but didn't make a sound or a complaint. He looked at the injured crew. Several had burns. He pulled out the water packets, some pain killers, and carbonic bandage cream. He moved to the closest person and handed her some water, and rubbed some of the cream on a burn on her arm.

Two women walked into the infirmary.

"We're from the S.C. Johnson. We have medical supplies for you."

"Are you medics?" Doctor Smith asked.

"We're marines."

"Take the supplies to Volaris over there and help him out. I'm in the middle of something."

* * *

In the engine room, John Dvorak and David the Mechanic were pulling wires out from the conduit leading to the superlight drive.

"These ones are melted," David said.

"So are these," John said.

"We should send in Crawler. He'll be able to map out the damage."

"Alright. From the look of these wires, the whole system could be fried. Let's not get our hopes up."

David nodded. He went over to a case and opened it. Crawler hopped out.

"Crawler, can you go into the conduit and map out all of the burnt-out wires?"

Crawler spun around in a circle, hopped back and forth, and ran into the conduit.

"I'll never get used to that," John said.

"Come on, it's adorable."

Three crew members from the S.C. Johnson arrived with a cart full of parts and tools.

"Oh good, so what did you bring?" John asked.

"A bit of everything. Oh, I'm Jacob Mobutu, an engineer on the Johnson. My colleagues here have some engineering experience as well."

"Okay, let's lay out the parts that you've brought and see what we can use. Crawler is in the conduit mapping the damaged wires."

"Crawler?" Jacob asked.

Crawler popped out of the conduit, paused to look at Jacob for a second, and then sped back to work.

* * *

The shuttle hatch opened and James Royson stepped onto S.C. Johnson's hangar.

"Come on, let's go to the cafeteria and get you something good to eat. Then we'll go visit the doctor so he can take a look at you."

The three kids stuck close together and followed Royson to the cafeteria. Balraj got a Titania Cola to drink and some bread. Shep got a chocolate ice-cream, and Bailey got a hot chocolate and some crackers. Smiles began to slowly spread across their faces. Royson took them next to the infirmary to visit the doctor.

"Oh, you kids have some tasty treats there," Doctor Chang said.

Shep smiled. Bits of ice-cream poked out through his lips.

"Come sit over here. I'll take a scan of each of you."

The three kids sat side-by-side on a cot. Doctor Chang scanned each of them and looked at the results. He then felt their hands, looked for swollen glands, and looked in their eyes.

"You're all a little dehydrated. I'm afraid you'll need to spend some time in the cafeteria drinking and eating. Doctor's orders."

"Let's go. I think I'll have an ice cream too," Royson said. He led them back to the cafeteria.

* * *

"Is there anything we can do to help?" Captain Bach asked.

"*Not really. Crawler has finished mapping out the damaged wiring. With the parts from the Johnson, along with some of our own, we'll be able to get enough power from the engine for regular* maneuvering and if we're lucky some very short distance flashes," John Dvorak said via the intercom.

"How short?"

"Just around the Uranus system. But the engine itself isn't damaged. I'm sure we'll be able to get all the parts we need from Horatio Station or the local colonies."

"Alright, I'll leave you to it. Let me know if you need anything."

"Thanks Captain."

The intercom clicked off.

"Well Smitty, what now? We can't just sit on the bridge while the rest of the crew – the ones who aren't hurt – work on patching this ship up."

"We could go over to the S.C. Johnson. Thank Captain Thomas. And join the interrogation of the people they're bringing back from the Labian ship," Smitty said.

"That's a good idea. And I'd like to meet those kids. We owe them – I don't know if they're old enough to really understand what they've done."

Jeremy Bach, captain of the least interesting patrol in the history of the universe, surveyed the bridge. They had been beaten up. They'd have to talk about brushing up on their battle tactics. But they were alive. That was what counted at the moment. Jeremy nodded.

"Let's go see those kids," he said.

"Captain, hold on," said Jerry Mulligan.

"What is it?"

"There's something wrong with Uranus."

"What?"

"The sensors are picking up a massive amount of energy within the upper atmosphere."

"Where? Put it on the screen."

The pilot put an image of Uranus on the screen. It was overlaid with an energy readout.

"That's odd," Smitty said.

"Some kind of storm?" Jeremy asked.

"I don't know. I've never heard of energy that intense in a storm – at least not radiating out into space."

"Dvorak, bring up the bridge screen at your console. Take a look at this," Jeremy said into the intercom.

"One second... Oh, that's not right," John Dvorak said.

"What is it?"

"The energy is off the charts. Look at those temperatures."

"So that's no storm?"

"That's no storm. It looks a little like the kind of thing I'd expect to see from a fission reaction. David, do you agree? David agrees. Wait, I see something else. Zoom in."

The pilot zoomed in. An area of white clouds was forming against the blue atmosphere. The clouds began to billow and rise up into a column. The clouds stretched toward space. They rose up into the thinner upper atmosphere. The clouds soon began to evaporate away as wispy tendrils of steam flowed off into space.

"What the hell is that?" Jeremy asked.

The clouds began to fall away entirely, and a shape became visible. A large, roughly cylindrical object was now slowly moving into space.

"What the hell is that!"

The object was covered by dark lines. There was an almost organic look to the pattern of the lines. The lines began to pulse with light. The pulsing got brighter and more frequent. And then, in one instant all the lines grew incredibly bright and the object flashed and was gone.

"What kind of ship was that? I've never seen a ship that looked like that before," Jeremy said.

"It was huge. I think now we know what the Labians were trying to keep under wraps."

"Smitty, what kind of ship can survive down there? What kind of ship can survive down in the depths of Uranus?"

TO BE CONTINUED
IN
ACTS OF BETRAYAL IN FARAWAY PLACES

CPSIA information can be obtained
at www.ICGtesting.com
Printed in the USA
LVHW030518200423
744764LV00005B/334